Barry Reed is a Boston lawyer specializing in medical legal cases. He is a member of the Board of Governors of the Massachusetts Academy of Trial Attorneys, and is Treasurer of the American Society of Law and Medicine. Mr Reed is married and has four child...

BARRY REED

The Verdict

GRANADA
London Toronto Sydney New York

Published in paperback by Granada Publishing Limited in 1983

ISBN 0 586 05404 9

First published in Great Britain by
Granada Publishing 1982
Copyright © Barry Reed 1980

Granada Publishing Limited
Frogmore, St Albans, Herts AL2 2NF
and
36 Golden Square, London W1R 4AH
515 Madison Avenue, New York, NY 10022, USA
117 York Street, Sydney, NSW 2000, Australia
60 International Boulevard, Rexdale, Ontario R9W 6J2, Canada
61 Beach Road, Auckland, New Zealand

Printed and bound in Great Britain by
Cox & Wyman Ltd, Reading

Granada ®
Granada Publishing ®

To those who wear the stripes of the law with honour

With thanks to Ken Gross

The smallest atom of truth represents some man's bitter toil and agony; for every ponderable chunk of it there is a brave truth-seeker's grave upon some lonely ash-dump and a soul roasting in hell.

H.L. MENCKEN

1

The priest had called him Francis. That was the way they worked, these priests – calling up lost saints, reminding you in their fashion of just who you were and where you came from. Pulling spiritual rank. You might be Frank in any number of high places, to any number of important people. But when the priests called you Francis, it felt like a crack on the knuckles.

'Tell me, Father, have you ever been in love? I mean with a real woman. Not with St Theresa or the Blessed Virgin. I mean with a black-haired girl who's a little crazy, if you follow me. Not a fantasy. A real flesh-and-blood woman.'

Galvin was staring out the smudged window of his office, overlooking Beacon Hill and the Common. It was never pretty in late March, when all the Christmas lights were gone and the snow died in lonely patches. Even the trees seemed bare and arthritic. And a little malice did not seem so out of place.

'I am talking about carnal lust,' taunted Galvin, drink in hand. He spoke to the window, not trusting himself to face the priest. 'The flesh. What some people call love. Did you know that in its more acute forms it actually hurts? Physically! I don't mean the act itself, although God knows what passes for an act of love these days. But just thinking of her. Remembering the details. You ache so bad that you don't care who knows. Not the bar association. Not your wife. Not even God. Know what I mean? Have you ever felt it like that? Bone deep? Have you ever really . . . Christ, I mean really felt it?'

'Don't mind me,' said the priest, fidgeting on the couch. He was smart enough to appreciate that Galvin was busy manoeuvring. Delaying. Avoiding the opening click in the business at hand. And he was willing to be patient and see where it all would lead.

Galvin tried to regain the edge. He fumbled with the one lawbook in his office without any dust on it. It was something by Blackstone, and it opened into a decanter of whisky. Galvin waved his glass vaguely in the direction of the priest.

' . . . felt it right there where you're sitting? Sure I can't interest you in a drink, Padre?'

'Not just yet,' replied the priest, pulling his wet raincoat onto his lap.

Galvin's boozy insolence lapsed into an awkward silence. He stood at the window, patting the drops of moisture that seeped through the sash. Particles of mildewed paint flaked onto the sill.

And then Galvin's hand fell to the bare radiator, jolting him. 'Shit,' he muttered, burying his hand in his jacket pocket, trying to conceal the pain. 'Sorry, Father,' he said, forcing a smile.

'Don't apologize,' said the priest.

'Goddamned landlords! I keep trying to get them to cover these grilles. Bastards. They won't keep the place up anymore. This was a pretty classy place when I first moved in. Hard to believe. But they kept it nice. Now all they care about is their fifteen goddamned dollars a square foot. That's what they get – fifteen bucks a square, and the elevator doesn't even work. And it isn't even all usable space. They tag me for the hallway and the bathroom and the broken elevator. Takes them a month to fix the son-of-a-bitch every time it shanks out. They have to lock the bathrooms like a methadone clinic. You'd think it was Roxbury Crossing.'

'Three floors isn't such a bad climb,' said the priest.

'Well, I'm not going to put up with it anymore,' Galvin sputtered, running out of anger, running down an embarrassed slope.

It had occurred to the priest, as Galvin raged, that he might indeed be his landlord. For Michael Thomas Brophey was no ordinary cleric. He was the eighth Bishop of the Diocese of Boston and, as such, presided over the Church's temporal domain: all 411 churches; all 231 schools, universities and colleges; all 12 hospitals and sanatoriums. There was also the matter of the investment portfolio. Not even Bishop Brophey or all the Church's financial wizards knew everything contained in that. He knew that the Church held substantial assets. In fact, the real estate holdings were extensive and included many of the older, statelier office buildings in this section of town. Of course, the Church employed management firms to run the properties. The truth was that Bishop Brophey didn't know whether or not he was Galvin's landlord, but he wondered if Galvin knew.

'Francis, my car is waiting and I haven't got much time. I've come to try and settle this awful business.'

'Do they call you Father?'

'Yes,' said the Bishop, fumbling through a briefcase. 'That's fine. You can call me Father.'

'I'm never really certain. I never know when to throw in an Eminence or Your Grace, or even whether I'm supposed to kiss your ring.'

'Why don't we leave it at Father? Just call me Father.'

'And you call me Frank.'

'Fine. I'd like to get to this –'

'I saw you play for Dartmouth.'

The Bishop smiled. He couldn't help himself. The memories were still sweet. Even now, at 42, more than two decades away from those unblemished autumns when he could pluck footballs out of the sky – even after all that time, the smile was pure reflex.

It must have been the junior year when the professional scouts had camped on his doorstep. They had sensed star quality. They had dangled fat contracts and the promise of immortality.

But Michael Brophey had sensed another kind of

9

immortality. His were abstract longings. There were always people to remind him of that junior year when he was the fastest runner with the surest hands. And when they spoke of it, the voices trailed off, like a regret. He might not agree, but he knew what they meant when they hinted that a sprinter was squandered in the service of God.

The hero of the gridiron had become a star within the Church.

He was the youngest member of the Roman Catholic hierarchy in the United States when he was picked to be the Bishop of Boston at the age of 39.

Not every one of the two million, eighteen thousand and thirty-four souls in the diocese fell under Brophey's spell. The Italians in East Boston and the North End regarded him as a colonial ruler from the Irish majority.

The stoical Poles in Revere and Chelsea were accustomed to being ignored. They accepted Brophey as an improvement over an Italian. But they expected little for themselves.

And the Irish never forgave him; they never forgave his Ivy League frosting or his liberal attitudes. Most of all, they never forgave his success.

Of all the flinty criticisms, only one had bothered Brophey. It was a snide cocktail-party remark that he overheard by accident. One of the upper-crust charity women was admiring the new Bishop's shy self-effacement. The man actually blushed under a compliment, she told one of her well-bred guests, who was poised over a tray of canapés. The reply came back with the same tasteful care with which she chose the anchovies: 'A man that shy must hide a great vanity.'

It singed Brophey's ears. He suspected that that one contained more than a little truth.

Galvin played with a dead cigarette lighter and the Bishop emptied his briefcase. They were taking the measure of each other, Galvin fending off the inevitable confrontation and the

10

Bishop trying to find an appropriate opening.

There was one item that Bishop Brophey left inside his valise. It was the file on Francis Xavier Galvin, Esquire. The Bishop had studied it before the meeting. Now he was looking for some artful way of letting Galvin know that he knew all there was to know about him.

Inside the folder was the report by the Grievance Committee of the state bar association, which was soon to be forwarded to the Supreme Judicial Court for action. Frank Galvin was about to have his legal head chopped off. When such findings were forwarded, it invariably meant disbarment.

The charges seemed a little flimsy, the Bishop thought when he read the report. Tame, even, compared with the routine transgressions committed within the Boston legal community. Galvin was accused of 'soliciting cases, financing litigation and conduct unbecoming a member of the Bar.'

These were the open charges. The paper charges. The real offence was inexpressible: a breach of manners. Galvin was guilty of flaunting an unauthorized romance.

No one pretended that the legal community in the greater Boston area was immune from adultery. Far from it. The majority of Galvin's fellow lawyers engaged in some form of hanky-panky.

No, if Galvin had merely been cheating on his wife, while maintaining the usual pretence of rectitude – tinged with some guilt, of course – there would have been the usual cover-up among his friends and peers.

But Frank Galvin, who had an indifferent wife and four alienated children stashed away in a heavily mortgaged colonial in Wellesley Hills, was wantonly, merrily and shamelessly cavorting with a 30-year-old Chinese American.

Lois Chen was the daughter of a prominent Boston restaurateur. She and Galvin had been virtually living together for almost four years.

No one except Galvin and Lois Chen seemed to approve of

11

the relationship. They went out publicly together, offending the Puritan remnant in every conceivable manner.

It was not only that she was Chinese, although that made it seem kinky in itself; it was not only that she was not spectacularly beautiful, although that only seemed to confirm the legal community's worst suspicions; it was not only that there was not the least sign of shame or apology in either of them, although they seemed to leave a social welt in their wake; it was not even that Galvin treated his wife as the mistress, sneaking her out to family dinners and such . . .

What truly galled the sober barristers of Boston was the fact that Galvin had lost all interest in his legal practice. He did not seem particularly upset when court appointments did not come his way. When some of his older and more reliable friends took him aside for a sound talking-to, he made no effort to change. He kept taking off in the afternoons. And all the while his practice was evaporating, he seemed to be enjoying himself.

That was going too far. That was when the members of the bar decided to take action.

The price of Galvin's digression was written everywhere for the Bishop to read: the cigarette lighter that wouldn't work; the windows that leaked and wheezed; the paint blistering on the walls; the Oriental rug beginning to fray. Even Galvin's custom-tailored suit was out of style, and the shirt cuffs would no longer stay crisp.

The lawbooks were still stacked in cardboard boxes, for want of legal scholarship – and worse, an eyesore, suggesting impermanence.

It was not hard to assess Galvin's precise predicament, for lawyers, like hookers, were judged by appearances. They stood inspection by the world every single day. They couldn't afford one off day or one cheap print on the wall. They depended upon illusion and attention to detail. A pair of scuffed shoes was a sure sign of decline.

And yet there was the memory of quality in the room. The office was located at the very top of Beacon Hill, which once all the best lawyers had hoped to scale. Through the massive French bow windows there was an impressive view of Park Street and the Public Gardens and the gold-domed State House.

If there was decay in the air, it was not without interesting lines of character and its own sad charm. The place might have fallen on hard times, but there was no mistaking the underlying substance. Bishop Brophey was not fooled by the neglect. It would take attention and some money to restore it – and the same thing, he thought, might be said of Galvin.

The Bishop interrupted himself and returned, as he always did, to the business at hand.

'I'm not here to offer absolution or listen to your confession. Save your anger for another time. I want to settle this matter of the lawsuit. I have releases here prepared by Monsignor O'Boyle. There's an agreement attached for a settlement of three hundred thousand dollars. I've been over this case with my staff, Frank, and this is a generous offer.'

There was an uncomfortable urgency in the Bishop's presentation. This was a distasteful duty. 'It's really more than a compromise, you know. A compromise suggests retreat. This is nothing like that. This covers everything. It's fully adequate. Morally and legally. In fact, I'm amazed at the generosity of the insurance company.'

Before Galvin could say anything, Brophey held up his hand. 'Look, Frank, I am also aware of your present difficulties. Let's just say that I was consulted. I'm usually asked for advice and counsel. Especially when the subject is someone like you, a bit underzealous in his attachment to Holy Mother Church.'

Galvin lit another cigarette from the stub of the last. He had moved away from the window and now leaned, half sitting, on

13

the front edge of his desk, facing the Bishop.

'Let me be perfectly candid. I don't like mincing words. First and foremost, I want this case settled. It only hurts to drag it on. I have read your motion papers and the briefs, and I was impressed. You are a talented man. A bit wasted. Thrown away, as it were. I'd like to make you an offer, but I don't want it taken the wrong way.' The Bishop cleared his throat and straightened his glasses. He took a breath.

'I would like you to join my legal staff. This is strictly on my own, you understand. I have not consulted with anyone else. But I like your spunk. You were pretty high in your class at Governor Bradford Law School, and you're still young. Just a few years older than me. You have tremendous potential. I hate to see such talent thrown away.'

'As you say, I have my difficulties.'

'Nothing that could not be managed. The derelictions don't seem so terrible.'

'You have a staff,' said Galvin, sounding a little nasty.

'Monsignor O'Boyle is getting along. He's seventy-five years old. We need new blood. We can use legal help. You know, the whole Church is under attack. We're fighting for our life. Our identity is being eroded. Our schools are closing. Our property is being taxed . . .'

'Your hospitals are being sued.'

'Yes. There are people who sense vulnerability in the Church. It's the wounded-animal thing.'

'You want me to throw away my practice? Give up all this?' Galvin gestured with a sweep of his arm.

'Frank . . .'

'Pack up my law books? I like it here, Father. I like the sunsets and the surprise on the days when the elevator works.'

'You can't win this suit, you know, Frank. I am here as a friend. You will spend a lot of your time and a lot of our time, and in the end you'll lose. You have to. Think about it. You can *afford* to lose. You're one man. It's one man's destiny. We cannot afford to lose. We have two thousand years and eternity to protect. We have the immortal soul of the Church in our hands. How can we gamble with that? How can we afford to lose when we are losing so much? What is the fate of one man against the whole Church?'

'I have a client to protect.'

'Protect your client, Frank. Protect that poor girl. I beg you. But fight us and you'll lose everything. Your case. Your client. Your licence. Take the three hundred thousand dollars. For the sake of your client. For yourself. You won't do better. I promise you. There are things here at stake that are greater than you or me.'

'I have an oath, Father. That may seem pretty thin measured against the fate of the Church. I'm fighting lousy medical care. I'm fighting for justice for one small girl who can no longer help herself.'

'You are going to ruin your client, Francis. And yourself. Good Lord, man, I don't understand your hesitation. I swear I don't. When I walked into this room, you didn't have a future. I'm offering you one. You should be on your knees.'

'Let me see the releases.'

Galvin took the blue-backed papers and held them under the light. He did not read them for information. He knew what they would say. It was out of sheer wonder:

I, Karen M. Ross, duly appointed conservator of Deborah Ruth Rosen, in consideration of $300,000 in hand paid to me by St Catherine Laboure Hospital . . .

The Bishop was right, thought Galvin. This would have been a famous victory. Yesterday. It was more than he had ever hoped to collect in the beginning. A great sum. And yet . . .

'Did Monsignor O'Boyle personally prepare these releases?'

'He did.'

Galvin handed them back to the Bishop. 'Please tell him that

I said that he can personally shove them up his ass.'

There was a flicker of rage that passed across the Bishop's face and left a shadow behind. 'I thought the Jesuits trained you boys better than that.'

'They didn't teach us to take bribes,' snapped Galvin. 'Did you think I'd sell out my client to save my own hide?'

'You have no hide!' the Bishop said. His hands clenched the arm of the couch and he was half rising, as if to lunge at Galvin. It was the first time in all the years he had been in the Church that he had felt such a physical urge to strike someone. He closed his eyes and composed himself. It was a great effort. 'We have misunderstood each other,' he said, standing now. 'That was no bribe, Francis. I was trying to save you. I felt sorry for you. But you are a stubborn man. Both offers are withdrawn. They will not be renewed. We will seek our remedies in court. I trust that this meeting was in confidence.'

He did not wait for an answer.

He swept up his papers and strode out of the room, leaving Galvin crumpled in a chair like a used tissue.

Outside, the Bishop dropped back into the seat of the waiting limousine. Monsignor O'Boyle did not like the look on the Bishop's face. The Monsignor had promised that Galvin would sign. He had guaranteed it. But first he had made the Bishop raise the offer from $285,000 to $300,000. When the Bishop asked why, O'Boyle had replied, 'These ambulance chasers have one thing in common: they're predictable. He's a typical guzinta.'

'A what?'

'A guzinta. If you offer him two hundred and eighty-five thousand dollars, he won't take it. A laywer's fee is always one-third. Three doesn't guzinta two eight-five very easily. They can't figure it out. But one-third of three hundred thousand is – short division.'

The Monsignor waited until they were in traffic. 'Well,' he asked, 'did he take the papers?'

'Yes,' said the Bishop.

'I knew it. I knew it.'

'. . . he took them and told me where to stuff them.'

'Oh, my God. Oh, Lord.'

'Take it easy, Brendan,' said the Bishop. 'Don't worry. We're in the right. We'll just have to let the lawyers handle it. Mr Galvin may be foolish, but he isn't spineless. Call the lawyers. Call them in the morning. Tell them I want this handled.'

The limousine stopped at the Chancery. Monsignor O'Boyle left. 'I'll see to it. I'll take care of it. Good evening, Your Eminence.'

The Bishop drove off. 'Jim, I'm hungry,' he said to the driver. 'Let's go for some Chinese food.'

2

'Goddamn it, Moe, I know you're in there!'

'Is someone out there?'

'It's me, Moe. Galvin.'

'Who's there?'

'Galvin. *Galvin.*'

The ocular peephole moved. Then Galvin heard a bolt being unlatched. Moe Katz had passed his three-score-and-ten, and his hearing was almost gone. It had been fading for twenty years or more, but Moe was a vain man, or a wise man – it was sometimes hard to tell the difference – and he would not hear what he did not choose to hear. He allowed himself to acquire a reputation as hard of hearing. It gave him advantages in the courtroom, getting things read back to him and giving him more time to think. It forgave things that he missed. But the chief advantage was a peace he would otherwise never have known.

It was, in fact, a metaphor come true. Moe Katz had spent a lifetime turning deaf at the undertone of Boston anti-Semitism. It was never really vicious or dangerous. Just a social migraine that he learned to live with. He did not hear the crude jokes and whispered insults. Deafness came as a blessing.

'Galvin,' he said, ignoring the wet raincoat, embracing his former partner, for he truly liked him. 'Come in. My God, you're drenched. Sit down. Take off your coat. Have a drink.

'So how did you know I'd still be here?'

'It's Friday night, Moe. It's only eleven o'clock. Where else would you be? You're still in temple.'

Moe chuckled, busy as he was, cracking ice, opening some

Scotch, making his guest feel welcome. He enjoyed such compliments, like a woman whose hairstyle attracts attention. Galvin had known Moe too long not to understand. The old man liked being shown his eccentricity. And this office was Moe Katz's passion. It was not so much that he liked the hard work. It was the atmosphere. The thick, musty texture of burgundy lawbooks. The rich wood of the shelves, and the fine leather of his chair. The soothing notion that somewhere in these offices were the answers to all the rules of behaviour in life. When he spoke of the law, even in the petty, run-of-the-mill cheap cases, it was with profound respect.

No, it was usually a safe bet that Moe Katz would be in his office late on a Friday night, like an art lover who could never tear himself away from a masterpiece.

'It looks to me like you could use this,' said Katz handing Galvin the drink.

'Why all the locks and bolts, Moe? You got a broad in here?'

'Those days are over for me, sonny boy. I don't collect any more horizontal fees. It's not a smart thing to let your putz rule your head. But that's your business, and I won't interfere. Enough said on that. The locks are there to save my life. The blacks are out there in the Common.'

He pointed across the avenue to the unlit park. 'They're out there now. They wait in the Common to see which lights are on. Then they come across and rob and kill us. Tonight, they're criminals. Tomorrow, they're clients.'

'Come on, Moe. Who'd steal anything in here?'

'Murray Friedman let three shvartzers in last week. A trusting guy. They came in and they held him out the window by his heels. Eighteen floors. They cleaned out his safe. They emptied his wallet and took his credit cards. They even took the typewriters and a couple of bottles of Haig and Haig. Then they put him in the hospital. Cracked his nose and knocked out five teeth and broke three ribs. No reason. They had

19

everything. Just like that. I get them coming in here every day. People just like that. My clients. I've been seriously thinking of packing it in. Murray will never come back. Right down the hall.'

'I guess I've been lucky,' said Galvin.

'Well, you're right next to the State House. You've got the Capitol Police patrolling the grounds. The only people who patrol around here are derelicts and muggers. I've had burglaries twice. I keep a loaded gun in my desk. Did you know that? I'd probably shoot my own pecker off. But I keep it in the desk and it makes me feel better. Ah, everyone's got problems.'

They both sat for a moment in the dim quiet, holding tall glasses of iced whisky. They clicked glasses and said 'Shalom' and let the effect of the liquor and the leather and the long friendship tranquillize the frayed end of a hard day.

'How's Harriet and the kids?' asked Moe.

'Fine, Moe. Fine.'

'Fine? That's all, just fine?'

There were certain ceremonies that Moe Katz observed ardently. He did not inquire to be polite. When he handed you a glass of whisky it was filled with all the hospitality he could muster. And when he asked about your family, he wanted to know. 'Son Kevin made All-East shortstop at Brown. Harriet's being sworn into the Third Order of Isabella – and this is very good Scotch.'

Katz leaned over and filled the glass. When Galvin asked about his family, Katz said fine and they both let it go at that. They didn't mention Moe's daughter, Rhonda, married to a Harvard Business School graduate, with two children now, and who for two summers had had a wild, dangerous crush on Galvin. It was during Galvin's bachelor days, and he had handled it gracefully. Without hurting her feelings. And although Moe was not supposed to know, and neither of them

20

even spoke of it, there was that lopsided debt between them.

Galvin drained his glass and crunched on the ice cubes. Moe looked older. He had always been small, but now he looked shrivelled. His face had become a spiderweb of lines. It was a face full of history.

Moe smiled at his old pupil. Galvin was no longer the perennial scamp. He was still good looking, and there was still the hint of a rogue in his smile, but he had crossed over some line halfway through his fifth decade, and the boyish good looks were beginning to collapse into character.

'How's the old litigation mill?' said Galvin, jiggling his glass for a refill. 'Keeping you busy?'

'I'll always be busy,' replied Moe. 'You know this practice. It's a candy store. I work nickel-and-dime cases out of a legal candy store twenty hours a day. When you take the crap no one else will handle, you keep busy. It's a living.'

'One more for the road,' said Galvin handing over his glass. Then: 'Moe, what do you hear?'

'What do you mean, what do I hear? You know I don't hear so good.'

'You hear pretty good when you want to. What do you hear about me on the street?'

Moe handed Galvin the glass. He took off his horn-rimmed glasses and polished them carefully with his waistcoat handkerchief. Then he studied the frames, holding them up to the light.

'I hear that you're headed for the lime pit.'

'It's all over, huh? Everybody knows?'

'Don't be a schmuck. It's a small community. When you break wind, everybody knows. And you've been breaking a lot of wind.'

'It's crazy. There isn't a lawyer in Boston who doesn't fool around. Boy, if everyone who ever tapped a secretary had to hand in his licence, we'd all be pushing apples. Hypocrites! Who's going to throw the first stone?'

'That's not the reason they sent a report to the bar overseers, and you know it. *You* don't just fool around. You have to pick the daughter of the guy who swings a lot of votes in the Chinese community – to say nothing of the fact that he runs the best restaurant in town. Mr Chen not only serves a very fine Cantonese cuisine, and delivers votes, but he raises a hell of a lot of early money around election time.'

Galvin tilted his head back and faced the ceiling. He laughed.

'What have you got to laugh about? You should be crying. Maybe even begging.'

'Moe, what if I told you that I can get out from under; not only that, keep my ticket, tuck one hundred grand in my pocket and practice gentleman law? What would you say?'

'I would say that I have given you too much Scotch whisky.'

'You think I'm joking. You think I'm joking, Moe? Do I sound like I'm joking?'

'It's one of your most endearing qualities, Galvin. I never know when you're joking. Whenever you came back from court and said you'd won a case, I thought you were joking. Tell me, are you joking?'

'I'm really serious.'

'But how could such a thing be? You must have something on Rutledge,' he said, referring to the chairman of the bar association's disciplinary board, the proper Roger Rutledge. 'You caught Rutledge making passes at young boys.'

'That's the trouble with you, Moe. You can't be serious. You know the case I have next week, the suit against Catherine Laboure Hospital?'

'Yes. I heard that you are suing God.'

'Matter of fact, Rutledge's firm is defending the hospital.'

'Well, God deserves the best. Daniel Webster probably isn't available.'

'Guess who came into my office not two hours ago waving a white flag?'

'Martin Buber?'

'No.'

'Martin Luther?'

'Come on.'

'I don't know any more Martins. Is it a Roger? Roger Rutledge?'

'Bigger than that.'

'Bigger than Roger Rutledge? Bigger than that you have to report.'

'Bishop Brophey.'

'Now we are talking serious. This man came to your office? What's he doing in this case?'

'Laboure is owned by the diocese, you know.'

'So? They carry malpractice insurance. What's the Vicar of Christ doing in your office?'

'Waving a white flag, if you can believe it. It's really funny. I should be out there holding up a bed sheet, what with all this disbarment business, and in comes the good Bishop offering me three hundred thousand dollars to settle the case.'

'It was probably just to administer Extreme Unction. You Irish are very strange like that: you enjoy wakes. He figures you're dead.'

Galvin was tilted far back on the couch, staring up blissfully at the ceiling, lost in that triumphant moment.

'Just like that! No waltzing around. Just, zingo: three hundred thousand dollars.'

'Three hundred thousand dollars?' asked Moe.

Galvin held up three fingers and nodded.

'So, naturally, you did the smart thing, the prudent thir You didn't take it.'

'How'd you know?'

'Because you wouldn't be here grinning like thar

23

just snuck off with a hundred-thousand-dollar fee. Because you're still on fire.'

'Moe! Moe! You should've been there. God, I wish I had a tape of that meeting. Christ, it was great.' Galvin was laughing hard now. 'He wanted to give me a pardon. A gold pass. Can you imagine that? He said he'd put the fix in with the bar association. And he could do it, too. All I had to do was settle the case. Then I could join his legal staff and have virgin nuns taking shorthand. It was as if he were offering me a new life.'

'Did you turn him down cold or did you say maybe you'd like to think it over?'

'Cold, Moe. No retreat. Burned all the bridges. I think I may even have insulted His Eminence. He came in there calling me Francis, you know, like I was still back in choir practice, and it got me mad. Well, if he was going to lay on his own spiritual mat, two could play that game. I started talking about sex.'

'I think maybe you caught something in the head at Iwo Jima. Not smart, Galvin. It is not smart to humiliate a man like Brophey. I judge him to be a man of great pride. He will want to get even. And he fights with pitchforks. You'll have a ruptured anal canal before he's through.'

'It's really funny, Moe. Laughable.'

'I hope that you are still laughing when you're pushing a cab down Tremont Street.'

'Hey, what's wrong with you? You're the guy who taught me to fight. I remember when I was a frightened young lawyer and I wanted to fold on a case, you sat me down here in this ~~nd gave me a lecture on not copping out. You told me to~~ ~~if I had to, but never fold. "Let the bastards~~ ~~~ht," you said. Remember?'

~~ty years ago when I didn't hear so~~ . I'm older. Smarter. I know when ~~ee you buried. I've seen too many~~ ~~be my age, Galvin, and it's a funny

glided in for a landing at Logan Airport, the tail-lights winking. The cabin portholes glowed in the dark sky.

'There's no such thing as never losing a case, Moe. Guys like Concannon settle when they sense a loss. Maybe that's why I had that visit from the Bishop. They have ten different angles and they work them all.'

'Did you come here for advice? Because if you want my advice, I'd say settle. Take the three hundred thousand and the free pass and the new start in life. Go back to Wellesley and grow old gracefully. Watch your kids go to college. Go to football games and get drunk with old friends. Give up the Chinese girl.'

'Moe – '

'I know you care for her. Just hear me out. I don't mean to insult you or cheapen this. I'm telling you reality. You are not thirty years old. You're fifty-something. Soon you'll be sixty and then you'll wonder what all the fuss was about. Your children will be old enough to hate you and you will hate yourself. What will any of this mean then? Let me get the Bishop on the phone.'

Moe picked up the telephone and stood poised, to make it easier for Galvin. 'I'll tell him that you were upset and that the visit caught you by surprise. You can see now that the offer was decent and fair. He'll listen.'

Temptation passed through Galvin like a sigh. And then it was gone. 'Put the phone down, Moe. It's too late. He wouldn't listen. Even if he would, I want this case. I want to try it. Those people turned my client into a vegetable and they think they can get away with it. They screwed up somebody's life and they think they can buy their way out for a lousy three hundred thousand dollars.'

'How are you going to stop them? They've got God and Concannon on their side.'

'I don't know. I've got a few angles. There were a lot of

29

nurses and doctors on duty that night. They can't all lie. I just know that I can't let them get away with it. Somebody has to yell Cop. You can't just turn someone into a cabbage and say, "Whoops! We made a mistake." Someone has to answer for it.'

'Galvin, Galvin,' said Moe, helping his friend on with his coat. 'You have no talent for surrender. Are you sure there isn't a little Hebrew blood in your background?'

'I don't know, Moe. Maybe *I* am getting a little hard of hearing.'

3

There was no putting it off. Today, after months of evasion, Galvin had to see his client.

It was Saturday, and Saturdays were long for Galvin. There were no football weekends in a one-man office. Saturdays were workdays. When he was first getting started, he hadn't minded so much. He'd even relished it – the unencumbered hours when he would loosen his tie and roll up his sleeves and whip the files into shape with inexhaustible energy. Afterwards, there was the reward of feeling virtuous.

But now there were hardly any files. And as he looked out the window of his apartment at the persistent storm, it seemed as if the weather matched his mood. The rain streaked down the windows, and the wind groaned through the cracks. Galvin scratched the stubble on his face and reminded himself to shave when he got to the office. Lois was sound asleep, and he let himself out quietly.

Billy Morrisey's pub lay halfway between home and the office, just on the lip of Boston's 'Combat Zone'. It drew an earthy clientele. Galvin occupied a special niche among the cab drivers and truckers and hard-hats. They came over and chatted about the Bruins and the Red Sox, but they called him 'Counsellor', conferring rank and a certain distance.

On Saturday mornings, Billy Morrisey expected Galvin. 'Pretty mean out there,' Morrisey said as Galvin shook off the rain and hung his coat on a wooden peg.

He slid a diluted Scotch across the bar, and Galvin downed the drink and mopped his head with a towel Morrisey had laid out.

'Thanks, Billy,' he said, watching as the bartender poured

him another Scotch and water.

Morrisey was nearing 70. He'd been in business for as long as anyone could remember. He knew all the secrets. He knew all the stories. He had known Galvin's father, Dr Jack Galvin. But the things that Billy Morrisey knew were never laid out on top of his bar. It became a subtle factor in the way he treated you. If he smiled at you and treated you well, it meant that Billy knew your story and you had passed some test of character. If he was brisk and businesslike, that too was a judgment.

Billy handed Galvin his third drink and withdrew to another part of the bar. Galvin cupped the glass in his hand, hardly moving. 'How's Moe?' asked Billy.

'Fine,' said Galvin.

Billy always asked about Moe. It didn't matter to him that the partnership had ended – he always associated Galvin with Moe, the Irishman and the Jew.

'He never comes in here anymore,' said Billy, dusting some imaginary speck from the bar.

Galvin put the glass to his lips and swallowed. The sleeve on his jacket was a little frayed. Moe would have been proud.

'Seventy-five-dollar suits have a certain integrity,' Moe had told him.

And it was true. Moe's lessons were all hard-won truths. Galvin respected the old man greatly. Which explained Moe's daughter. If he had not taken advantage of Rhonda, a real knockout, it had been only partly a matter of honour. When it came to sex Galvin had very little honour. But he owed that to Moe; he owed Moe his career, and more.

It had its roots in an accident and a strange quirk of timing. There was also the matter of the immovable object and the irresistible force; that is, Galvin's Irish stubbornness against the pervasive cruelty of the Boston aristocracy . . .

It was the summer of 1945, in the wilting heat of August, and yet there was a peculiar buoyancy in the air. The war against Japan was about to end, and the streets of Boston were filled with breathless servicemen awaiting official victory. The civilian population was in a giddy mood after four years of casualty lists. The evidence of the impending celebration was everywhere. On the MTA, even the stone faces of the commuters were bright with anticipation.

All except one young man. He had been wounded at Iwo Jima and walked with a slight limp. The leg would soon heal. He was not so sure about his spirit. The youth felt bitter, cut off from the great jubilance about to burst across the land.

It was pure luck that Moe Katz spotted Galvin on the crowded subway platform that noontime. Moe was a little frantic. A world war might be about to end, but he had to be in two places at the same time. At two, he was due back in court for the dismissal of charges against a client accused of passing a bad cheque. He couldn't afford to be late. Someone could change his mind: the district attorney, the complaining witness or even the judge. At the same time, Moe had to see that a subpoena was served on a miscreant husband. If he failed, the man would surely flee the state, and Moe's client, the wife, would lose her alimony and child support.

The problem was that in the general atmosphere of reverie, no one wanted to work, or even seemed capable of serious employment. All the city marshals had their hands full. Then Moe Katz spotted the sober-faced young man, Frank Galvin, standing at the Park Street station. It was such a wild chance, such an improbable thing; but Moe gave the stranger the subpoena and $5, and a powerful trust was born.

It was Galvin's first encounter with the law, and it changed his life.

Galvin became Moe's apprentice and the bonding went deeper. Within limits and as far as it could go under the circumstances, Galvin became Moe's surrogate son. Moe paid Galvin's way through four difficult years of night courses at Governor

Bradford Law School, a diploma mill willing to embrace anyone with the price of tuition.

Galvin responded with uncommon devotion. He performed the expected legwork, serving summonses and researching cases, and volunteered for extra duty. He ran out for cigars and coffee. He made certain that Moe remembered to eat, and he stayed with him long into the night, listening to Moe lecture and complain and ramble on about legality and human behaviour. He was a patient and grateful audience. For Galvin was learning the law in the trenches, and his bitterness was transformed into vitality. When Moe Katz plucked Galvin off the subway platform, the youth had been angry and disgusted. He was ripe for self-destruction. Not suicide, because he was not the type, but serious, prolonged, deadly drinking. He might have wound up on the docks during the day and in an alley at night. It was Galvin's nightmare.

When Marine Corporal Galvin came back from the South Pacific, he was unprepared for defeat. But that was what it was like. He had run smack into the same obstinate snobbish rejection that had been the despair of his youth. An antibody of Ivy League preference had formed around the best jobs to keep out riffraff like Galvin.

Galvin had worn his Marine Corps greens. Still rejection. Then he put on his dress blues, with ribbons – the Purple Heart, Pacific Theatre, Combat Infantry, others of lesser rank.

'Maybe in six months,' the official at the Bay State Colonial Bank had told him with that familiar vague sneer of finality. Things hadn't changed. He reverted to civilian clothing – double-breasted grey sharkskin, white shirt, grey felt hat. He was still out of place.

Moments before Katz had seen Galvin at the courthouse subway station, a man named Hainsworthy at Massachusetts Life & Casualty had halfheartedly interviewed the young man, taking calls and chuckling to friends about social blunders at a recent cocktail party. He had held the application at arm's length and offered Galvin what he termed a career opening in the mail room. Fresh from Iwo, Galvin took it for the insult it was. He was still wearing the aftermath on his face when Moe Katz saw him. Maybe Moe even sensed some affinity in that expression. Some memory of Brahmin disapproval.

The wound would never heal. Every time Galvin seemed on the verge of social acceptability, he would hear the man offering him a job in the mail room.

But there was another voice inside Galvin that whispered caution. He was wooed by the thought that he would finally be safe when he achieved the proper degree of respectability. There was, in that interior voice, the suggestion that his life would be 'solved' if he could just make enough money, make the right connections, become part of the Boston aristocracy.

The two voices were in an endless war. The advance of one was always at the expense of the other. It meant, inevitably, that there were never any unqualified victories in Galvin's life. He didn't even know whom to root for. He liked the Red Sox only when they were losing.

So it was, so it had always been from his childhood. He carried the memories like a fuse. When he brooded too much, or when he was deep into his whisky, the fuse would start burning and he would talk about his father, the late Dr Jack Galvin. He gave his life on the altar of public service, the son would say. A fine broth of a man, that, he would add, falling into a kind of sentimental brogue. A doctor during the great Depression. Not like the country-club doctors nowadays, with their Medicare annuities and nursing-home write-offs. A family doctor. A humble man who made house calls and had no head for business. He took whatever fees he could collect, and that wasn't much in the Depression. You brought home roast chickens and jellied hams and jars of preserves. And if you didn't starve, you didn't get rich.

Frank Galvin grew up on those home-cooked fees that his father collected for delivering half the infant population of the

South End. And there was a spot deep inside Frank Galvin which was reserved for the memory of his father. He remembered most of all the mornings when he awoke in the dark, before dawn, when his father had been out on one of his urgent missions. He would wait up for him, and when he heard the car, he would come down and make his father a cup of tea in the stone-cold kitchen.

His father's eyes would be bloodshot, he'd sigh wearily, but he was too keyed up to sleep. They would sit at the kitchen table, father and son, hardly speaking, snug together. Upstairs, Mary Galvin was still asleep, and those moments alone like that with his father were jealously held islands to Frank. He would be curled into a blanket and his father would sip tea and smoke one cigarette after another and Frank knew that there was no other part of their lives so private.

Frank took it for granted that he would go to Georgetown and then to Harvard Med. It was not something they ever spoke about.

In many ways, the intimacy was an imaginary one. Frank realized that later, after everything fell apart. He had assumed too much. He had placed his father on a remote, inaccessible pedestal. But then, everyone did. Jack Galvin, after all, was a doctor. His work was too important to be interrupted by such mundane things as mowing the lawn, or taking his son to a baseball game. He was a doctor. He didn't have to check Frank's homework or ask his wife how the day had gone. He was busy saving lives. In comparison, everything else seemed trivial.

So no one noticed that it was all too much for Dr Galvin. Frank didn't really understand what went wrong. He never saw the symptoms, or else he misread them. But somewhere along the way, his father's stamina broke. Other doctors could take a day off or build an investment portfolio or worry about a golf score. But Jack Galvin was too sensitive, or too weak. Frank could never decide which.

Jack Galvin was haunted. Each death became harder to bear. They all died, after all. All the patients. Sooner or later. They came to him, the new patients, with their pleading eyes, and it became exhausting to lie. The best he could offer was a reprieve. And then there would be the inevitable, inexplicable death. A young child would die for no apparent reason, and all the medicine and all the technology seemed a waste. At night, he lay in bed terrified of sleep. Each time he closed his eyes, the dead patients would come to visit him. They would come as he remembered them in life. Nothing grotesque. Not accusingly. Just persistently.

He started drinking gin to get to sleep. Then he began to miss morning rounds. He forgot about office hours. He would start out on a house call and never get there. He became reluctant to take on new patients.

The decline didn't take long. New patients stopped coming. Old ones dropped off. Colleagues began whispering about his 'problem'. They had to cover for him during the most routine procedures. The gin that was so hard to detect became impossible to conceal. He no longer walked to work – he staggered.

Soon, they took away his hospital privileges. That seemed to break the last thread holding him together. He went from gin to beer to cheap wine and finally straight to medicinal alcohol. At the end, he was shooting up with Demerol and morphine.

They found Dr Galvin one dreary morning in a mud-splattered hallway near the Old Howard Burlesque Theatre in Scollay Square. When the police returned the few pitiful effects to his wife – a cracked black bag and some worn-out instruments – she never cried. 'He's *been* dead awhile,' she said coldly.

Dr Galvin was 36 years old when he died.

The Boston Medical Society paid for Jack Galvin's funeral. It was more than the society had ever done for him in life. Frank, who was 9 at the time, bore the brunt of his mother's disappointment. She was 29 years old, but she retired forever from life. She never took off her widow's weeds, and every hint of sex or desirability or passion was erased from her life. It was not so much her love for Jack Galvin that made her behave so; it was spite. She turned the old brownstone into a boardinghouse, reminding Frank that that was what her husband had forced her to. That was where it all ended. The admonition so meaningfully unspoken was not lost on her only son.

Frank Galvin buckled down and set about making good. He hawked beer at Fenway Park and sold programmes at Harvard Stadium. He shovelled snow for the street department and spiked railroad ties on the Boston & Maine. He even got through four years at Boston College-Intown in the midst of a world war.

He was imbued with an awesome sense of purpose and responsibility. It was as if his father had left behind a pile of unpaid promises that had to be met. He owed the world a success.

It made it easier when he sold insurance policies and collected bills and finally joined the Marines. The war had come as an interruption in his headlong quest for vindication, and he was not about to ignore even that responsibility. He picked the roughest service.

The reality of combat and the possibility of death were a sobering shock. The wound was an embarrassment. He was shot in the leg by one of his own buddies when they ran screaming onto an undefended beach. There was no glory. There didn't even seem to be much purpose. He was listed in the casualty report as having been hit by 'friendly fire', as if the torn flesh could tell the difference.

Galvin was shipped home on a blood-caked hospital ship with all the other disillusioned casualties. At night, he listened to them die as the overworked nurses attended to the sure survivors. Somewhere in the ocean, when the shock had worn

38

off, men woke up to the fact that they had lost legs or arms or had been crippled for life, and a pall settled over the ship. Galvin's wound was not overly debilitating, but heroism and life were not what he had thought they would be.

The law seemed a perfect solution to all of Galvin's personal and professional quandaries. There was, built into the practice, cynicism.

Galvin found that he could succeed in life and still not burn himself out. He would be saved from moral immolation. He didn't even mind the menial work of his apprenticeship. He welcomed the running and fetching and the antidote of Moe Katz to the academic platitudes he was fed in school. Moe Katz came at the law like a lover who knew all of the beloved's flaws and fallacies yet felt she was too dear to ever be abandoned.

Moe would sit back in his chair late at night after all the others had gone home, holding a glass of whisky in one hand and a cigar in the other. He sampled them each to remind himself of the pleasures of taste while he spoke softly about the beauties of the law.

'You'll see,' he would say, 'all the things that happen in a courtroom. It's a world in itself. A whole new world. The lawyers are like the players. They come into court wearing fancy suits and old suits. It doesn't matter. They look like Spencer Tracy or Adolphe Menjou. It doesn't matter. They can even stick a finger in their nose and you think that this is a real zhlub. Then he opens his mouth and the most beautiful things come out. Out comes Oliver Wendell Holmes. Beauties. Great lawyers in tattered suits! It makes you want to cry. Then they have the great theatrical lawyers. The actors. They strut up and down in front of the jury, showing their cuff links and watching their own reflection in the eyes of the audience. Not a crease in their clothing.

'But I'll tell you the best. The best! The best aren't the great dressers or the great actors, not the great theoretical lawyers.

The very best are the lawyers who do their homework. The guys who come into court with the case down cold. Beginning to end. Can't be fooled. You know, you never really surprise a good lawyer. He never asks a question if he doesn't already know the answer. He comes prepared. This is the guy who'll kill you every time.'

None of it was lost on Galvin. Galvin watched and learned and culled from Moe's great store of wisdom, extracting gems that glistened with what Moe would call 'probative polish.'

Moe's witnesses could all remember particular dates, especially when they were crucial to his case. It was seventeen days after Palm Sunday, or three weeks before Kathleen Mary's First Communion. They were just coming from Mass or on their way to something holy and pure. A jury would accept a plausible psychic mnemonic from Moe's clients.

There were many axioms. Galvin learned not to look too good when he went into court. He had to give the cab drivers and bartenders and hod carriers someone to identify with.

'Hold your hat in your hand when you ask for justice,' counselled Moe. 'And don't forget – seventy-five-dollar suits have a certain integrity to them.'

Such advice stood Galvin in good stead for the many years that he remained with Moe Katz. Until he acquired a taste for better suits.

'One more for the road, Counsellor?' asked Billy. It was his way of saying that it was time to go. It jarred Galvin back to the present.

'I've had enough, thanks,' replied Galvin.

As Galvin shouldered into his raincoat, Billy leaned closer, his leathery face full of concern: 'If I can be of any help . . . '

'Help?' Galvin shrugged as he buttoned his coat. 'You just keep my nook warm. That's all the help I need. And Billy, don't cheat yourself on the tab.'

But both Billy and Galvin knew that the morning round was on the house.

The rain slackened by evening. Galvin's headlights caught the sombre concrete entrance to the building, and he hesitated before turning off the ignition. Through the blurred windshield, he stared at the name over the entrance: HOLY GHOST HOSPITAL. It was getting dark, and the lights went on in the building. He had spent all day going over the files. There was no longer any possible delay. He climbed out of the car into the rain and cold and night.

The lobby was brisk and efficient. It tinkled like ice.

'I am Frank Galvin,' he told a receptionist. 'I believe you're expecting me.'

A young nurse came up and smiled and took his hand. He felt as if he were being consoled. 'I'm Deborah Ruth Rosen's lawyer,' he said.

'Yes,' she said. 'Please have a seat. I'll get the supervisor.'

There were no casual visitors to the chronic-care facilities. There were only the duty bound. And no matter how careful the preparation, they were invariably stricken by the ordeal they were about to undergo.

'Mr Galvin,' said the voice, and Galvin jumped. 'I'm Stacy Curtis, the supervisor of nurses at the Cardinal O'Connell Wing.'

'I'm Mrs Rosen's lawyer,' he stammered.

'I know,' she said, accustomed to the self-consciousness of visitors. 'Debbie's had a good day. She'll be glad to see you.'

There were plastic flowers in a dry vase on the nightstand and a crucifix on the wall.

On the high hospital bed, under the pulleys and tubes, like a puppet lay his client. She barely left an indentation on the mattress.

Galvin's files said that Deborah Ruth Rosen was 5 feet 3

inches tall and weighed 110 pounds. But people shrink in coma. They collapse into a foetal position, as if withdrawing from life back into the womb. First the fat goes. The liquids keep alive the vital organs, but there is no excess food for fat. Then the muscles atrophy and disappear. The body seems to fade into skin and bone.

After four years, Deborah Ruth Rosen had become the size of a 10-year-old child. The staff had come to treat her as a child. 'Debbie, dear, you have a visitor,' said Miss Curtis. 'It's Mr Galvin. An old friend.'

Across the bed stood another nurse, watching Galvin's face. Galvin didn't move. A pair of doll's eyes bulged from bony sockets. Thin lips quivered and saliva drooled from a withered mouth.

'She's happy to see you,' said the other nurse. 'She salivates when she's pleased.'

The liquids dripped into her veins from bottles strung over the bed. Her waste drained into discreetly concealed receptacles. A respirator wheezed for Deborah Ruth Rosen. The smell in the room was not human.

'Would you like to be alone?' asked Miss Curtis.

The light reflected from the carefully combed strands of hair. The eyes stared blankly at the ceiling. He moved closer. He touched her cold hand. Looked at her thin, cracked lips.

He moved his lips as if to say something. But no words came. Then he turned and left.

4

At the very moment when all the tactical and strategic talent were ganging up at Rutledge, Guthrie, Cabot & Moore – the upper-crust law firm with authentic Winslow Homer seascapes on the wall, where the switchboard did not ring, but instead emitted a polite ping – at the same instant as they converged to plot his downfall, Frank Galvin confronted himself.

One hundred grand! He had been awake most of the night agonizing over it. He now sat in his office nibbling on a pencil and mulling the offer. As he rolled the figure around in his mind, he bit harder, splintering the pencil. He put his feet up on his desk and stretched back in his creaking swivel chair. A few files stashed on the radiator behind him toppled to the floor.

One hundred thousand dollars!

Galvin looked around him, struck by the dinginess of the office. The afternoon sun caught the flights of dust like searchlights spotting enemy bombers. The ceiling was all cracked, and every time the door slammed, plaster dust broke loose, collecting in little puddles along the bookcase and on top of the filing cabinets.

It was dismal, he thought. How come he had never noticed before?

He stared at the telephone, which did not ring.

'Peg,' he said, flipping the secretarial intercom, 'get me Bishop Brophey's number. Try the Chancery on Lake Street.'

'Brophey? On Lake Street? What do you want with His Excellency?'

'Peg, why do you always repeat what I say?'

'Repeat what you say?'

'Just get me the number. Don't ask questions. Not now. I'm not in the mood. Please, just get it. And don't tell me it's unlisted.'

'The Bishop. Right. Don't get heartburn . . . Got it right here in the Brighton directory: Algonquin 9635. Jesus, Mary, such an ordinary number. For a Bishop! I'd have expected something a little more appropriate to his rank. Goodness, even the Patriots football team has something classy. Commonwealth 1776.'

'What would you say to Paradise 1177? Or Intercourse 7711?' Galvin prattled, a tinge of humour returning to his voice. 'Did you know, Peggy Twomy, that there are two towns in Pennsylvania called Intercourse and Paradise? Paradise is next to Intercourse. Those who know say the two are very close . . . Are you still there, Peg-o'-my-heart?'

'Not funny – and speaking about obscenities, did you know that the IRS man was in again yesterday? Second time in two weeks. Wants to look at the Chinese rug you listed at six thousand eight hundred dollars under Office Fixtures. I'm sick of covering for you, Galvin. You'd think I was Rose Mary Woods or someone. I'm out of excuses. I already told him it was out at the cleaner's. Yesterday I said your wife took it for the weekend – you know, like visitation. He started quoting the US Code, Title Eighteen. Gets you one year in the federal penitentiary for lying to an official of the US Government. I tried to laugh it off.'

'Well, how'd ya do, Rose Mary?'

'He wasn't laughing. He's coming back Monday. I suggest you borrow the Ming back and at least have it rolled up in the hallway.'

'Loyalty, Peg. Second-finest quality a secretary can have. After they passed out your loyalty, Peg, they threw away the mould.'

'Don't give me that, Galvin. You've always had more than your share of loyalty from me. Been fronting for you for years.

Be nice if it was reflected in the pay envelope . . . What's the first-best quality?'

'Big tits.'

Galvin scribbled the Chancery number on a scratch pad and stared at the phone. He tilted back farther in his chair, dislodging a few more files. Then he crumpled the scratch paper and slam-dunked it into the wastebasket.

It was four o'clock. Peggy would be deep into her Gothic paperback, which she would not let go until the 5 P.M. exodus. She was not overburdened by work – the phone seldom rang, there was little dictation – so she could finish a Mary Stewart novel in two days. But she was burning with curiosity.

'Do you want me to try getting through to the Bishop's executive secretary?' she said sweetly over the intercom.

'I'll handle it.'

Peggy pretended not to hear. 'I happen to know Monsignor Kerrigan. He played tackle at BC with my uncle Al. Used to be curate at Lady of Good Counsel in Quincy. He's very friendly with Monsignor O'Boyle, who's the Bishop's right-hand man –'

'Thanks, Peg. I can handle it.'

Peggy Twomy did not stand for that kind of treatment. It was the family-kitchen tactics brought into the office. There was, in their relationship, the abrasive devotion of any domestic couple.

'That man was in for the rent yesterday' – her voice testy. 'I told him you were in court. He said he'd have you in court again. You're three months down now. He said that made you a tenant in sufferance, but he's doing all the suffering. He wants you to meet your obligation by Friday or vacate.'

Galvin listened with eyes clenched.

'I'll be leaving at five. There's nothing on for tomorrow. Oh, by the way, there was a message. The China Doll wants you to call.'

'Thanks, Peg. You're all heart.'

'Galvin,' she said in her best weary-but-adoring motherly tones, 'I'm really worried about you. You might try dropping into St Anthony's shrine on Arch Street and make a general confession. The shrine's run by the Franciscans, you know. They've kept their feet on the ground. Not like the Jesuits. You can get some real solace down there.'

'I appreciate that, Peg. Say the Stations of the Cross for me and don't forget to take down the mail.'

She would not bother him again. At $250 a week, Peggy Twomy was a little too expensive for his budget. The little work that she had to do she did poorly. But she had been with him for nine years. She needed the money. And she knew all his secrets. He could be comfortable with her. And his pride just wouldn't allow him to bring in an answering service – a dead giveaway of the fiscal skids.

Galvin reached into the bottom drawer of his desk, scuffled under the camouflage of papers and pulled out an almost-empty bottle of Scotch. He drained it into a used paper cup, shaking out the last drop before slipping the bottle into the wastebasket. Then he reached behind two volumes of Williston on Contracts and pulled out an unopened bottle of Jameson and Sons. He sat at his desk and held the bottle up to the light, watching the reflection dance on the wall. Then he christened it with a few healthy swallows.

'Ten hundred hundred!' he said out loud.

The hiss of the radiator, the Scotch and the twilight had put him into a reflective mood. He gazed at the papers on his desk and saw that the morning mail had grown pink with dunning letters and bills.

Galvin took another pull on the Jameson's and tried to retrace his road to the ragged edge. He had tried to check things. As clients became scarce and fees dwindled, he had started drafting wills without charge, hoping to become the attorney for the estate. He had begun placing ads in law journals, then in the *Boston Globe* and finally in the gossip tabloids, claiming to be a legal clinic.

He attended wakes: wakes in West Roxbury, Everett and Chelsea; in Revere, Hyde Park and Jamaica Plain; occasionally venturing to bedroom towns like Arlington and Melrose and as far north as Swampscott. A ten-spot to Tippy Larkin of Larkin Brothers Funeral Home in Southie would get him the double handshake in front of a bereaved widow.

'He's a grand Irish lawyer, Mrs Canavan,' Tippy would say. 'You might need some help against the trucking company that did poor Hal in.'

But Galvin knew that it was a hell of a way to practise law. It was demeaning. And he suspected that Larkin and the others he tipped generously stoked many similar fires.

To look busy, he scheduled all his appointments for 11 A.M. But even then it was ghostly in the waiting room. So he made it 11 A.M. on Tuesdays. Even then it was lonely and depressing. When the telephone did ring, it was usually the landlord asking for the rent or the lawbook company threatening legal action.

Galvin reached into the wastebasket, fishing past the sticky remnants of several lunches, plucked out the crumpled note bearing the Chancery number and carefully flattened it out. No doubt about it, he thought, a very prosaic number. He smoothed it on his desk, as if he were performing an art restoration.

He was alone now, without the bravado for Moe Katz or the defiance for Bishop Brophey or the impatience for Peggy Twomy; alone with all the bills and the empty calendar and the silent telephone and the wrinkled paper with the easy way out.

It was Moe's fault. All Moe had taught him was Yiddish whiplash. No diversity. He should have learned something about condominiums and tax shelters and federal regulations.

He blamed no-fault insurance. Dried up a good source of business. The little cases. The bread-and-butter fees. A few phone calls, a friendly insurance adjuster and it paid the rent and secretary.

The Governor called it insurance reform. What a crock. All it did was drive all the poor people out of court. There were no fast-buck cases anymore. And if anybody needed the fast buck, it was the poor. The courts were now playpens for the rich; nothing but tax litigation and corporate disputes.

His attempts to diversify had been sad and futile. He had hustled around, like the rest of the whiplash lawyers, setting up tax shelters and cash-flow dodges for his friends. Most fees he collected in worthless stocks. He had no head for business.

He knew now that it had been a mistake to leave Moe Katz's office nine years ago. Moe had seen the day of the individual practitioner coming to an end. Survival, Moe had advised, depended on sticking together. That, or knuckling under to the big law firms, keeping your nose clean for the gold watch and a final handshake. It had not been an acrimonious parting, although there were wounds. Moe had never uttered a word of reproach, but Galvin knew he was hurt.

He had nurtured, schooled and dressed Galvin. Taught him legal moves and feints. In a way, Galvin was Moe's alter ego, the son he'd never had. He loved Galvin's irascibility, his stubbornness, the way he'd rail against the Yankee Establishment.

There had been a farewell party at one of the better lobster houses. It was a miserable, drunken affair in which sentiments were thick and overdone. They had slugged drunken toasts to each other, talking about love, never mentioning the anger.

When Galvin had driven Moe home, the old man wouldn't leave the car. There was something he wanted to say, but he didn't know how to say it. They sat there, the two men, alone in the cold car for ten minutes.

'My father was a Shylock,' said Moe Katz. 'You didn't know

that, did you? Nobody does. He worked in the Fall River mills, but his real job was lending money to the other people who worked in the mills at great interest rates. That was how he put me through law school. He acquired this great respect for the law because he was outside of it.'

Galvin did not speak, and he did not look over to his friend in the passenger seat.

'It happens to a lot of people, you know,' Moe continued. 'There are things they cannot have and so they want them even more. I see this. My father had a great love for the law. It didn't come to me until late in life. You see, I already had the law, so I didn't see it the way that he did. I take clients now who are Shylocks. Sleazy people. They bust kneecaps for money. I think, maybe this would have been my father. I try to see the law through their eyes. Through his eyes.'

'Are you hitting me for a loan?' said Galvin.

Moe laughed. 'No, schmuck, I just want you to remember that what you want may not be what you think.'

Getting his own office had been a little like running away from home and setting up his own apartment. It was filled with an exhilarating sense of sin. He'd had it decorated by Kerry Collins, an artsy friend who was into crafts. They had played at the decoration like lovers, shopping around for foamy prints and lobster traps and fishing nets and ship's lanterns. It looked like something out of a whaling museum.

At the end, when she realized that she was not going to be part of the decor, Kerry had presented him with a bill.

'That's all I am to you anyway,' she'd said, handing him the itemized account of her time – 'just another tradesman.'

'You mean you want me to *treat* you like any other tradesman?' he said, matching her indignation.

'No more. No less.'

'Very well,' he said, wounded.

And he was true to his word. Like any other such bill, it never got paid.

For a while, it looked as if Galvin might succeed. He wore pin-striped suits and button-down collars, and he carried an unopened umbrella on sunny days. He attempted to blend into the State Street image.

But he was a prisoner of a powerful streak of rebellion. The men in the blue-ribbon firms were too controlled, too inbred. Galvin occasionally got stinking drunk and would spit in their eye. On one occasion, he threw up on the doorstep of the Harvard Club. At the time, the club was holding his application for associate membership. The board of directors, who never spoke above an arched eyebrow, simply filed the application in the inactive file. He never got the lucrative probate appointments that membership in such an organization would ensure.

He attended local bar meetings where lawyers got together and lied to each other about how well they were doing. He lunched at Locke-Ober and managed to become enscrolled on the rolls of the Clover Club, Boston's élitist society of Irish-tinged professionals, where he dined on Saturday nights. He tried. He listened and backslapped and laughed and applauded and dished out insincere accolades until he would get drunk and make a fool of himself. He could join, but he could never belong.

As the sun disappeared behind the Prudential Tower, Galvin felt the weight of a great silence. He was alone. He glanced at his watch. It was five forty-five. Peggy was long gone.

The lights from the adjacent John Hancock Building winked on and off as the night cleaning crew moved through the building. Galvin sighed and got up and began shutting off the lights. He put the wastebasket into the hallway. Then he straightened the magazines in the reception area. They were all a year old.

'A hundred thousand dollars!' he said.

He started to leave, then stopped and went back to his desk. He picked up the paper with the Chancery number on it, folded it and put it into his pocket, and left.

5

On Monday nights, the cocktail waitresses at the Harbor Lights Lounge at the top of Somerset Towers got dressed up as SPARSs and WACs and Army nurses. The piano played nonstop – 'I'll Be Seeing you,' 'Rose of San Antone,' 'Let's Remember Pearl Harbor,' 'Wild Blue Yonder' and 'We'll Meet Again.' Monday night was World War II night at the Harbor Lights Lounge, and it was Apple Blossom Time.

The hot pilots and the boys who had been company clerks and the iron men of Bastogne had been equalized by time. They wore their beer bellies like chevrons. In the dim lights of the lounge, under the spell of the liquor and the old songs and the old uniforms, they were all still heroes. Fat and fiftyish, the bald eagles flew again.

Galvin liked it there, where they still rolled out the barrel, even if he was not one of the backslappers. He liked being there, slumped over the bar, sucking in beer and whisky chasers, standing under the model Spitfires and model Messerschmitts, listening to all the old songs sounding so brokenhearted, coming as they did from the throats of men and women parched for that lost sentiment.

'You look as if your side lost,' said the young voice behind Galvin's ear. You could be fooled by such voices, if you allowed yourself. 'Do you have a light, General?'

Galvin didn't say anything. He reached for a book of matches on the bar and lit one, and as it flared, he saw her. Stunning – pure silk. She was not one of the regulars. Not one of the weary old camp followers, still trailing some whiff of glory. Still trying to look 25. On World War II nights, they were always kind to each other at the Harbor Lights Lounge.

52

The women called the fading men boys. And the men hid the disappointment of the first sight. They always called them girls.

But this one singed Galvin's finger. She was tall and willowy, and held together in graceful curves and manner. He burned his finger on the match.

'Good thing I didn't ask for a ride home,' she said.

She smiled a smile that was full of self-confidence and understanding. She knew that she was attractive and realized that her presence was an incongruity. But she was smart enough to sneak past it.

'It's no use,' he said. 'It will never work out between us.'

'Oh, and I suppose that's my fault? Like the match?'

'Of course,' he said. 'Not that it matters. But I blame you. I blame you because, well, just look at yourself. That's a terrible thing to do to a man like me.'

'What's a terrible thing to do to a man like you?'

'It's like holding up a recruiting poster,' he said. 'You make me feel like a wart.'

'Maybe if we tried to talk things out,' she offered.

'Great,' he said, extending his hand. 'The name's Frank. I always think it's important for people to get the names straight when they're trying to work things out.'

'Donna,' she said stoutly, firmly returning his handshake. 'Couldn't agree with you more, Fred.'

'No, no. Frank. As in Francis.'

'Don't be silly. That's a girl's name. I'd say that you were Fred. And a damn good Fred, unless I miss my guess.'

'Swell, Margie. Now how about something to drink?'

'You know me, Fred.'

Sometimes the chemistry is just so. Sometimes the lines of humour and sensitivity intersect perfectly. He liked her instantly. Even if she did make him feel like a wart. Not that she was taller. But he had to stand erect to match her height. It destroyed his slump.

And then another piece of magic – the bartender was right there to take the order. There were people who spent an hour trying to get his attention. But here he was, smiling and asking what'll they have. Galvin took it as an omen. He should be playing poker, he thought.

She wore gloves. When she reached for the white wine, she had on chic leather gloves. Like a pilot. Or a hit man.

They paused for the drinks, as if they were waiting for a traffic light to change. There was no urgency in the silence between the sips.

'I take it,' she began, 'that you are a veteran of The Big One, as WW Two is referred to around here.'

He nodded.

'Where did you serve?'

'Well, I tried to do my bit for everyone. Started out in the RAF and then I was in the Luftwaffe. I commanded a U-boat, but the food was awful. I ended up in tanks. Great grub.'

'You must have an interesting résumé.'

'Most people think I'm fickle. There are even some who question my patriotism, if you can believe that. There I was doing a thankless, dirty job and those shirkers don't even say thanks!'

'They're just jealous,' she said, holding up her wineglass in a salute. 'I would be proud to serve under you.'

The bartender took this as a signal for a refill.

Galvin still wore his wedding ring. There were occasions when Galvin slipped it off, but it left a discoloration – a ghost, he called it – and that was more damning than the thing itself. Besides, it was demeaning to sneak it on and off. Not that it counted for much with Galvin. He didn't even know whom he wore it for anymore – whether his wife or Lois Chen.

He saw her glance at the ring and then look away.

'We check our compunctions at the door,' he volunteered bravely. She smiled. 'It's a friendship ring,' he said.

'Not that it matters,' she said.

'You'll let me have my mystery, won't you?'

'And me mine,' she said, emptying the glass.

'No such thing,' he said. 'I'm a dangerously jealous man.'

He took their drinks and moved to a corner table. He felt exposed at the bar, with every man making one sortie past his beautiful companion.

'I've been here before,' she said, looking around the room clinically.

'Oh?' he said. 'And where did *you* serve?'

'I served drinks all through collège. I was a cocktail waitress. And I went through the whole war in little snatches, between the bar and the tables. I've been from Tarawa to the Rhine and back again.'

'Here's to old soldiers,' he said, flagging another round.

'I never really understood it,' she said, half to herself. 'I never understood the *appeal* of that damn war. You know, my father would choke up every time he saw a John Wayne movie. There was no such thing as too corny for him. He saluted when the flag went by, and he stood up for the National Anthem. With such pride! With such fierce pride! Almost as if he was mad about it.'

Galvin drank his whisky and chased it with his beer. In his mellow glow he couldn't decide which side he was on. Part of him was with the father and the sheer dumb hopelessness of such feelings. And part of him understood the girl's bewildered cynicism.

'It's very strange,' she said. 'It feels so lonely here.'

'I know what you mean, kid. But I'll tell you something: I'm lonely at singles bars.'

She nodded. She understood. She smiled.

'It's pretty romantic, though,' she said, looking up at the model dogfights. 'It must have been something when people could still be heroes. All the men coming home decked out with ribbons and medals. Block parties and all. It really must have been something.'

'Yeah,' he said. 'It was something.'

'You know, I still get choked up over the sixties, when I was in college. We were all crazy and angry and innocent. Lying down in front of draft boards, and marching. Marching in Washington and in the Common. There were always marches. I'll bet we marched as much as the Third Army.'

'Not quite,' he said, and he was beginning to get a little annoyed.

'Sometimes I see someone I went to BU with – you know, one of the long-haired dopers – and there he is all slick and neat and carrying an attaché case. Mr Clean. We look at each other and he sees me and there is that smirk of recognition.'

'It's not the same thing,' he said.

'No,' she said, catching his tone. 'It's not the same thing. You know what I used to wonder when I worked here? I used to wonder how the veterans of the Wehrmacht spent Monday nights.'

He shrugged. He was fighting off the effects of five Scotches and a lot of beer. She was saying something. And she was beautiful. He looked up and smiled and tried to pay attention.

'Did you fight the Japs?' she asked.

'No,' he lied, unsure of why he lied except to keep the terms of the relationship fundamentally dishonest. 'I was a Remington Raider.'

She looked puzzled.

'I was a company clerk at Fort Dix in New Jersey,' he said. 'It was rough. We had a German cook that I engaged in combat. He used to serve eight eggs for twelve guys. No one can say that I was not provoked. He could have been sending those missing eggs to relatives in Germany for all we knew. I threatened to hit him with my typewriter. It was a Remington. That put him straight. We got our eggs after that. Listen, those Remingtons can take out an eye.'

She was laughing now, and there was nothing Galvin liked better than to make a pretty woman laugh. All other reactions could be faked. Interest could be faked. Affection could be faked. But a phony laugh was easy to spot. He could always measure his progress by the laugh, and she was laughing so hard that she was crying.

'You know, Frank – '

'Call me Galvin. Please. Only people I don't trust call me Frank. Call me Galvin.'

'What about Francis?'

'Only bishops call me that.'

'Donna St Laurent, as in the seaway. I like Donna.' She held out a hand, and it was a pact. They had passed an initiation.

'I like Donna too,' he said.

'What do you do, Galvin?'

'I chase ambulances.'

'That's an expensive suit for an ambulance chaser,' she said.

'Oh, this,' he said fingering the lapel. 'I stole it from Filene's basement. Watched it for three weeks. No one bought it. They mark it down every week. So I got it for half price. Couldn't afford to pass it up. You get ninety days to pay. A real steal.'

'I'll bet you're a trial lawyer.'

'No. You almost can't be a trial lawyer anymore. Not with no-fault. The good, triable cases are few and far between. It's like a ballplayer who sits on the bench too much. You get rusty.'

'Have you tried any really big cases?'

'Some.'

'I'll bet you have a good batting average,' she said.

'Fifty-fifty,' he replied. 'I have my days. It's not always in your control. Sometimes my clients tell the truth and we win. Sometimes they stretch the truth and we lose. Jurors know when someone isn't levelling. They can usually ferret it out. Then we all head for the showers.'

'You mean to say that you take cases where your client is lying?'

'My dear young woman, I have even won such cases.'

She shook her head. 'Isn't there something wrong with our judicial system when that happens?'

'Come, come. Even liars deserve a day in court. And I am not a jury. I cannot always tell. Someone comes to me and says he was rear-ended on Beacon Street and has a bad back or a bad neck. Should I tell him he's a faker? Do I know for certain? Who can see pain? And then there's the other matter of my bar bills and the instalments at Filene's, to say nothing of my alienated wife and all my girlfriends.'

'But sometimes the faker wins,' she persisted. 'Isn't that what you just said? Is that right?'

'So?'

'My God, I can't believe this. You're telling me that someone who is faking it, faking symptoms, deserves to win a malpractice suit?'

He didn't remember mentioning the word 'malpractice'. Maybe he had. Something flickered far off, but he ignored it.

'That's not what I said.' He held up his hand for a fresh round of drinks. By now he knew that it was not his own magic that improved the service, but Donna's presence. He was feeling a little too sober for his own liking and ordered a double.

'Look,' he said, 'it is a basic precept of the law – everyone is entitled to a day in court. Even a murderer is entitled to a defence. And it has to be a good defence. The best defence possible. Otherwise it would be a charade. As a consequence of that, once in a while someone is going to be acquitted who shouldn't be.'

'Do you mean that?'

'Of course I mean it,' he said impatiently. 'Think about it. You're pretty bright. Who shouldn't get a good defence? What category? Will you make one category exempt? What would happen? Child killers are exempt. From now on anyone accused of child killing doesn't get a defence. What happens when the cops catch the wrong child killer? Suppose they pick you?

'No, everyone gets a lawyer,' he continued. 'Everyone gets the best defence possible. Because they just may be telling the truth. Once in a while, someone who is guilty will walk away. But that's the price we pay. Better to err on that side than the other. It is really better to let ten guilty men go free than to convict one innocent man. Because when you go the other way, it slips. When you accept the one innocent man getting convicted, pretty soon it's ten innocent men to get one guilty man. Pretty soon it's a roundup and it gets very sloppy.'

'You made a speech,' she said pulling away her handbag.

'I haven't eaten,' he said. 'It makes me loquacious.'

'I haven't either. It makes me hungry.'

'Well, then, how about sealing our newfound friendship with dinner? What do you say, Donna St Laurent as in the seaway?'

She smiled. 'How about Chinese?'

He flinched. 'How about Italian?'

6

This man Galvin was like a cinder in the eye of J. Edward Concannon.

'What do you plan to do?' the Bishop had asked after reporting Galvin's rejection of the settlement.

Concannon looked out the window of his private office thirty floors above the Charles River, where only the best legal talent nested, and said almost wistfully, 'He doesn't leave us much choice, Your Excellency. We'll have to destroy him.'

The Bishop shuddered. He didn't want to hear any more. No one liked hearing the bloody details. The weekend was over: Galvin had not reconsidered. Now it was in the hands of the lawyers. Concannon let the Bishop leave.

But as Concannon stared at the burgundy folder with the outline of the case in it, he could not shake off an annoying little speck of feeling for an old fighter pilot. It was an intuition of danger.

Why wouldn't a man who was on the brink of disaster accept a parachute?

It was nine o'clock, and Concannon buzzed Miss Crane, the evening receptionist, and asked her to please get Mrs Concannon on the phone. As he waited for the connection, Concannon walked across the expanse of Belgian broadloom, so thick and finely textured that it never showed a footprint. He stood at the floor-to-ceiling windows watching the Charles meander from the Mystic River Basin. On the far bank the Harvard and MIT quads glowed in the night. It was a pilot's-eye view, transcending the chaos and clutter of life.

The intercom buzzed. 'All three phones at your home are busy, Mr Concannon. Shall I keep trying?'

'Thank you, Miss Crane.'

Apart from the case folder, the burnished rosewood desk was almost bare. There was a black onyx pen set from the American Bar Association with gold engraving:

To John Edward Concannon
The Nation's Outstanding Lawyer of 1979

It was strategically placed, the inscription facing the clientele.

To the left of the pen set was a small silver frame with a picture of his wife and four children. It was an old picture – taken a decade earlier at the poolside of his Marblehead estate. For Concannon, the picture had become a family coat of arms. It unfailingly reminded him of just who and what he was.

The children of the picture were no longer small. They had scattered to colleges and careers. But Kim had hardly changed. With some alterations for style, the picture could have been taken at breakfast. He had married an American aristocrat.

It was not only the fact of money and attention that kept her looking so young. What kept her intact was patrician obstinacy. To be sure, Kimberly Cushing Concannon had her own special hairdresser and her own special couturier. She was diligent with youth lotions and daily exercise. She crowded her days with fatuous committees and useless charities.

But that didn't explain it. Her beauty secret was in her eyes. They were steady and defiant. They held time in abeyance. She was simply not yet ready to grow old.

If there was anything in the world J. Edward Concannon admired, it was that much control.

'Mrs Concannon on line five.'

'Hi, Kim. Tough day. I may be a little late. Keep the Clarks and Fletchers busy. Tracy Clark likes margaritas, but try not to let her get going too soon. Keep the Chivas on ice for me. Be there as soon as I can.'

'I'll handle it, dear.'

In the war, a man learned to weigh such promises. You got to know whom you could count on and whom you couldn't. On top of the matching rosewood credenza was a picture of a boyish-looking John F. Kennedy. The autograph read, *To Ed – That 109 would never have gone down if you'd been riding shot gun.* It was signed *Jack.*

Jack Kennedy had been through the war and knew whom to trust. Concannon was proud of that. He and Kim were alike in that too. If she said she would handle something, he could count on it.

'Mr Concannon,' came the thin voice from the side door.

'For Christ's sake, Cummings, don't be so goddamn timid. Come in.'

Concannon did not particularly enjoy the terror that he evoked from the staff who worked for him. But he believed passionately that he had to keep them tough. He demanded quality performance, nothing less. As a taskmaster he showed no mercy. It was the war again. The soft pilots never returned.

'It's that Canadian National Airlines case,' said Cummings. 'The judge wants pretrial briefs in by eleven tomorrow morning.'

'What's the problem?' Concannon said crisply.

'The problem, sir, is that Pam and I are having a dinner party. We've been planning it for six months. I'm late already. A lot of important people are going to be there. Potential clients.'

'Who?'

'People from Channel Three. Michelle Robbins, the theatre critic. Jeff North, the State House reporter. Peter Phillips of *Eyewitness News*.'

Concannon's pale-blue eyes narrowed as he measured his young associate. Seconds dragged by.

'Let me tell you a few things about your guest list that I'm sure you're unaware of. Boston is, after all, a small town, and there isn't much that goes on here that I don't know about. If I don't know, I find out. It gives one an edge. Shelley Robbins is hanging on to her job by her fingernails. North dances in whatever political wind blows his way. I happen to know – and keep this to yourself – that Phillips is going to be axed. They aren't potential clients. If you told me that David Carrington, who owns the network, was coming, or even Chet Fullerton of the FCC, I might have some sympathy. Shelley Robbins! Christ, she only keeps her job by screwing every producer in Boston.'

'I could get a ten-day extension,' stammered Cummings. 'Judge Nolan will grant it. The court always grants an initial request.'

'There'll be no extension,' snapped Concannon. 'It's a sign of weakness. We do not ask for extensions in this office. If the other side requests a continuance, if they are not ready, that's their problem. We will be on the firing line at eleven tomorrow morning. If you have to work all night, then you will work all night. It's as simple as that. It will be proofed, typed and ready to go.'

The young lawyer accepted defeat.

'You and Mrs Cummings have a lovely home in Swampscott. Right on the water, and I believe you have your own docking facilities with a thirty-six footer.'

'A thirty-footer,' Cummings said diffidently.

Concannon paused, annoyed at the interruption, wondering if Cummings simply lacked judgment or just wasn't getting the message.

'You know, Brad, not many men your age are so advanced. I like your style. To men like us, these things – yachts, planes – they aren't luxuries: they're necessities. And we keep these amenities because the job comes first. So unless you can see some other way of getting the thing done, which I cannot, I suggest you call your wife and tell her that you will not be able to make the dinner party. I will be back here by seven A.M., and I want it ready by then. You'll brief me on the results, and at 'ten thirty we'll grab a cab and see Judge Nolan.'

'I'll have it done,' said Cummings quietly as he turned uneasily for an exit.

They didn't understand, thought Concannon. But then, there weren't too many of the fighter pilots left. He walked slowly towards his desk, pausing near the door. There on the wall, amid all the dry diplomas and testimonials, was the glossy print of the 89th Fighter Wing of the Eighth Air Force. He studied it as he had countless times before. They had called themselves 'The Wild Geese', after the Irish patriots who fought for Napoleon against the English. The young faces with the uncomplicated grins were all Irish: Harrington, O'Brien, Cullinane, Kelley, Neville. And there, with one arm hanging possessively on the prop of his Mustang, *Garry Owen* enscrolled on its cowling, was the 21-year-old squadron leader, Major Ed Concannon.

Most of the others were gone – lost in flames over France. But Concannon had survived. He had lasted through sixty-five missions over enemy territory. There were twenty-nine swastikas on his fuselage. But the price had been high.

He was sweating now, lost in that cloud of thirty-five years ago. He had been returning from a mission when he spotted what appeared to be a crippled FW-190. He started to roll in for the kill; then he noticed the face of the pilot. Frightened. Young. And so, in a gesture of ancient camaraderie, he dipped a wing and rolled out and headed for the Channel. The German, however, had feigned difficulty. He closed in behind Concannon and riddled the P-51 with dual machine guns.

Instinctively, Concannon put his plane into a banking stall. He slipped and skidded in the airstream, checking his dive with a quick thrust of the stick. Shoving the throttle to the fire wall, he came up under the 190 and pumped a burst of fire into the German. He continued strafing the plane as it spun towards the earth and crash-landed in a field. Then he made two more passes at the downed fighter, strafing it until it exploded.

He never spoke of it. And he never made the same mistake again. He never softened an attack, and he never relinquished pursuit until the kill was certain. The other members of the squadron noticed the change. But they simply said that he had taken a more businesslike approach to his job.

Later, when he returned to civilian life and became a lawyer, he applied the same tactics to his work. He did not merely take on a case. He covered every angle. He considered every possibility. He saw all the traps. He never relaxed, never stopped to savour his accomplishments. He fought with cannon and machine guns and battering rams. If one method didn't get results, another surely would.

Concannon won. That was all that mattered. In the courtroom he had no peer. He could try any type of litigation: criminal fraud, first-degree murder, a stockholder's suit, antitrust. Few trial lawyers, including district and US attorneys, would risk their won–lost records for a go at Concannon. His fees were stiff, but his track record was undeniable. He was the Establishment.

Concannon, who had once turned his back on what he believed was a disabled German fighter, opened the burgundy folder again. What did this man Galvin have that could hurt him?

Inside the carefully catalogued file were copies of trial briefs, depositions, evidentiary documents and the investigative findings. There were summaries and background material and digests of everyone and everything within the *Rosen* case's circumstantial orbit.

The attorney who had prime responsibility for the pretrial preparation was supplied by Roger Rutledge of the firm of Rutledge, Guthrie, Cabot & Moore. Rutledge, who represented the diocese in all legal matters, had retained Concannon to try the case. Bishop Brophey approved. He knew he was getting the best.

Rutledge had certain research advantages. There were no fewer than 140 graduates of Harvard and Yale and Columbia and Stanford law schools shuffling briefs for his firm. Not merely the cream of the crop, they excelled in every way – law-review brilliant, physically attractive, names deep rooted in political and fiscal traditions. It seemed as if they had been picked to beget a new race.

The attorneys assigned to assist Concannon had been selected with utmost care.

'Quite frankly, I don't see all the time and energy being poured into the case,' said Roger Rutledge at the briefing by his associates. 'Our fee is going to be horrendous. This man Galvin is not even listed in the lawyers' directory. Who is this man?'

Two of the assistants looked at each other and nervously cleared their throats. It was then that Rutledge noticed that his principal assistant assigned to the case was missing.

'Where is she?' he asked.

'I believe she's out doing research,' said Marvin Kaplan, one of the brighter lights in the firm.

'Damn,' said Rutledge. 'First one thing, then another. You know Concannon's a fanatic on detail. A wild man. Fighter pilot in the war. Can't fool with such a man. Where's she off to when I need her?'

'I think you can count on the fact that she's on the case,' said Kaplan. 'Donna St Laurent is on top of the case, if I know her.'

7

He could hear Sam, their 2-year-old, crying in the background. He cupped the telephone closer and sank deeper into his lie.

'I'm sorry,' he said. 'I don't have a choice. I'm stuck. Try to understand. These things happen. Everything hit the fan at the same time.'

She was as silent as midnight, and he kept walking out into the darkness.

'This fucking case is killing me. Killing me. I swear to God, I'd like to just give it up. Take the money and run. I'd really like to do that. Wish I could. And you know how dumb Peggy is; well, she screwed up all the papers. All the notes for the voir dire. The motion papers. Everything. I have to redo the whole goddamned mess . . .'

It wouldn't have been so bad except for the fact that Lois had often sat on the other side of the lie. She had been at Galvin's elbow when he made precisely the same kind of telephone call to his wife.

' . . . And the typewriter is broken, so I'll have to work at Moe's place. So you won't be able to reach me later because he shuts down his switchboard. You know how it is when you're Jewish. But I'll call you later, sweetheart. As soon as I can get a minute, I'll break away . . .'

'I don't want to hear this,' she said coldly.

'What? Huh?'

'I don't want to hear this shit, Galvin.'

There was no reproach in her voice. Just ice.

'Look, honey, I know how you feel. But it can't be helped. I have to get these papers ready. Don't you know what's going on here?'

'I think so.'

'They're trying to kill me! For God's sake, they want me stuffed for Thanksgiving. You think this is some kind of a game? Are you crazy?'

By now Galvin had worked himself into a mild state of indignation. After all, he *was* in a professional pickle. No doubt about that. How did Lois *know* he was lying about working late? He could have been telling the truth. It was possible.

'I would wind up pushing a cab down Tremont Street!'

That did it! Now he was really pissed. The mere vision of himself pathetically sitting in an unwanted taxicab on Tremont Street was enough to unleash a flood of self-pity. And anger. After all, Lois couldn't know that he was waiting for Donna St Laurent to come out of the ladies' room. Not for sure.

'You think I *like* to stay up all night retyping everything that dumb broad fucks up during the day? You think it's fun working all day and then working all night? You think I like doing something that she could easily have done right the first time?'

Now he was getting annoyed at Peggy.

'She's so lazy!' he went on, working himself into a frenzy. 'What am I supposed to do? You want me to lay down and die? You want to let these insurance bastards roll right over me? This is the biggest case of my career. If I don't win this one, I've had it. We've both had it. Sammy, our future . . . And what about that poor Rosen girl? . . .'

And then he heard her slam down the telephone.

Bitch! he thought. Women are all the same. Orientals. Supposed to be different. Can't do enough for their man. Christ. What crap. Just too goddamned American. Too Wellesley College. Never had to worry about a thing in her life. Never had to get up in the morning and stare into a bleak future. All those income trusts and untapped capital. She would never really understand hunger. Not just some pang in the pit of your stomach. But the pain. She'd never taste it.

And thus he rid himself of any possible guilt for what he was about to do. It was her own fault.

'Everything all right?' asked Donna, who stood far enough away from the phone booth so that Galvin could take whatever tack he wished.

'Just checking my service,' he said, smiling, sweating. 'It's like being a doctor. You always have to be available.'

'Well,' she said good-naturedly, 'what do you expect from a man who chases ambulances?'

Later, as they sat at a corner table at Seafare in the Faneuil Market district, he ordered a second bottle of wine. The two dinners lay half-eaten between them. Galvin was smitten and he could not eat, and he would not be able to sleep later. He gushed and stumbled in the opening throes of a brand-new love. He recited his own form of poetry – a kind of macho boasting.

There was a sense of compatibility as they watched the late-night singles manoeuvre. They listened to the laughter and honeyed voices that went with the decor. Polished oak with exposed brick, spider plants and Boston ferns cascading from wooden beams. Galvin poured some more wine.

'You have to be a great lawyer,' said Donna.

'Is that a woman's intuition?' asked Galvin.

'No. It's a fact. I can tell about people. I always know.'

'Tell me a little about yourself,' he said. She smiled and sipped her drink. He was enthralled. What difference did it make what she did? Ad exec; schoolteacher. She wasn't a hooker – that was certain. He signalled the waiter for another carafe of wine.

'What do you really think of me?' he said, finally.

'Well, I think you're a lot better lawyer than you make out. I think you've probably had an interesting career. When is your next famous case, Galvin?'

He looked at her for a moment. 'Funny you should ask,' he

said. 'As a matter of fact, I do have a big one on next week. The biggest case of my career, as a matter of fact.'

'I knew it,' she said. 'You gave me that feeling. On the brink of something. I'm almost psychic.'

'I am going up against the whole Roman Catholic Mother Church,' he said. 'And all the doctors and all the lawyers in the entire Western Hemisphere.'

'My God!'

'Not quite. But I'm taking on St Kate's, which is the same thing to a lot of people. Especially around here. I'm taking on St Catherine Labouré Hospital, two doctors, the operating-room team and whoever else gets in my way.'

'Oh,' she said. 'The malpractice case. That's when you sue the doctors for bad medical treatment, isn't it?'

Again Galvin felt something odd. 'Yes,' he replied. 'We like to say the doctors goofed. It's easy to say. Proving it is something else. People don't like to think doctors screw up. They'd rather believe in voodoo. So it's hard to prove – it's like pushing a car uphill with a rope.'

'Can you push a car uphill with a rope?'

'See what I mean? It's even hard to visualize.'

'C'mon, Galvin. You wouldn't bring suit against all those people unless there was some way to prove it. How do you prove something like that?'

'Ah, there's the kicker. It's not easy to nail a doctor. Especially one with juice in the Church. If a lawyer screws up – say, blows the statute of limitations or misses a lien on a title – there are ten thousand lawyers standing in line ready to testify against him.

'But with doctors,' he continued, 'it's worse than the Mafia. They have a conspiracy of silence. A code. The man in white is a folk God. They call it the Lazarus Syndrome. He can saw the wrong leg off the Pope and everyone gets deaf, dumb and blind. He can leave Kelley clamps inside a guy's stomach and the College of Surgeons will swear that it's accepted medical

70

practice to store a little hardware inside the abdomen. They really stick together, these guys. The medical Mafia. At least, the Cosa Nostra makes no pretence about its benevolence. But these guys are full of pious bullshit. They lie and call it honour.'

'So how can you sue them?'

He swirled the last of the wine around the bottom of the glass.

'How can you not?'

'Seriously, Galvin. If it's so impossible, how can you bring a suit?'

'There are ways.'

'How?'

'There are a few doctors out there who don't suffer from indigeo testicularis. Not many. But a few.'

'From what?'

'Lack of balls.'

'Oh.'

'Of course, it's not easy. You have to find someone willing to take on all the medical societies, the AMA even. Someone who can stand up to the polite professional death threats that go with the territory. Doctors do not cross easily. I know.'

'Isn't it unethical to go shopping around for an expert?'

Something tugged at the back of his mind. He hadn't used the word 'expert.' It was a term of art, as they say in the legal profession. He let it pass again.

'No,' he said. 'Good medicine is universal. A few years ago most states had what was called the "locality rule." Before one doctor would be allowed to testify against another, he had to be familiar with the standard of care practised in the community where the alleged wrongful conduct occurred. And if they practised substandard surgery in New Bedford, well, that was the norm, the standard of care. We had one case right here in Massachusetts in which one doctor couldn't testify against another doctor in the next

71

town four miles away. The locality rule. Totally absurd. Thank God, that's been overturned. Now there is no geography for good medical practice. It's the same everywhere. A doctor from New York City can testify that some doctor in Boston was guilty of bad medical practice.'

'Is that what you're doing in this case?'

'Absolutely. You couldn't get any local doctor to testify against St Kate's. That's like asking the Bishop to throw rocks at the Pope.'

'What kind of malpractice case is it?'

Galvin held up his hand for the waiter. 'How about me getting you something a little more tropical – say, a sombrero or a margarita – Miss St Laurent?'

'Are you trying to ply me with liquor?' she smiled. 'Vodka gimlet on the rocks.'

There was, in the delay before the drinks arrived, the possibility of changing the subject. But the inertial effect was hard to overcome.

'I'm fascinated with your case, Galvin. As you lawyers say, what are the facts?'

'Tell you the truth, I expect to hang them with the largest malpractice verdict in the history of Massachusetts, perhaps the United States. I'm suing for fifteen million.'

'Ow! Fifteen million dollars! That's a lot of malpractice.'

'Well, I'll tell you, I have a client. A little Jewish girl. Twenty-eight years old. Just a housewife. Two kids and a third on the way. Routine pregnancy. Routine delivery. And when they got her to St Catherine Laboure Hospital, they turned her into a vegetable.'

'How?' she asked. 'How did it happen? Wasn't it just an ordinary OB case?'

'Well, it should have been. It was an OB case, all right, and it should have been routine. But they fucked it up. Gave her a general anaesthetic. They clamped an inhalation mask over her face. Everyone's standing around talking about the weather or the yacht-club dance while all the time she's upchucking into the mask. She drowned in her own vomit.'

'How awful.'

'Only no one knew, because her face was buried in the mask. She stopped breathing. Her heart stopped. And they fiddled around for seven or eight minutes trying to figure out what to do. All the time, the life's being sucked out of her. Finally some genius took off the mask and they saw what had happened. But it was too late. After four minutes without oxygen, you become a zucchini.'

'That's terrible.' She wrinkled her brow with a show of concern. 'But tell me, Galvin, doesn't that happen sometimes? Isn't that what is known as an act of God?'

'Oh, sure. I've been getting that crap ever since the Sisters of St Joseph had me at St Brigid's grammar school. Kid gets hit by a truck – act of God. A 727 goes down over Syracuse. Kills a hundred and eighty passengers. Blame God. Rough weather. Doesn't make any difference that someone back at Logan was supposed to check the squall lines, maybe keep everything on the ground. Hell, no. That's not economical.'

'Galvin, I really mean, it's awful, but isn't what happened to the woman a normal medical risk? I don't see where the negligence comes in.'

'Normal? Is there such a thing as a normal risk? If it's a risk, then it's one no person should have to run. A patient goes into the world's finest hospital – no problems, healthy, minor procedure, doctors and nurses hanging from the ceiling – and bang! She comes out in a box, or worse, a living corpse.' He was holding her hand, leaning close. Then he backed off.

'We call it negligence when they fail to do something they were supposed to do. Call it lack of diligence. I call it dereliction of duty. First of all, the reason you're not supposed to eat before an operation is so that you won't throw up into the mask and trigger just what happened, respiratory and cardiac arrest. If she had eaten within a few hours, they should

73

have given her a spinal instead of a general anaesthetic. That's just first of all. Second of all, they should have gotten her heart going within four minutes.'

'Is there someone who will say all this? I mean, besides yourself?'

I can have her, thought Galvin. Whoever she is. Whatever her game. I can have her.

'What happened to the girl?' asked Donna, breaking away from the pause.

'She's an exotic plant,' said Galvin, fingering a cactus plant near their table. 'They keep her in the hospital, with tubes sticking out of her nose and her arms and her belly. She's kept at a constant temperature in an antiseptic room. They move her a bit to avoid bedsores. They clean her constantly, but the stench is unbearable. She coos and drools like a baby. She's able to blink her eyes, which is how we know she's conscious and aware of what has happened to her.

'She blinks once for yes and twice for no. And she cries. The nurses come in at night to wipe away the tears and spittle. She'll never improve. She'll be that way until the day she dies. Unfortunately, that won't be for quite some time. She has a good heartbeat. Kept in a controlled environment. Constant medication. I.V. feeding. Sooner or later, though, she'll get pneumonia. Her lungs will fill up with liquid and she'll drown.'

He signalled for another round. Donna held her hand over her glass. She had had enough. Galvin shrugged and said to make his a double.

'Who have you got to prove all this?' she asked.

I can have her, thought Galvin. It was the first sense of real power he'd had in a long time. He feigned fatigue. Forced a yawn. His head nodded.

'Boy, am I bushed,' he said.

'C'mon, Freddie, my battling barrister. We'll catch a cab to my place,' she said. 'No one should drive after sixteen

Scotches. They might lift your licence.'

Galvin caught her half-smile.

'Where'll I sleep?' he mumbled.

'Next to my cactus,' she said.

8

By the time he left Donna's apartment, Galvin was still infatuated with her. He was also still frightened of her.

They had both been surprised and shaken by the success of the physical encounter. He had been worried about performance, and she hadn't expected much. Instead, from the moment he got her alone and brushed her cheek tenderly with the back of his hand, it was out of control. They couldn't even wait to get undressed. They pawed and groped at each other as if they were both wearing mittens. It didn't matter that he was clumsy. He got the parts uncovered and began the coupling. If she noticed, she didn't seem to mind. She was equally caught up. They were both on fire.

He managed to get them both undressed in the midst of the conflagration. While Donna, to her own surprise, babbled and murmured and groaned and lost control of herself completely, Galvin juggled the complicated set of interdependent tasks. 'Don't come!' she kept pleading as Galvin fumbled with buttons and the impossible lock in a remote part of her bra. He was grunting and sweating in frustration and passion and hoping that she would not suddenly notice his ineptitude.

'Don't come – oh, please don't come!' she cried as he began to curse and mutter under his breath – all of which had the same general tone of heat as great passion. His hand, caught behind her back in the tangle of her bra strap, had begun to fall asleep.

He muffled her plea by locking his mouth on hers, as he rolled her and rocked her from side to side in an effort to work her free from her skirt.

Some primordial urge surged within her. She met him like a savage.

It was no coincidence that the moment of climax arrived at the same instant as the removal of the last shred of clothing. It was a sock that Galvin had to twist around to remove from his left foot.

When it was all over, Donna was surprised that she was naked. She could not remember getting undressed.

'Who is this brave doctor who is willing to take on all the powers of Boston and heaven?' she asked, running her finger lightly over his heaving chest.

He didn't hesitate. 'A guy from Long Island. An anaesthesiologist on the staff of a hospital in the Hamptons.'

She propped her head up, leaning on her closed hand. Galvin lit a cigarette and watched the languid smoke curl upwards.

'What makes you think that he'll stand up to the pressures?' she asked innocently. 'There are bound to be pressures.'

'Oh, there'll be pressures, all right,' replied Galvin. 'They play rough in Boston.'

'You've got something up your sleeve,' she said.

'I always hide an ace,' he said. 'Or two. And *I* cut the cards.'

'I'll call you Gaylord instead of Galvin. Gaylord the Riverboat Gambler . . .' she said, as she drew imaginary circles just below his rib cage. 'What's the ace? The doc from Long Island?'

'Not just a doc,' Galvin said, 'but a doc who can't be intimidated. He's seventy-eight years old and he's past caring. What can they do to a seventy-eight-year-old guy?'

Plenty, she thought. They could do plenty. She was going to ask for his name, but decided to quit while she was ahead. She didn't really need his name. How many seventy-eight-year-old anaesthesiologists could there be in a tiny Long Island hospital?

She yawned.

'I better go,' he said, hoping that she would invite him to spend the night.

'Yes,' she said pleasantly. 'I have a big day tomorrow.'

'Don't get up,' he said. She watched him with a satisfied smile as he buttoned his shirt, sat down to put on his socks and struggled into his shoes. 'I'll find my way out.'

He bent down and kissed her lightly, pulling the crumpled sheet up over her exposed shoulders. He made his way through her foyer, where prints and photographs lined the wall. One print caught his eye. He squinted at it in the dim hall light as he unlatched the safety bolt. It was a university degree with a gold seal. DONNA MARTINA STRELENSKI, it read in Old English lettering. BACHELOR OF LAWS, COLUMBIA UNIVERSITY SCHOOL OF LAW, JUNE 2, 1973. He let himself out quietly.

It was four in the morning when he left, dazed with his good fortune and without a place to sleep. The janitor of his office building found him slumped against the broken elevator. He ignored Galvin on the first two rounds, thinking that he was a derelict. But at 6 A.M., he recognized Galvin's snoring and poked him in the ribs with his shoe.

'Elevator's broken,' he said, a little nasty.

Galvin sat up with a start. 'Oh, it's you. I lost my key. Could you let me into my office?'

'Not supposed to do that,' said the janitor.

'I know. But I lost my key.'

'My orders are not to let *anyone* in,' said the janitor. 'I could lose my job. They keep getting in, break the elevator, steal anything.'

'But you *know* me, Pat. It's me, Galvin. I promise I won't steal the elevator.'

'Mr Solomon is always telling me not to let anyone in. If he caught me letting you in, I'd lose my job.'

'Pat, I'm tired. Let me into my fucking office!'

The janitor recognized desperation when he heard it. He had taken Galvin to the end of his patience, but he enjoyed that kind of brinkmanship. After all, how many people can a janitor drive to exasperation?

'Okay, Mr Galvin, but remember, it's your responsibility.'

'What's my responsibility, Pat?'

'If anything is missing.'

'Right, Pat.'

He fell asleep on the couch. The janitor dusted ceremoniously, emptying Peggy's ashtray, lifting up a roll of postage stamps that had carelessly been left on her desk and placing it in his pocket.

Donna lay awake staring at the ceiling. She was annoyed. Rutledge had called him an opportunist. He was that, all right. And careless. Small time. A little ridiculous. His attempts at urbane sophistication were ludicrous. Still . . .

What a character! She couldn't sleep. Why should she feel bad? He had a moral and ethical code as thin as rice paper. But it was like the sex. Despite all indications to the contrary, it had been great. Despite the fact that he was no good and a loser, she liked him.

It would not be easy to betray him. But she would manage.

9

Two days before the trial, as Galvin burrowed in for one more hour of sleep on the remains of his office couch, the final briefing for the defence took place in Concannon's offices high over Boston Common. The various staffs assembled around the long boardroom table like the Allied generals and admirals on the eve of D-Day. There was almost a pre-battle tension in the air.

'The first thing to keep in mind,' said Concannon, opening the meeting and putting everyone at ease, 'is that we are the good guys.'

There was an appreciative chuckle around the table.

'And in Boston,' he continued, 'the good guys always win.'

The chuckle broke into sustained laughter. A secretary moved around the room serving coffee, now that the mood had softened. The ones who laughed hardest and longest were the ones in most peril. The medical staff from St Catherine Laboure Hospital. They were clustered at the far end of the table, as if they expected sheer distance to put them out of the range of danger.

The leader of the medical team was Dr G. Rexford Towler, Boston's leading gynaecologist and chief of surgical gynaecology at St Catherine's. A learned writer, erudite speaker, he was rumoured to be a prime candidate for president of the American Medical Association. Dr Towler smoked a pipe, and it was said among the wags on the hospital staff that he sent up emotional smoke signals with it. When his mood was tranquil, the pipe lolled between Dr Towler's lips, and there would be an occasional lazy curl of smoke from the bowl of the pipe. But in a crisis, he puffed like a locomotive.

At the legal conference, Dr Towler's handsome profile was obscured behind a cloud of smoke.

On Dr Towler's left, supporting his chin with folded hands, was Dr Dan Crowley, chief of anaesthesiology. Dr Crowley was a man totally absorbed in his career, and the other aspects of his life suffered. He was 47 years old and in the breakup stages of his fourth marriage. To his left was the third co-defendant, Carolyn Nevins, the anaesthesiology nurse, her auburn hair tied back in a tight coif.

'Without minimizing the stakes in this case, I think I can reassure you about the outcome,' Concannon said, addressing the group. 'Frankly, I'm surprised it has gotten this far. I don't even understand why any lawyer would take on a malpractice case, especially one like this. Doctors shouldn't have to worry about such things. It encourages defensive medicine. But the opposition persists. I would like to think that we will set an example here and put a stop to such harassment once and for all.' Concannon was telling them what they wanted to hear.

The door opened and Donna St Laurent came in. Dressed in an exquisitely tailored two-piece suit, she arrested everyone's attention. She was ten minutes late, but moved with assurance. As she sat in her assigned seat, she smiled at Concannon.

'We were just going over final tactics,' said Concannon, and she nodded.

'First, we should not all arrive together at the courthouse,' Concannon counselled. 'We should come in separate taxicabs, and we should arrive at staggered intervals. I don't want potential jurors to see an armada. Also, there should be absolutely no laughter while the trial is in progress. This is serious business, and we are taking it seriously. Don't even discuss it on the outside. When you're in the elevator or at lunch, you can be overheard. One flip remark can destroy a case.'

There was nothing remarkable in all this, but it established

Concannon as the leader and it set the tone for the trial. Even the obvious sometimes has to be uttered.

'Right now, I want to go over the case with the doctors and nurse. Miss St Laurent, will you stay. And Roger, please remain with your associates, Mr Kaplan and Mr Carrington.'

Galvin would attempt to win sympathy for himself as the underdog. Concannon had a different strategy in mind. Five of the most talented lawyers in Rutledge, Guthrie, Cabot & Moore would provide logistical backup. But they would be behind the enclosure taking notes, checking case citations and points of law as they arose. Human-interest stories about the medical profession would start surfacing in the *Boston Globe* and *Herald American*. Possibly a series on hospitals, on nurses, on the long hours put in by those succouring the sick and ministering to the dying. Heartwarming statistics. No mortality rates. A profile on the handsome Dr Towler was already scheduled for Sunday's magazine section. At the defence table would be Concannon, Donna St Laurent and two young male lawyers – one Jewish and one the son of United States Senator Carrington from New York. Concannon knew how to neutralize an opponent's advantages.

'Now, Dr Towler,' began Concannon when they were alone with the immediate staff, 'let's go over this one more time, if you don't mind . . .'

The doctors and Nurse Nevins did not understand or appreciate the legal forum into which they were thrust. They listened attentively as Concannon began his interrogation. It was not the gist of a story that Concannon had to know. He was taking it apart under an electronic microscope. He was turning the details over and testing them chemically, emotionally, legally, morally. A woman is admitted to a hospital. She is asked certain preliminary questions. Routine. So many checks on a preadmission form. When had she last eaten? The answer is recorded. Who was the woman? What was her condition when she got there? Could she understand the questions? Who took the history? Was she listening? It is all a complex chain of events, and each link has its own story. Each link is bound to the next, so an attorney must know it all and be able to dissect it and put it together again.

Already Concannon had enlisted experts from five of Boston's leading medical institutions who were prepared to testify that Deborah Ruth Rosen had received the best medical care available. Men from University General, Boston Presbyterian, Harvey Cushing Clinic, Beth El Memorial and the New England Medical School had studied the charts and depositions and scrutinized every aspect of the case. There was a striking unanimity of opinion. They found 'the conduct of the defendant doctors and of the operating team consistent with standards of good medical practice.'

There was, of course, the undeniable fact that the patient was now a vegetable. But the experts were ready to face that. They were, after all, colleagues, subject to the same professional peril. Doctors, they would report, cannot be responsible for untoward results as long as they did their best. The full professors, published anaesthesiologists and esteemed surgeons were prepared to defend the record. Sometimes, for reasons that cannot always be explained, it happens. Something goes wrong. No one is to blame. It happens . . .

'I am going to put you on the witness stand,' said Concannon, and Dr Towler's pipe billowed forth. 'And I am going to ask you to tell the jury what happened in your own words. For now, I want you to tell us the history, the presenting diagnosis and exactly what you did in the care and treatment of your patient. Relate it just as if we were the jurors. Okay, Doctor, go ahead.'

'Deborah Ruth was recommended to me by a colleague, Dr Sheldon Rabb, because of a previous difficult delivery.' Dr Towler was a distinguished-looking man. The silver streaks in his hair added a scholarly dimension to his presence. He spoke carefully, and his voice had the timbre of a veteran doctor-politician. At conventions and assemblies, at colleges and before Congressional committees, Dr Towler had learned to sound like a television anchor-man delivering the news. 'Deborah Ruth had other complications. She was diabetic. Low haemoglobin. She was subject to snycope – fainting spells . . .'

'That's fine, Doctor, fine.' Concannon . nodded encouragingly. 'I like your using the first name. I'd drop the "Ruth". Sounds too professorial – like she's a med student and you're calling on her for a recitation. Might be well even to call her "Debbie". Our reports indicate her intimate friends called her that. Refer to her as "Debbie". Nice. To you she wasn't just another statistic. She was a person with a name. And you knew her well enough to call her Debbie. You liked her.'

The doctor looked pleased.

'And remember,' Concannon counselled, 'jurors are ordinary people. Lay people. Not particularly intelligent. High school educations, if that. Overexplain. Use simple terms. Be helpful. Give homey illustrations. When you describe the heart, tell them that it's like a pump, about as big as your fist. And hold up your fist. And it opens and shuts, opens and shuts. And do that with your fist. Open and shut. I don't want to interrupt when you're on the stand, so keep in mind that things must be brought down to a level that they can understand. Okay?'

'Okay,' replied Dr Towler.

'You're explaining it to cab drivers and bartenders. Make plenty of eye contact. Look at them when you're speaking. Not at the judge or at me. Talk *with* the jurors like you'd talk to your friends. All right, Dr Towler, please continue.'

'She was a serious operative risk, Debbie was. I was particularly worried about her low haemoglobin. This is a red flag. You see, the blood is like a river carrying ships downstream. The ships are blood cells, and these cells contain valuable cargo called oxygen. All living tissue, the brain and muscles and the skin, all need oxygen to survive . . .'

'Uh, Doctor, you should keep it simple, but you mustn't insult the jurors. It's a hard balancing thing, but I'm sure you can handle it. You have to be folksy without appearing condescending.'

Dr Towler shifted uncomfortably in his chair. 'Well, her oxygenated blood was deficient. It was only two-thirds normal. The brain and other vital organs just weren't getting enough oxygen.'

'Good,' said Concannon. 'You don't want them to forget that you are a professional, either. The right tone is one of awed intimacy. I know it's not easy. But you've got it now.'

'As I say, she'd had a lot of problems during her last pregnancy. That's why she was referred to my office. It was a difficult case. I saw her for the first time in April. She came to my office with her first two children. Howie, who was three, and David, who was two . . .'

'Oh, that's perfect,' said Concannon. Everything checked. Concannon had already thoroughly interrogated Dr Rabb. The previous breech birth, Deborah Ruth's heart trouble, her low haemoglobin, fainting spells – it all checked. Dr Rabb was prepared to testify that he had suspected complications in future pregnancies and that was why he, an OB-GYN with considerable experience, on the staff of Beth Israel, had referred the case to Towler. He would so testify, emphasizing that since he thought the case was beyond him he had consulted the best. If Beth Israel and Dr Rabb had ducked this difficult case, why saddle Dr Towler, Dr Crowley and St Catherine Laboure with the responsibility?

'I did a thorough workup then,' Towler continued. 'The last child, David, was a breech birth. That's when the buttocks are presented first, rather than the head. In her seventh month, she began having fainting spells. Medically, we call this syncope. That's when Dr Rabb checked her haemoglobin. And she also had diabetes mellitus. That's when the body has trouble processing sugar because of faulty operation of the pancreas. Thus, extra sugar gets into the blood and urine. So her system was quite depressed and severely compromised. In addition to all that, she had an old heart murmur. Her aortic valve – that's the main valve which allows the blood to be pumped from the heart through the entire body – well, that wasn't functioning as smoothly as it should have been. All of these factors made her case difficult. A risk. One that we could handle. There was nothing that, by itself, was too dangerous. But –'

'I think, Doctor, we should leave that kind of speculation out,' said Concannon. 'The jury should hear the list of difficulties and draw their own conclusion. Also, we'll save a few nuggets for our opponent's cross-examination. To be sure, the plaintiff's attorney will question you about her prior difficulties and ask you to explain –'

That was enough for Dr Towler. His pipe flared, and a great puff of smoke exploded out of his mouth.

'They go too far,' he said getting up, smacking the bowl of his pipe into a large ashtray. 'Too far. I don't have to explain myself to ignorant oafs.'

He stalked out of the room. Concannon watched him go and then gave Donna an eye signal. He was like a quarterback sending out someone to intercept a dangerous pass.

'We'll take a break,' he told the others in the room.

Outside, Donna caught Dr Towler at the water fountain. 'I appreciate how difficult this is,' she began.

'How could you?' he shot back. 'Do you know who I am? Do you have any idea of my stature in the medical community?'

'Doctor,' she said grimly, 'I understand perfectly. It is that stature which we are trying to preserve.' She softened. 'I know how hard this is, but we are trying to help. We're on your side. Truly.'

She smiled – a reassuring, supplicating smile – and he relented. He came back into the room and sheepishly resumed his seat, reloading his pipe.

'As I was saying,' continued Concannon, 'the plaintiff's attorney will question you about her prior difficulties and ask you to explain. This is the time to run with the ball. To score points. We will drive home the point that disease entities in combination pose the gravest risks. Always dangerous. Okay?'

'Okay. I see what you mean.'

'And Dr Crowley and Miss Nevins, this goes for both of you.' They nodded agreement.

'Go ahead, Dr Towler.'

'I followed Debbie's case closely. I saw her every two weeks in my office at the hospital. We kept pace with the lab work. Her electrocardiograms were normal. Her blood counts were tolerable. I tried to build her up physically. Prescribed Vitamin B-one and made certain that she got a lot of rest and watched her diet.

'When I got word from the service that Debbie was starting labour it was close to five A.M. I was dictating notes on another case. I was still in my office at the hospital. I alerted Dr Crowley, and the team assembled –'

'Who was there? Who were the members of the obstetrical team?'

'Carolyn Nevins was the nurse-anaesthetist. Janet Stevens was on scrub and assist nurse. Barbara Cosgrove was the floating nurse. Oh, and there was also Mary Rooney, a general nurse in obstetrics. She was an institution at St Catherine's.'

Concannon was looking out of the window at Boston Harbor. It seemed as if he might have been daydreaming, but even with the averted look, he listened carefully.

'What did you observe about her appearance when you first saw her?'

'She was pale,' replied Dr Towler. 'She was in pain. I thought she might be in danger of going into shock, and so I ordered her hydrated. That is, I got an I.V. started as soon as possible. She was on a stretcher in the prep room, and I went in and tried to reassure her . . .'

'Why? Why did you bother to stop and reassure her when you had so many other things to do to get ready?'

'People are frightened when they enter a hospital. No matter how well prepared. No matter how innocuous the procedure. It's scary. So when they look up and see a friendly face, it is a comfort. I always try to be there . . .'

'Nice. Very nice. What happened then?'

'Dr Crowley came over to say hello. He told her that he was going to give her a general anaesthetic. He told her that she would be going to sleep. I think he mentioned the name of the agent – nitrous oxide.'

'Not you think, Doctor. This leaves you vulnerable to cross-examination, to the charge that you're guessing or don't really know. Answer it with certitude. "Dr Crowley chatted with her briefly, telling her that he would administer a general anaesthetic – nitrous oxide. She said that would be fine." '

Dr Towler looked uneasy. Smoke from his pipe rose in quick, short jets. He was the one who commanded attention, lectured others. Taking orders made him uncomfortable.

'Dr Towler, it's really quite simple,' Concannon went on. 'Look at it this way. You were right there during this conversation?'

'Yes.'

'You heard it?'

'Yes.'

'You and Dr Crowley were standing next to Debbie in the prep room, right?'

'Right,' said Dr Towler quietly.

'Then what happened?'

'We took Mrs Rosen –'

'Doctor, please, Debbie.'

'Yes, of course. We took Debbie into the operating room.

Nurse Nevins started the I.V., adding 0 point four milligram of atropine to dry up secretions. And then Dr Crowley began inducing the anaesthesia.'

'Everything was routine? You had her coming along nicely despite her past medical difficulties?'

'It couldn't have been more routine. She was breathing regularly. It was all going smoothly. The vital signs were good. Blood pressure. Respiration. Pulse. I had just completed the episiotomy – a little incision in the vaginal surface to ease the delivery – when Debbie began getting cyanotic. I couldn't understand –'

'I beg your pardon, Doctor, but we don't know what that means . . . cyanotic.'

'I'm sorry. Her skin coloration. She was turning blue. It signals a lack of oxygen in the blood. And then Nurse Nevins and Dr Crowley said something. Her blood pressure fell to forty over twenty. Her pulse was weak and thready. There was no blood in the vaginal incision. She had stopped bleeding. She stopped breathing. Someone yelled, "Cardiac arrest!"'

'To give the jury some idea of the time frame, how long did all this take?'

'Seconds. Quicker than it takes to tell it. I immediately signalled a Code Blue. That's an emergency call. I pushed a red button next to me, specifically used for this purpose.'

'Okay, what did you do?'

'We are all trained in emergency procedures. There's a crash team at St Catherine Laboure that automatically responds to a Code Blue. It's a specially trained disaster unit. We had two problems. An emerging infant. And a dying patient.'

'Doctor, you did everything that could humanly be expected,' said Concannon. 'You brought forty years of medical experience to that instant of crisis. Everything known to medical science was applied. You literally reached down into the Valley of Death to pull Debbie back. Isn't that true, Doctor?'

Dr Towler's voice broke. 'Yes,' he said, choking. 'That's

true. We did our best. We did everything possible to resuscitate the patient. I began compressing the heart mechanically with the heel of my hand until the crash crew arrived.

'The brain is so fragile. There is just four minutes to restore cardiac action to get oxygenated blood once again coursing to the brain. That's all you have. It's an area as big as a softball. Contains millions and millions of cells. They all need oxygen to survive. They must have it continuously. After four minutes, they begin to die. They cannot be brought back. It is irreversible. Once a brain cell dies, it's gone forever.' The doctor paused to compose himself.

'I kept compressing the chest cage. Pushing on the sternum – the breastbone. This stimulates systole, or contraction of the heart. It simply squeezes the blood out of the heart and into the aorta – the great blood vessel leading from the heart into the circulatory system. When you take your hand off the chest, the heart's resting state – diastole, or dilatation – begins. The blood flows back into the heart. It fills. Then contraction expresses the blood out into the circulation again. We keep the heart pumping manually.'

'And this is how you get the oxygen circulating to the vital organs when the heart isn't functioning by itself?'

Dr Towler nodded acquiescence.

'What about the rest of the team?'

'It gets a little hectic. Dan Crowley cut an airway into the trachea, bypassing the upper respiratory orifices. That got air directly into the lungs. You have to keep the air passages clear. Then the crash team arrived and took over while I attended to the birth of the infant. Contractions had stopped, and there was a great danger of the baby strangling without oxygen.'

'Yes? That was the sequence?'

'Well, Dr Crowley had already removed the anaesthesia mask and we could see what had happened. She had aspirated vomitus –'

'Okay. Now, this is crucial. This is central to the whole case. You cannot even seem to sound as if you're trying to make it sound evasive. No euphemism. No bullshit. She threw up into her mask. That's it! It may sound brutal to you, but it's going to sound a lot worse if you sound as if you're avoiding naming the thing.'

'Yes. Dr Crowley removed the mask and the vomit poured out. My God! There was no doubt then of what had happened. She had thrown up into the mask, clogging her trachea. No oxygen was getting through to her lungs. She was drowning in her own vomit.'

Donna was taking notes as fast as she could. She was a professional, and the facts had to be taken down. Recorded. Some part of her mind was horrified. She could visualize the scene; she could see them pulling the mask away and the flood of vomit pouring out. She could see Deborah Ruth Rosen dying on the table while her baby was being born.

'Did you determine what caused the cardiac arrest?' asked Concannon.

'Yes. Primarily, it was caused by the patient's aspiration of vomitus into the anaesthetic mask, but it was also due to other factors. Low haemoglobin; suppression of blood pressure and the heart rate by inhalation of the anaesthetic. This happens. There's no way of guarding against it. Also vagal stimulation. The vagus nerve is really a cranial nerve, meaning that from its origin in the brain stem it passes through the cranium, or skull. However, it courses through the body even down to the abdomen. It wanders all over the anatomy. The Greek physician Galen named it in the second century; it means "vagrant" or "wanderer". It even controls cardiac activity. Press on the vagus nerve and you slow the heart rate. Again, the emerging infant, the trauma of childbirth, can cause traction on the vagus nerve.'

'Were you able to tell that she was aspirating vomitus prior to removing the face mask?'

'Not really.'

'How about the cardiac arrest?'

'That is something that you cannot guard against. It's a rare event. But it happens. It can occur even in innocuous surgical procedures. It can happen at the dentist's during a tooth extraction. Some patients are hypersusceptible. The system reacts against the anaesthetic. Sometimes it happens for reasons no one can explain.'

'You cannot predict, then, when this is going to happen?'

'No. It happens to patients who have had the same anaesthesia agent before without reaction. Then, for some inexplicable reason, this time there is an adverse reaction . . . like being stung by a bee. One person hardly feels it – some slight skin irritation for a few seconds. Another person – same amount of toxicity – goes into anaphylactic shock and dies.'

'Please go on.'

'Nurse Nevins began to bag-breathe Debbie. She forced pure oxygen into her lungs.'

'Dr Towler, from the time you first detected cyanosis until bag breathing commenced, how much time elapsed? And Doctor, if I ask you this question, or if the plaintiff's attorney asks you this – and he will – we have to be fairly consistent. The question of time is crucial. This goes for all of you – Dr Crowley and Miss Nevins. I want everyone to agree in a general way. No one was looking at a watch during this crisis. No one was counting the seconds. This was a Code Blue emergency. Everyone had an assigned task and was carrying it out precisely as designated. No one was standing around watching the clock. So we will all agree that about two minutes elapsed, give or take ten seconds, from the first sign of cyanosis to the initial bag breathing. Two minutes. Remember that. If you forget everything else, remember two minutes.'

During a break, Donna pulled Concannon over to the window.

'Send them to lunch,' she said.

'What?' asked Concannon, somewhat annoyed.

'If we knew who Galvin's expert was, could it help?'

'It might,' he replied. 'It would give us time to get book on him early. He might be vulnerable. He might be incompetent. We wouldn't have to check him on the fly or find out things after he testifies and Galvin sends him to Puerto Rico on a vacation so we can't recall him. It's a nice head start. Why? *Do* you know?'

'Send them to lunch,' said Donna, who now saw bright possibilities for her future.

10

The waiter moved with the silence and grace of an underwater swimmer. He laid out the asparagus spears in one long, sweeping motion, then painted them with hollandaise sauce. Donna felt pampered.

'His name is Lionel Thompson,' said Concannon, returning to the private dining room. Donna had told him about the 78-year-old star witness, and Concannon had excused himself. She sipped wine while he was gone. She assumed that he would put staff on it, as if ordering artillery fire on an enemy position.

She didn't tell him about the other thing. She didn't tell him because she wasn't sure herself. It was a suspicion. A suspicion about a suspicion. It had been almost too easy with Galvin. She had a feeling that there was more to it. But she wouldn't say anything yet. She wouldn't risk the ridicule of hearing it called 'woman's intuition'.

She sipped the dry white wine and gazed out the window of the penthouse dining room, stretching her legs luxuriously under the table – as if she were in a warm bath. This was her kind of world. She debated, as she waited for Concannon to return, whether or not to tell him. She was not certain that the price was right. Besides, it would weaken the value of the first message.

'I don't want to know how you found out,' said Concannon, raising his wineglass to toast the occasion. 'Suffice it to say you have succeeded where many of your male colleagues have failed.'

The implication stung. Concannon might seem brilliant and

suave, but there was a certain clumsiness about him. Or was it arrogance? She wasn't sure. She swallowed more wine and felt the heat in her cheeks.

'Does the fact that I'm a woman seem the only relevant resource about me?' she asked, smiling slightly.

Concannon looked up. His fork was poised. He dwelt on her long, tapered fingers gently caressing the lip of the glass. 'It's not something that is easy to ignore,' he said.

She raised her glass slightly in salute, and almost at the same instant the waiter refilled it. He had managed to compound the insult with another compliment. He was a formidable man, this Concannon.

'Just as a matter of interest, Mr Concannon, I was third in my law-school graduating class. Columbia.'

'Are you from New York?'

'Yes,' she said too quickly. 'Grew up in Queens.' She caught herself, feeling suddenly déclassé. She was disarmed. She would not like to tangle with him in the courtroom; bed perhaps, but not the courtroom. Suddenly she pitied Galvin.

'Tell me,' he said, 'why did you move to Boston? Doesn't New York have a lot of decent law firms?'

'Oh, I did some graduate work here. Got my Master of Laws at Harvard. I always was a good student. They tell me I have a photo-retentive memory. Great for exams. But mostly I was running away from my mother.'

'Really?'

'I have an Old World mother,' she said. 'She's one inch high and she lives in the back of my head and she shakes her finger at everything I do. She wants me to get married. She sits up there wagging her finger at me and telling me to get married. It's not easy living with a tidy-bowl mom.'

'That sounds pretty normal.'

'Oh, it's normal, all right. It's just very hard to live with. If I were working in New York, I'd have to live at home. Unless I was married. Even then I might have to live at home.'

'And you don't want to get married.'

'Mr Concannon, I do not wish to get married. Not that I take that as a proposal.'

'What's wrong with marriage?'

'I have a lot of friends who are married. One or two are even happy. Maybe. Generally, it doesn't work out. Not if a woman wants a career.'

'It can. If the people are mature.'

'I don't know any men that mature. Most men want you glazed and stuck in the suburbs. Forgive me, Mr Concannon, but marriage is a one-man show. The woman winds up wearing a silver-lamé bathing suit, stiletto heels and mesh stockings. Her job is to help the magician pull the rabbit out of the hat.'

Donna studied his face, his rugged, chiselled features. Surely he was interested in her. Surely his attentions went beyond her legal investiture.

'More wine?' he said, pouring.

After lunch they reassembled downstairs in the expansive conference room. There was a danger of lapsing into complacency. Fine lunches and expensive furnishings and lavish settings lulled people, and Concannon did not intend to let that happen.

'I can't emphasize this too much; I want to be clear on the two-minute thing,' he said. 'You don't all have to say two minutes on the nose. If the plaintiff's attorney says, "Could it have been two and a half minutes?" answer, "Yes, but I think it was closer to two minutes." If he says, "Could it have been three minutes?" answer, "No. Definitely not that long. My best judgment is two minutes."

'And if he says, "If you weren't consulting a clock, how could you be so certain of the time?" your answer is that you are basing the estimate on experience of thousands of operations and deliveries.'

Concannon moved his watch and held it up. 'Now, the plaintiff's attorney may actually time you to test your accuracy. He may lay his watch on the jury rail and say, "Now, Dr Towler, or Miss Nevins, or Dr Crowley, I will say "Start" when the second hand is on zero and I want you to say "Now" when you think two minutes have elapsed." It's an old lawyer's stunt. People get rattled on the witness stand and usually foul it up and end up far too short. But this is where we can score some points of our own. If he starts the test, I'll let him. Now, don't look at your own watch. Don't look at the courtroom clock, which has no second hand. The jurors will be glancing at their own watches. What you do is count to yourself. One. Pause. Two. Pause. When you hit one hundred twenty, say "Now". You'll be surprised. You won't be right on the nose. I don't want exactitude. But you'll be reasonably close. That lends credibility to everything.

'One other thing,' he added. 'Don't move your lips.'

There was a touch of buoyancy in the room as the afternoon session progressed. Dr Towler's pipe smouldered placidly. Nurse Nevins smiled now and then, and Dr Crowley's knitted brow began to relax. Donna watched the cool confidence of Concannon and wondered how she could manoeuvre him into a dinner invitation. She wondered if he cheated on his wife. She wondered what he would look like in the morning, rumpled and unshaven. Occasionally she caught a glimpse of Roger Rutledge, whose eyes would wander in her direction.

'Okay, let's get on with the narrative,' Concannon said. 'Assume you're still under oath, Dr Towler. What happened next?'

'The Code Blue team was there,' said Dr Towler. 'The defibrillator was brought in, and Nurse Richards attached the electrodes from the machine to Debbie's chest. This took a few seconds. We attempted to shock the heart back into operation. Ignite the electrical spark, so to speak, that keeps the cardiac muscle beating rhythmically. It didn't work. Dr Menninger, the crash-team cardiovascular surgeon, next injected a stimulant – epinephrine – directly into the myocardium – that's the heart muscle – and that did it. As a last resort I was prepared to perform a thoracotomy . . .'

'A what?' asked Donna, looking up from her notes. 'I'm sorry, I didn't quite catch that.'

'A thoracotomy,' said Dr Towler, barely masking his annoyance at the intrusion. 'T-h-o-r-a-c-o-t-o-m-y. That's when you open the chest surgically. With your hands, you grab hold of the heart muscle itself and squeeze it several times. This sometimes works when everything else fails. But we didn't have to go that far. We got a heartbeat from the stimulant. We watched it on the monitor. It grew strong. Debbie's colour returned almost immediately. Her vital signs stabilized and appeared normal.'

'Okay,' said Concannon, leaning across the table, drawing everyone closer. 'Now we are at another crucial question. This is the heart of the case. No pun intended. No levity from here on in. But it's apt. Everyone has to remember this. I'll ask it this way. "Now, from the instant you first recognized the signs of cardiac arrest until you restored the heartbeat, how much time elapsed?" This is the most important time element of all. If you remember nothing else, you have to remember this. Approximately four minutes!'

Concannon pushed his chair back and banged his fist on the conference table for emphasis. 'Four minutes. No less. Maybe a little more. Say four minutes thirty seconds. Why do I say four minutes?'

Dr Towler began to answer.

'No,' interrupted Concannon. 'Let me tell you why. This is the defence. The crux of our case. You must understand what I am about to tell you. You can give it back to me in your own words when you are on the witness stand, but this you must understand . . .

'What happened was a tragedy. Cardiac arrest. Brain damage. A rare event. But it does happen and it cannot be prevented. Regardless of your heroic efforts. For some inexplicable reason the heart stops. Resuscitation procedures are instantly commenced. You attempt cardiac compression, suctioning, intubation, bag breathing, electric shock, direct myocardial stimulation. Sometimes the heart responds. Sometimes it doesn't. Like a faulty motor on a cold morning. But no one can guard against cardiac arrest. And it is no one's fault if resuscitation efforts fail.'

Concannon had control of everyone's attention. He spoke with assurance. He was the wing commander.

'The human brain,' he continued expansively, 'is an exquisitely delicate organ. It lives hand to mouth on oxygen. There is no reserve supply. It uses twenty percent of the body's oxygen. Yet, it is less than one percent of the total body weight. But it is a furnace that must be continually stoked. Shut off the fuel supply, and there is serious trouble. There is a very thin margin of safety. And that margin is four minutes.

'A human being can last weeks without food. Days without water. But without oxygen, you die in minutes. The brain goes quickest. Four minutes.

'Deborah Ruth Rosen lives in a near-vegetative state today. Her electroencephalograms are practically flat. She was in a coma for sixty days. She lies in bed like a cabbage. And she has lain like that for four years. So we know that she must have suffered tremendous brain damage while she was on the operating table. She had heart stoppage and oxygen starvation.

'If we say that the deprivation was for three minutes, then all the leading medical authorities would testify that she would have only mild neurological deficits. So we are not going to state that the elapsed time was three minutes or under because it just couldn't have happened that way. The end result is too severe. We have to remain credible.'

'The four-minute rule is a little more flexible than that,' corrected Dr Crowley, who was lighting a cigarette with a stub from the last. 'Calder Jones in New York says three and a half minutes, tops.'

'I know,' said Concannon quickly, 'and Hans Schopen at the Mayo Clinic says four and a half to five minutes. But those are the inner and outer limits.' He had done his homework and was not about to tolerate nitpicking sophistry. 'Let's agree on the four-minute rule here, among ourselves. The plaintiff will not be able to dispute the defence if we agree that four minutes or, tops, four minutes thirty seconds went by. No medical authority of any consequence will challenge the cause and effect.'

'Mr Concannon' – Dr Crowley spoke gravely – 'you will note on the anaesthesia chart that we forgot to record exactly, by checking the five-minute intervals, just how long the heart was at a standstill.'

'This is just my point,' said Concannon. 'I'm well aware of the anaesthesia chart. Nurse Nevins started to record the vital signs after ten minutes went by. There's a ten-minute lapse in recording. Two five-minute intervals went unchecked. Why did they go unchecked for ten minutes? Simple. This was an emergency situation. Everyone had a job to do. Nurse Nevins, you weren't sitting around with a stopwatch and pencil. It was actually four minutes that elapsed. Not ten.'

'We did do our best, Mr Concannon,' cried Nurse Nevins, who had been silent for most of the session and was now holding back a flood of emotion. She struggled to keep control. 'All of us. We all did our very best. My God, doesn't anyone have any idea what it's like in there?'

'It's all right, Carolyn,' said Dr Crowley, touching her hand.

'These people understand.'

'But they make it sound like we did something wrong!' she cried. 'Mr Concannon is making it sound like we have something to hide and we have to conspire to cover it up!'

'No,' said Concannon firmly. 'Not cover up. But win. I have no doubt of who is right and who is wrong. I'm fully aware of what went on in that operating room. But the courtroom is *my* operating theatre. I know how that operation is performed. There are rules and ceremonies, just like a hospital. You people scrub, and we prepare. You're not being coached to lie. I'm not telling you what to say, but how to say it. If you just go onto the witness stand cold, without the antiseptic scrub of my conference here, your story will become infected. The opposition will pull tricks and stunts to try to rattle you. But if you are on the stand and he asks for the two-minute test, for example, you will have a clear head and you won't panic. My aim is to give you the confidence to be able to tell the truth. We don't want any surprises. And remember, you know more about the subject matter – medicine, your specialty – than he does. You have the advantage.'

'I'm sorry, Mr Concannon, but this has been a terrible strain,' said Dr Towler, half rising. 'We are not accustomed to such . . . to such . . . I don't know what else to call it – to such anger.'

'I understand,' said Concannon.

'I think we all feel a little better now,' added Dr Crowley.

There was a knock on the conference-room door and an assistant brought in a note. Concannon called Donna aside.

'Your Dr Thompson is a bit of a quack. He went to New York College of Medicine and Husbandry . . .'

'I never heard of it,' she replied.

'Well, it's now defunct. It was an old diploma factory off Broadway in Manhattan where MDs and horse doctors took the same courses for the first two years. He's not even board certified. No teaching experience. No hospital affiliations except the East Hampton Hospital for Women, where he has guest privileges.

'Originally from Kingston, Jamaica. Practised there for years. About five years ago he got some sort of professional reciprocity to practise in the States . . . Also' – Concannon repressed a grin – 'he's of the Negro persuasion.'

'I guess you'll be able to handle him on cross,' she said.

'Maybe he won't even get to the batter's box,' said Concannon. 'I know a few people in the Long Island Medical Society. Maybe a discreet phone call or two will keep the bastard home.'

Concannon's eyes flashed with a new zest. He sensed victory with one quick thrust. 'Roger,' he said, turning to Roger Rutledge, 'I believe we will settle Galvin's hash once and for all thanks to Miss St Laurent.' Concannon smiled at Donna.

'And Roger', he continued, 'please have that young lawyer of yours – you know, the black football star from Stanford, Wilson Gayner – sit in with me at the counsel table in place of Curt Carrington. And if it's okay with you, I'll call "Kip" Keough at the *Globe*. A nice story on Wilson might be timely. Football fans don't forget their heroes.'

'I guess that settles Mr Galvin,' Donna said.

'I don't know,' Concannon replied thoughtfully. 'It seems pretty flimsy, basing a whole lawsuit on one cardboard expert. Are you sure there's nothing else?'

'What else could he have?' she replied.

Later, when she called Galvin's office, Peggy Twomy said she had no idea where her boss was.

'Is this Miss St Laurent?' asked the secretary.

'Yes,' said Donna, surprised. 'Yes, it is.'

'Well, Galvin left a message for you. But if you want my advice, honey, you'll hang up now.'

Donna looked at the receiver quizzically for a moment.
'What's the message?' she asked.
'He said you'd be able to reach him tonight at the Plaza.'
'The Plaza? What Plaza?'
'The Plaza Hotel. In New York.'

11

'Let me make sure I've got everything clear, Galvin. You can't go back to your office because there are two guys with three subpoenas waiting for you. You go to trial day after tomorrow and your expert witness is waffling. You haven't seen your wife in three weeks. And you're cheating on your mistress. You may even have compromised your case to this bimbo that you met last night. I don't get it, Galvin. What's the problem?'

'I think I love her, Moe.'

Galvin sat dejectedly on the couch in his old partner's office, squirming like a guilty truant.

'Who?' cried Moe. 'Which one? No, don't even tell me. I don't want to hear it. It's probably someone you met on the elevator coming up here. I swear to God, Galvin, you keep this up and you'll add three years to my life. I don't want to die until I see how everything turns out.'

'Don't laugh, Moe. I need help.'

'Don't laugh? Don't laugh? Are you crazy? Galvin, if you don't laugh at this you're in big trouble. This is too serious not to laugh. My advice to you is to laugh before it's too late. In a few years, you'll look back on all this and cry. Right now, laugh! It's your only hope.'

'I could also use a drink.'

'Help yourself,' replied Moe, forgetting for the moment his native hospitality. He was stunned by the sheer complexity of Galvin's plight. 'You know where I keep the shnapps.'

Galvin's hand shook as he poured the Scotch into a paper cup.

'I was in my office about an hour ago,' he began, shaking his head in disbelief, 'you know, taking a nap on the couch. God, I've been working so hard on this fucking case. Day and night . . .'

'I know about the nights,' said Moe. 'I've seen some of the effort you put in after dark. If you worked that hard during the day, you'd be Chief Justice.'

'. . . Anyway. So Peggy buzzes and says there is a very important call but the guy won't leave his name. She really loves drama. "Just tell him it's Dr X," the guy says.'

'Dr X? Wasn't that a guy in New Jersey, accused of killing a few patients with curare a couple of years ago?'

'Different X,' said Galvin. 'This is my guy in New York. You know, my medical expert.'

'In the Rosen case?' said Moe.

'Right. But I didn't know that. He sounded very shaky. And he was talking in code. Like he was part of the Plumbers' Unit. "Do you recognize my voice?" and that kind of shit. Then he says, "You know why I'm calling?" and I say, "I can guess."'

'Boy, what nuts. Don't you even know what your man sounds like?' chided Moe.

'Well, yes, when I know who I'm talking to. But I was sleepy and all I heard was "Dr X" and you know how it is when you pretend to understand what someone's talking about, but you don't and you figure you'll catch up. My Dr X, Moe, was scared. Really scared. His voice even trembled. They got to him, Moe. Imagine that – they got to him. The bastards! Well, he explains how he has guest privileges in anaesthesiology at a Long Island hospital. East Hampton Hospital for Women. He's seventy-eight years old and it's the last place in the world he can practise medicine. He says he doesn't need the money, but he's afraid to retire. Doesn't want to rot on a porch.'

'That's not hard to understand,' said Moe. 'People die quickly when they retire. Look at Max Gross. He was eighty-two years old and they had to help him into the courtroom.

But he wouldn't retire. Finally, he had to quit. They took away his driving licence. He was coming home from court one day and he stopped for a red light.'

'What's wrong with that?'

'He was on the expressway and the red light was on an overpass. Poor Max. He couldn't get to court anymore without a car. So he had to retire.'

'Then he died, huh?'

'Who said he died? He's fine. I'm playing poker at his house tonight. You should be in such good shape at his age. You should even get to be his age. What a terrible thing to say about poor Max!'

'Moe! Moe! Listen to me! I'm in big trouble. He tells me that he won't be able to testify. He's whispering into the telephone and he tells me that one of the guys in the county medical association passed along a friendly tip that he shouldn't get involved; it would cost him his privileges.'

'Sounds like someone in Concannon's office is onto your witness. Is he vulnerable?'

'Who's not vulnerable? Christ, everyone's vulnerable. Could any of us stand some close scrutiny? Would you even want to?'

'Sounds like it's all over for you.'

'Not quite. I talked him back into it.'

'How did you manage that?'

'Well, he tells me he's coloured and has grandchildren and likes to go sailing weekends off the Hamptons –'

'What colour? Turquoise? Vermilion?'

'Moe, there's nothing funny in this. He's black. Tells me he's black. I could've died. Imagine flashing a black MD as an expert in Suffolk County.'

'Boy, those Micks and Poles from Southie and Chelsea will love you. Not to mention my landsmen from Mattapan. And why in hell did it take this long to find out that he wasn't Harvard crimson? Talk about preparation. Christ, didn't you ever meet the guy before?'

'No, I didn't,' Galvin sighed. 'I got his name from one of the national law journals. You've seen the ads: Anaesthesiologist. Specialist. Will review malpractice cases. Available to testify. Plaintiff or defendant. No name, just a New York PO box.'

'Boy, Galvin. Really some ace you've got up your sleeve!'

'You see, Moe, I gave him fifteen hundred dollars two years ago. Talked to him a few times on the phone. Never knew he was black. It never came up. He gave me his report indicating Catherine Laboure et al. are in the soup and tells me he'd be available when the case comes to trial. He had a dignified English accent, like he's from Oxford or Eton or someplace. That's what threw me.

'Well, he's from Jamaica – not Jamaica, Long Island, but the island in the Caribbean. And he tells me he graduated from some medical school in New York City. He returned to Jamaica, practised for years in Kingston – tropical diseases, obstetrics, surgery, anaesthesiology, everything.'

'How about witchcraft? The islands are big on voodoo.'

'Do you want me to continue, Moe?'

'Please continue.'

'So he recently returned to New York. Say, five years ago. His family was there, and he got admitted to the New York Medical Society without having to take his boards. Sort of a reciprocity deal. Now he's shaky because they're checking into his credentials.'

'That's funny, Galvin. Laugh!'

'Well, Moe, he's coming. Got him booked in at the Parker House for the weekend.

'It took some doing to get him to come. He's real pissed off. Christ, if he was some Uncle Tom from South Carolina or Georgia I'd be in trouble. But these islanders are proud, Moe, like us Irish. Maybe an omen. Well, I give him the old Black Panther stuff. The "us against them" routine. I tell him I don't care what colour he is. Could be purple for all I care. I'm back with the Irish rebellion, back with Parnell and Collins and De Valera, Kevin Barry and the Easter Uprising. How we Irish were known as the Niggers of Europe . . . and how the English stuck it to everyone. Stripped the land, sent the Irish to Tasmania to work in prison colonies. Sent the blacks in chains to Jamaica. I tell him about Toussaint L'Ouverture, the black general in Haiti, leading the slaves against the English.'

'The French,' Moe corrected.

'What's the difference? They're the ones in power. They do the kicking. And we're getting kicked.'

'Why should he risk his licence for a lousy fifteen hundred?'

'"You know," Thompson says, in that soft Limey accent of his, "what can they do to me? Really. They only tolerate me around here because they're short of anaesthesiologists. I'm old. They'll stop me in a year or two anyway. Sooner, if some MD wants to level off and move out here. They killed this Rosen girl and I'm not going to let them cover it up, Mr Galvin. Tell them they're in deep trouble."'

'Those were his words, Moe. Christ, you should've heard him. Jesus, he's sore!'

'He'll be a helluva lot sorer when Concannon puts him in the shredder,' Moe said. 'Not certified, never took his New York boards . . . and what makes you think Judge Sweeney will let him testify? That prick Sweeney may find he's about as qualified as a candy-striper. And I wouldn't blame him.'

'Well, Moe, I've got to go with what I got. I'll qualify him all right. Christ, half the cardiologists around here, the OBs and surgeons, aren't board certified. And there's nothing like having an expert witness who's on fire.'

'Galvin, you're fighting submarines with a flamethrower.'

'And I told him the whole case hung on him. That without him, there wouldn't be a case. Meanwhile, as we're talking, two city marshals show up. They have subpoenas from the bar association and from my landlord. I am trying to sound rational and pathetic for Dr X while Peggy is running back and forth shrieking that they're going to take away her typewriter. It was like the Marx Brothers.'

'How did it end up?'

'Dr Thompson said he'd come, so I told him I'd go down there and take him back personally. An escort.'

'What do you need from me?' asked Moe. 'Carfare?'

'I need a friend. What you said before is probably true. Concannon knows about this guy. I don't know how. I was going to spring it on him at the trial as a surprise. Thompson would testify. On and off the stand. Just like that.' Galvin snapped his fingers. 'By the time they started to check on him, he'd be off the Hamptons doing a little fishing. But now I've lost my surprise, and I have to assume I'm being watched.'

'And so?'

'So I had planned to make another stop in New York. But if they're tailing me, I can't do it alone. I need help.'

'You want me to pick up your mail?'

'I want you to skip tonight's poker game.'

'I have a feeling that you are going to ask more than that.'

'I am going to ask you to catch the shuttle into New York. The next one. And I am going to ask you to see someone for me.'

'So you have more than this one expert for the case?'

'So far, he's all I have. But with your help, Moe, I can pull this out. I'll write down the name and address and I'll explain it to you on the way to Logan. I'll be in New York too, but we can't see each other. You'll understand it all –'

'I don't know if I want to get involved, Galvin. You're not exactly on a winning streak. And besides, they got a contract out on you.'

'If you don't, I'll understand. But I wouldn't ask if I could do it myself. And there's no one else in the world I can trust.'

109

'I hate airplanes. I hate New York City. The cab drivers are worse than in Boston.'

'So you'll do it,' said Galvin.

Moe held his breath for a few moments, then exhaled. He took a paper cup and drank two fingers of Scotch whisky. 'Print the name and address, Galvin. And be careful. You have such terrible handwriting I could wind up in Cincinnati.'

12

Mary Rooney had been expecting Galvin. When Moe telephoned instead from the airport, she was suspicious and annoyed.

'It's about the case,' he said. 'I'm working with Frank Galvin.'

'What case?' she said. It was a hard, flinty reflex against strangers. 'I don't know what you'd be talking about.'

'It's about a case when you were working in Boston. When you were a nurse at St Catherine Laboure Hospital four years ago.'

She knew what case, all right. Moe had worked with such people before. As a lawyer, he ran into them all the time. People with built-in insulation. Mean, working-class hard-liners, who had to be broken like spies for any information.

'Please, Mrs Rooney –'

'It's Miss Rooney, if you don't mind.'

'I'm sorry, Miss Rooney. It's just that I'm tired. I'm an old man. And you know what case I'm talking about.'

'Come on down if you're comin',' she said grudgingly.

'Thank you, Miss Rooney,' Moe said gently. 'I'll be right over.'

The subway was a mistake. He should have taken a taxicab. He rode all the way down to 14th Street holding his breath. The train was filled with junkies and psychopaths. One grinning maniac kept walking up and down the subway car opening and closing his fly. Moe was the only one who looked at him. That was a terrible mistake. He had broken the code. There was an unwritten code on the subway: you were not supposed to notice. Normal people were supposed to read their newspaper or paperback book or stare into space. They were supposed to avoid eye contact with the maniacs. No matter what.

But Moe noticed. And it was as if he had thrown away his immunity. He had become a fair target. He had entered the psychopath's world.

Please God, only let him hold on for a few more minutes, Moe prayed. Sooner or later, this one will explode. No question. Only let it be later.

When the train pulled into the 14th Street subway station, Moe practically ran to the exit. The young maniac stayed on the train, grinning lasciviously at him through the window. With just a smile, he had brutalized Moe.

'I almost got killed on the subway,' he said when she finally let him in. 'I don't know how people can live here. Maniacs running around with their flies open!'

'Why didn't Mr Galvin come?' she asked.

Moe was still breathing hard from the stairs and the tension. He had not taken off his coat. He sat at the kitchen table bundled up against rejection.

'He couldn't,' said Moe. 'He would if he could, believe me. But he couldn't.'

'Well, ye've wasted a trip, Mr Katz. I don't have anything to tell him.'

'Just let me catch my breath,' he said. 'I thought I was going to get killed.'

Mary Rooney recognized discomfort. She had spent a lifetime ill at ease. 'Would you like a cup of tea?' she asked.

'That would be very nice,' he said.

She moved around the kitchen preparing the tea with one hand. With the other, she clutched her cardigan tight.

Since she had retired from St Catherine's, she had grown even lonelier. She had moved to New York City to be close to her sister's children. They were all that was left of her family. But it was clear that they regarded her as an intrusion and a

112

burden. They never came to visit and she felt uncomfortable in their homes.

She often regretted her sudden retirement, although at the time it had seemed the only thing to do. She preferred to remember what it was like working as an obstetrical nurse. It's the only department in a hospital where more people leave than come in, she would say.

And the job itself was always a joy. There was a momentary intimacy, during the great drama of birth. There was hardly ever any aftermath. Not like in the other departments, like medicine or surgery, where you watched them die. In OB, there was mostly gratitude and joy.

And if she was noticed or remembered at all, she liked to think that she was a flickering image – the nice, sweet old nurse cooing them to sleep.

The incident had poisoned it. She had been on the lip of retirement anyway. Forty years in the delivery rooms was enough. But the incident had pushed her over the edge, and she'd left and moved to another city, where she spent most of her time in the kitchen brewing tea against the chill in her bones. And wore her sweater like a shield.

'Will you be taking milk?' she asked. 'I don't have any lemon.'

'Just a little sugar is fine,' said Moe. 'Do you miss working?' he asked her.

'I miss my privacy,' she said.

'I don't like to disturb a person's privacy.'

'But that's what you lawyers do, isn't it? I'll tell you the truth, Mr Katz, I don't take to lawyers very much. They suck a person's blood. They do. Suck a person's blood. Do nothing as far as I can see but cause trouble. They build nothing. They create nothing. They live off misery. Meanin' no disrespect, Mr Katz, but they're a devious lot.'

'I couldn't disagree with that,' said Moe.

'I know what ye're here about,' she said. 'It's the Rosen case.

Someone's suing the doctors and the hospital. And someone's going to get rich. But it won't be Deborah Rosen. It'll be some lawyer, now. Won't it?'

Moe sipped his tea. 'You may be right, Mrs Rooney – I mean Miss Rooney,' he said. 'In fact, in most respects, I agree you with. How do you like that? I couldn't disagree. The *business* of a lawyer is trouble. It's like a cop. A lot of lawyers abuse it. There are lawyers who string along a client. Create trouble. I wouldn't deny it.'

'So what are we talkin' about?'

'We are talking about something entirely different.'

'Mr Katz, don't get cute with me.'

'You know, that girl is a vegetable.'

'I know that. I know all about it. So what's your lawsuit going to do about that? Are you going to bring her back to life with all that money?'

'There's more at stake than money.'

'I know that, too. There are reputations and lives at stake. You think a lawsuit doesn't hurt people? Let me tell you, Mr Katz, you can do more damage with yer lawsuit than anyone did to Deborah Rosen. People have to have confidence in a hospital. A hospital can die, just like a person. What good will it do to destroy the hospital? It won't bring anyone back, will it?'

He was up against a great wall of pride. And loyalty. She had spent forty years being proud and loyal to the doctors. There had been things she had seen over the years that were wrong. But what was that against the great good that she had also seen?

'If you had seen something wrong, you wouldn't tell me, would you?'

'No,' she said. 'I wouldn't.'

'There's more to this than you know,' he said.

'There always is.'

'What about the children? No one can help Deborah Ruth.

That is true. But there are still the children. Shouldn't they be considered?'

'It's not somethin' I'd like to talk about,' she said.

'If you don't want to talk about it, then you don't want to talk about it. But whether you talk about it or not, they are still there.'

'Well, what about the children, Mr Katz? They've lost a mother, but no one can make that up to them. Not you. Not I. Not Mr Galvin. And your lawsuit won't bring her back.'

'No,' he agreed. 'A lawsuit can't bring back a mother. No one can bring back a mother, as you say. But it can do other things.'

'I don't know what ye're talkin' about.'

'Let me just make a small point. For my own sake, so I can go away with a clear conscience. You can reject the idea and throw me out and I'll go away and never bother you again. But just humour me for a second.'

'What is it, Mr Katz? I know ye'll get it out anyway, so you might as well have at it. What's this *wee* point that will ease your conscience?'

'What is it that a mother provides for her children?' he began with a debater's flourish. 'A mother provides love, and warmth – and *protection!* Protection, Miss Rooney. The fierce lioness who won't let anyone near her cubs. Try to touch an animal's young and the mother is always there, guarding them. Protecting them . . .'

'I don't see, Mr Katz, where this is leadin'.'

'Be patient for one more minute, Mary,' he said, and paused for a sip of tea. 'You haven't got a cookie, have you?'

She took out a box of biscuits. It wasn't the same thing, but he shrugged and took a few anyway, to go with the tea.

'Protection, Mary. Helpless children who no longer have the security of a mother to take care of them.'

She fussed with more tea for herself. Then she took a seat at the opposite end of the kitchen table, facing Moe, as if to debate.

'Do you know how they live now?' he asked. 'Do you have any idea of what their lives are like? Well, I'll tell you. There are three of them. Eight. Six. And four years of age. But they don't live together. They are broken up and shunted back and forth between aunts and uncles and distant cousins. No one wants them.'

'What about the father?'

'The father! That bum. Do you know that he never went to see Deborah after the . . . uh, what happened? Not once. Never! He shipped the children off as soon as he could. Sooner. It wasn't even decent.'

'But legally –'

'Legally? Legally, he's fine. Legally he has remarried and he doesn't work. His new wife supports the two of them. Legally.'

'He doesn't support the children?'

'Not a penny. He's washed his hands of the whole thing. No one wants any part of them. No one.'

The implication was not lost on her. She knew that he was accusing her of turning her back on them too.

'But the aunts and uncles?' she said.

'They do enough to keep the children alive. They feed them. They provide a roof, in turns. Every three months the children uproot and live with another set of relatives. They live somewhere for three months and then they are sent on the circuit. They don't make friends, because they know that they'll be leaving soon.'

'My Lord!'

'I'll tell you the truth: psychologically, they are becoming very withdrawn children. They don't smile. I went to see them with Galvin. They're very polite. They sit quietly with their hands folded in their laps, like they don't want to make anyone mad . . .'

'Oh, that's awful!'

'Psychologically speaking, I would say that they are becoming more and more like their mother.'

'Is that true, Mr Katz?'

'Well, Mary, they live with people who watch every crumb that they eat. Can you imagine what it's like to live with people who don't want you? Can you imagine when people begrudge the very food that you eat?'

No one had to tell her what it was like to sit at sullen dinner tables. She knew the shrivelling feeling of being unwelcome. She knew, as she watched the private and secret things that passed between couples, the lifelong want of someone to trust.

'Yes,' she replied quietly. 'I can imagine that.'

They had more tea, and Moe talked about this neighbourhood that he had once known. He backed away from the topic with a lawyer's instinct for sensing an internal struggle.

'Ten, fifteen years ago. Maybe twenty. We used to come to New York City for a convention and the first thing we'd do is go to Greenwich Village to see the fags. Nowadays we have our own fags in Boston. But in those days, it was still unusual. There was a kosher deli at Broadway and Thirteenth Street. Best corned beef sandwich in the whole world. The best. And pickles! I never tasted such pickles. My mouth is watering just thinking about it . . . I didn't see that deli when I came down. Is it gone?'

'The neighbourhood's changed,' she said. 'I used to be able to go to Mass every day. My sister's boy, Kevin, used to take me to early Mass at St Matthew's. But they changed his hours. He's with the fire department. He can't take me. I wouldn't go myself. Too dangerous. A man followed me home a few weeks ago. He looked nice. He was white. Young, too. He followed me into the hallway and started saying filthy things to me. *Me!* An old woman . . .'

'It's hard when no one wants you,' he said.

She was thinking of the hospital and the delivery room and

the spiritual feeling it had always evoked. The long, cleansing scrubs to prepare. The ritual and devotions of the doctors and nurses – priests and nuns – and then the miracle. Birth.

'You were there, weren't you?' said Moe. 'In the operating room. You were there?'

'Yes,' she said. 'I was there.'

'And something went wrong.'

'Yes,' she said flatly. 'Something went wrong.'

'What went wrong, Mary? What was it that turned Deborah Ruth Rosen into a living corpse?'

'How will the money change things for the children?' she asked.

Moe sat back a little and let out his breath. He knew that he had Mary Rooney.

'There is an uncle who lives in California. Deborah's brother. A nice man. He has just finished school and gotten married. He wants to take the children, but he can't afford it. He married a girl who already has two children and he doesn't want to deprive them. You can understand.'

'He would keep all three?'

'Yes. He would keep all three. But more important, they would never be a burden again. They would be paying their own way. Even little children know when they are welcome.'

'I don't know anything firsthand, you understand. I was there, but there were other nurses . . .'

'Mary,' he said, 'we go to trial tomorrow. The hospital has marshalled the biggest law firm in Boston against us. So far, all we've got is a hunch and a prayer. If *you* don't help, we will be roasted alive. Deborah Ruth Rosen will continue to rot with minimal care. The children will continue to move around from place to place, hand to mouth. If you have anything at all that could help us, for God's sake, please tell me.'

'Have some more tea, Mr Katz. I'll be right back.'

She went into another room where she kept the telephone. He could hear her dialling. Then she closed the door. When she came out, she was smiling a sad smile.

'As I said, Mr Katz, I wasn't the only nurse on duty that night. There was an admitting nurse. I think you should meet her. She's been waiting a long time to meet you.'

13

She was waiting in the Palm Court when Galvin came down from his room. She was nursing a vodka gimlet and listening to the string trio's medley of Richard Rodgers tunes.

A captain in black tie approached and offered menus. But Galvin said they would be drinking for a while. At a nearby table there was the muffled squeal of well-brought-up children being offered the pastry cart.

'So,' said Galvin.

'So,' echoed Donna. 'Surprised?'

'No. Not really. Just disappointed.'

'But you left a message. Didn't you think I'd come?'

'I knew you'd come,' he said. 'I was just hoping you wouldn't.'

'That's crazy.'

'That's me. Crazy. Chasing ambulances and hopeless women.'

The trio slid from 'Mountain Greenery' to 'I Wish I Were in Love Again', and Galvin finally smiled. Atmosphere was important to him. When he stayed in New York, he stayed at the Plaza. He would sit in the Palm Court, with its elegant fronds and exquisitely embroidered women, and it would enhance whatever mission he happened to be on. The strings provided the background theme. An ordinary seduction, which might even have been sordid elsewhere, was promoted by the setting to an epic romance. An advantage became a conquest. A court decision slightly in his favour became a benchmark in his career.

The Plaza heightened the proportions.

A timid failure could even become tragic.

'I would think you'd be flattered,' she said. 'Here I come down from Boston and you have the gall to be disappointed! I chase you to another city! What are men coming to?'

'Their senses, I guess. Oh, I'm flattered, all right. You say you chased me down here?'

'Caught the first plane.'

'Flattering. Very flattering. And I believe you. I believe that you followed me down to New York because I'm a great kisser. I believe it. I also believe in the Easter Bunny.'

She knew something was wrong, and she played for time.

'Well, what do you think, Galvin? Why *am* I here, in your clutches?'

'Because you love me. No doubt about it. You're crazy about me.' Then he leaned over to whisper. 'Let's go up to my room and screw. They only allow that in the rooms. They're very strict in this hotel.'

She laughed. 'Can I finish my drink first? A girl's got to get in the mood.'

There *was* something else. Now she was positive. He was not here simply to fetch Dr Thompson. There was something else up his sleeve and it made him very cocky. This was not the same fumbling Galvin who had trouble with his zipper. He was smarter than she gave him credit for. Although she had sensed something all along. How long had he been on to her? She would have to find out. She would have to find out what else he planned to spring in court.

Her poise suddenly fell into her throat. Concannon would blame her. Galvin was her assignment. That had been clear from the start. She resented it. But she had always understood it. Somehow, she had to retrieve the situation. But first she had to find out how things stood.

'Can we be friends, Galvin?'

'What happened to lovers?'

'Friends are harder to find.'

'Do I have a choice?'

'I'd like to be your friend,' she said.

'You screw all your friends?'

She sighed. 'Buy me another drink, sailor, and I will tell you how Mr J. Edward Concannon plans to carve you up and serve you for breakfast tomorrow.'

The waiter stopped by. He had been hovering just out of range, waiting for a break in the apparently intense exchange. Waiters at the Plaza were trained like dancers to step into and out of a conversation without disturbing the rhythm. Galvin ordered two double Scotches and one more vodka gimlet. He was feeling a little crazy, and the liquor might work either way. It could sedate him or send him through the roof.

And he couldn't take his eyes off Donna. He studied her more carefully. She wore a beige silk blouse and probably nothing underneath. He could sense her movement under the silk.

'Okay, friend,' he said, 'now let me ask you something.'

'Shoot.'

'Don't tempt me . . . Do you always betray on the first date, Miss St Laurent?'

She was not certain whether or not she was supposed to laugh.

'Because,' he continued, 'I'll tell you the truth, I like to wait awhile myself. I like to get to know someone. I think there has to be a relationship first. Build up a little trust. You know what I mean? You can't really betray someone *meaningfully* until you know them.'

She laughed.

'But you!' he went on, ignoring her reaction – 'you're amazing! You seemed to have skipped all those complicated in-betweens. None of that quiet-courtship stuff. No getting-to-know-you period. Just bang! If you'll pardon the pun. Just Wham! Bam! Thank-you-ma'am! Boy, I really gotta hand it to you . . . Donna Strelenski, as in the Pulaski Skyway. Aspiring young Portia . . .'

'Look, Galvin, you wanna play games all night or can we talk turkey? I would like to discuss business.'

'Business? You wanna talk business? What business are we in tonight, Tokyo Rose? You wanna sell some atomic secrets?'

'Cut the shit, Galvin. You're starting to piss me off. Who do you think you are, with this holier-than-thou horseshit? Fuck you, Galvin. Get off my case.'

'Careful,' he said, looking around and noting that they were beginning to affect a few eyebrows. 'I believe your true colours are beginning to run. You're really not the sensitive kid who agonized and marched and bled because the nation's soul was out of sync. Scratch Donna St Laurent, and underneath she's just your everyday crass imperialist, trying to make a buck.'

'Come off it, Galvin. I know a little bit about you. I know exactly what kind of person I'm dealing with.'

'Really. What kind of person is that? What kind of person are *we* dealing with?'

'Let's say you're not exactly Sir Thomas More!'

'You have me there. I'm not Tom More. I'm not even Ralph Nader. But then, my dear, you're not exactly Rebecca of Sunnybrook Farm, are you? Closer to Lady Macbeth, I'd say.'

Galvin stopped paying attention to her. He was genuinely hurt. He had liked Donna from the moment he first saw her. Now he shifted in his chair and surveyed the room. Over his shoulder he watched a balding, heavily jowled man in his late 60s fondling the leg of a girl just out of her teens. At first, Galvin thought that he might be an uncle or a cherished family friend. But the old man grew progressively red in the face from excitement as the girl grew progressively red from embarrassment. She pulled her afternoon shopping bags about her as if to insulate herself from further attack. Large coloured bags with Bergdorf, Saks and Gucci labels.

The old man had hair like puffs of cotton, and it only served to highlight the flame in his cheeks. Such things were not uncommon at the Plaza. There were always old gentlemen flirting with coronaries and healthy young girls with shopping bags. They flew in together, from California, or Chicago, as once they had flown in from Venice: the old gentlemen fawning gratefully over the young girls, who affected an exaggerated hauteur.

It was Galvin's secret wish to end up like that.

'Hey!' said Donna, offended, looking back over her shoulder to see what it was that had stolen Galvin's attention. 'Hey! I'm talking to you!'

'Sorry,' he replied, 'but I was trying to annoy you.'

'The point is that I was telling you that you are a hypocrite.'

'Not so,' he said. 'I'm healthy as a horse.'

'A hypocrite. Hypocrite! Not a hypochondriac.'

'Oh. Well, that's different. So?'

'So? So you can stop acting as if I had personally arranged for the Crucifixion. Let me ask you something, Mr Self-righteous.'

'Okay. But I reserve the right not to tell the truth. What's a little deceit between friends?'

He was out of Scotch, and when he held up his glass a busboy plucked it out of his hand. The waiter leaned in and asked if they would have another, and before he knew it there were fresh drinks on the table. The string quartet started up again. Soft Old World stuff. Mendelssohn, Liszt. 'Intermezzo,' the theme from *Elvira Madigan*.

'Galvin,' she bristled. 'You've got the morals of a pig. You'd screw a dead snake.'

'I would?'

'Don't try to tell me,' continued Donna, 'that you never took advantage of some star-struck legal secretary to get information. Don't try to tell me that you haven't diddled some tootsie in the pursuit of your career.'

'You're asking me,' he said, 'if I have ever had a roll in the hay with some skirt to further my career or a particular case. Is

124

that about right?'

'You got it.'

'Have I ever gone to bed or had carnal knowledge with someone who was party to a case while it was under adjudication: is that a fair and accurate rephrasing of the question?'

'What's the matter, Counsellor – is the premise too complex?'

'Sex for pay, huh?'

'C'mon, Galvin. Answer the question. A simple yes or no.'

'I'm thinking.'

'Don't give me that. I didn't do anything that you haven't done a hundred times. Admit it.'

'I'm trying to think!'

'It's just because I'm a woman. Your ego got a little bruised. You wanted to believe that you were still the champ of World War Two. You thought I laid you because I liked you. Isn't that true? Am I any worse than you and the ten million other sharks in this business?'

'Yes,' he said. 'Goddammit, yes! It's different. You're a woman! That's what's different.'

'It wouldn't have worked any other way. Let's face it, if they'd sent a man you'd've gotten suspicious.'

'The thing is,' he said, 'the really shitty thing about what you're doing is –'

'Yes?' she said.

'You're still doing it!'

She smiled in spite of herself. She smiled against her best interests. She looked away but she continued to smile.

'You work for Concannon,' he said.

She nodded. 'I am opposing counsel,' she said. 'One of several opposing counsel.'

'No kidding. A lawyer, huh? I thought you knew too much for a secretary.'

'Law degree and all. Are you impressed?'

'Let me put it this way: why should I bother to sit here when I know I'm in the presence of my enemies?'

'Maybe we can work a deal, Galvin. I know things that you don't know. You know things that I don't know. It is possible that it may be to our advantage to know when to quit. If, for example, I tell J. Edward that your case is sound and he should settle, he may listen. He could get the offer increased.'

'But you already know my case,' said Galvin. 'Will you go back and tell Concannon to give me two million dollars?'

'You don't have to tell me the whole thing, Galvin. Just enough so that I can be useful. So I can go back there and know what I'm talking about.'

'How about dinner?' said Galvin. 'I'm really getting hungry. We can discuss it further.'

'There's a lovely French restaurant on Fifty-seventh Street,' Donna said. 'This is my town, remember? We can lay out the ground rules with some Chateaubriand for two.'

'Got a better idea,' he replied.

'Oh?'

'It's called room service.'

He called Dr Thompson from the telephone near the men's room. The doctor said he had a fear of flying.

'Meet me at Penn Station,' said Galvin. 'We'll take the train up. But we gotta get going tonight.'

'When am I due on the stand?' asked Dr Thompson.

'Probably day after tomorrow.'

'Have you booked me a room?'

'The best. At the Parker House.'

'Okay. Penn Station. What time?'

'Can you make it by eleven?'

That would give him ample time to pack and drive into Manhattan.

'I can make it. Is the room confirmed, Galvin? I don't want to sleep in the Common.'

'It's confirmed. If worse comes to worst, you can sleep with my girlfriend.'

It was a satisfaction for Galvin to imagine Donna's reaction to being stood up. As the train clicked north on tracks that sounded as if they'd been oiled, he smiled, thinking of her waiting in the unpaid-for room at the Plaza Hotel.

The train emerged from the tunnel and raced off towards the Connecticut shore. Galvin sat back, reclining the musty green velvet seat as far back as it would go. Jesus, he thought, assessing Thompson now as his medical expert. He's really black! Would this cause problems with the jurors? Would they accept him as an authority?

'Tell me, Doctor,' he said, 'what's the L.B. stand for?'

'Lionel Ballestra. Named after the Ballestra family, which has run Jamaica for a hundred and fifty years.'

'L. B. Thompson,' Galvin said out loud. 'There must be some way to impress the jury with your distinguished background.'

'You mean, you don't want them to think I'm just some renegade nigger.'

'I never use words like renegade,' said Galvin.

14

Galvin was flustered. He couldn't find the pleadings folder. It was 10:15 A.M. and he was due in Judge Sweeney's chambers in fifteen minutes.

The intercom buzzed.

'It's Harriet,' said Peggy.

'Who?' said Galvin.

'Your wife. She's on twenty-one.'

He picked up the phone, holding it by his shoulder while he tried to straighten the file with both hands. 'I'm really jammed,' he said. 'The case goes on in ten minutes. Can I talk to you later?'

'I want to talk to you now, Frank. I haven't bothered you in weeks, but I have to talk to you now. I just can't go on like this . . .'

The intercom buzzed.

'Hold a sec,' he told Harriet.

'It's Lotus Blossom on twenty-two,' said Peggy.

He punched 22. 'Hi, sweetheart. Listen, I gotta be in court in five minutes. Can I call you back –'

'Galvin, you better take a second now, you son-of-a-bitch! You talk to me now or I'm getting out of your miserable life and taking Sam with me!'

The intercom buzzed.

'Hold on for just a second,' he told Lois Chen.

'Some woman who calls herself Lady Macbeth on twenty-three. She says she knows you. Sounds like it, too.'

He hit 23. 'What is it? I gotta be in court in two seconds.'

'I just wanted you to know that I'm not angry,' said Donna.

'Terrific.'

'And there's nothing personal in what is about to happen to you.'

She hung up. He punched 21.

'Sorry, honey, but everything's crazy today. Now, what's all this about you and Sam getting out of my life?'

'This is Harriet,' said his wife, after a brief pause to take the situation in. 'I am happy to hear that your girlfriend has reached the same conclusion about you that I have.'

Then she hung up.

When Galvin picked up 22, Lois was gone.

This is not a good omen, he thought. This is not an auspicious way to begin the case. Maybe I should start getting chest pains. Tell the court I'm sick.

The intercom buzzed.

'Judge Sweeney's law clerk just called,' said Peggy airily. 'The judge wants to make certain that you'll be in his chambers. Just about now. Otherwise, he's going to dismiss the case. That's what the law clerk said – throw the case out of court. And assess costs and your adversary's legal fees to Francis X. Galvin, Esquire. That's what he said. Listen, Galvin, would you mind if I took the rest of the day off? I'm getting a terrible headache!'

He finally found the case folder. Nothing was in the right place, but it would have to do. He stuffed two bulging manila envelopes into his briefcase and started out the door. The phone rang. He knew he shouldn't answer it. But Galvin always had trouble ignoring a ringing telephone. It was Dr Thompson.

'Get a good night's sleep, Doctor?' asked Galvin.

'I've been doing a lot of thinking,' said Thompson. 'Fact is, I didn't sleep at all. I just don't know about testifying. That's the truth, Mr Galvin. I just don't know. Frankly, I think it'll ruin me on Long Island.'

'Don't do this tò me, Doc. We went all over this on the train last night. Not now. Goddammit. If you choke on me, Doc, we're all done! Finished! Look, I'm really late. Jesus Christ, think of Deborah Ruth. Think of her three little kids. I'll call you from the courthouse. Listen, Doctor –'

'Yes?'

'I need you, Doc. Don't let the bastards scare you out of this case. Don't let them get away with it! You know what went on. If you can't make it, we'll fold our tents right now. Please, Doc. Please! Goodbye.'

He didn't wait for an answer. The phone rang again as he started out the door. It was still ringing when he locked up and hustled down the stairs. If he hurried, scout's pace, running to every other telephone pole, he could make the courthouse in eight minutes. He began a fast walk. But as he passed the State House, he stopped for a moment before the statue of Mary Dyer, the Quaker martyr who died on the scaffold. Mary Dyer, who loved God perhaps a little too strangely for the Puritan Establishment. 'Mary Dyer,' he whispered, 'help me!'

At ten thirty in the morning, the Suffolk County Court House always swarms with traffic. The corridors are clogged, and the elevators go up with the passengers holding their breath.

Through the hectic swirl walked a small, middle-aged woman. The sea of lawyers parted before her, because Elizabeth Ann McLaughlin masked a great power in her benign appearance. She carried her artillery into Judge Sweeney's chambers, doors flung open before her, smiles lighting her way. Miss McLaughlin was the court stenographer.

The veterans and pros all knew and courted Miss McLaughlin. For it was within her power to make or break a case. She could even decide an appeal. Whatever went onto the tape of her stenographic machine was the permanent record of the courtroom proceedings. She could, they all knew, with a key word here and there, help a friend and punish an enemy. And she was a dangerous enemy.

She could put a cough into the record. She could eliminate a gesture. Clean up a judge's charge. Or clutter it.

Concannon was a particular pet of Miss McLaughlin's. She regarded him as a credit to her race. And he always remembered to ask about her ailing sister and had nice things to say about the way she looked. She was not fooled by such tactics – she had been around enough courtrooms to recognize theatrics. But she was willing to be charmed. She gave him every benefit when he was before the bar.

Concannon, for his part, knew that Miss McLaughlin was precise and careful in the mornings. By the afternoon she was tired and cranky, feeling the effects of her arthritis. He timed his crucial cross-examinations for the morning sessions.

With Galvin, it was another matter. She had heard the scandal whispered in the cloakrooms, and she disapproved. When she took a case with Galvin in it, she would wince, or groan, or address the Court. 'Judge, tell him he's going too fast,' she would say. She wrote her disapproval into the record.

Galvin arrived at the courthouse out of breath and seven minutes late. 'His Honour will see you now,' said Jeremy Callahan, the bailiff. Callahan had the serious drinker's forbearance, and when he smiled at Galvin it felt like the kiss of death. Judge Sweeney was waiting impatiently, his black robes flying behind him as he paced back and forth. Judge Sweeney was a bully. He used his office like a club. Had it not been for the generous political contributions of his father-in-law to the party and his subsequent appointment to the bench, Eldridge Thayer Sweeney would have been an obsequious junior partner in some obscure law firm. And he would have remained meek and mired for the rest of his life.

But the judicial robes made him feel like a Black Belt in legal karate. He lectured lawyers far more learned than he about points of law of which he knew little or nothing. He was constantly reversed, even reprimanded, by the Court of Appeals, but the effect was to make him nastier and angrier. He argued hotly against the breakdown of law and order as he sent black burglars to prison for as long as he legally could while paroling white-collar criminals or giving them occasional wrist slaps. He was fanatic on punctuality, demanding it of everyone but himself. Lawyers were known to fake heart attacks, peptic ulcers and yellow fever to transfer out of his clutches.

Concannon wasn't worried. He could handle Sweeney. In fact, his only concern was that Sweeney would bend over too far in his direction. The judge, who could be remorseless with an inept loser like Galvin, was inordinately deferential to a winner like Concannon.

Judge Sweeney was 75 years old, and he was impatient with lengthy court fights. He liked to break the backlog, move the cases along. He would always call the lawyers into his chambers before the start of a case for what he liked to call a 'little judicial head banging'. It was usually the plaintiff's head that got banged. 'What in hell are you doing here?' he would bark. 'You're not going to tie up this court at a thousand dollars a day with this crap, are you?' He would lean over and call the defence lawyer by his first name. 'Tom,' he would say, very chummy, 'throw in another hundred dollars to sweeten the pot,' then turn to the plaintiff's attorney and say, 'Take it and run.' Under that kind of pressure, cases were usually settled.

For assorted reasons, the spectators' benches in his court-room were popular with young attorneys and court personnel. You never knew, they would say, what Sweeney was going to pull next. Lawyers from Suffolk to Berkshire County had their

132

favourite Sweeney stories. He was famous for the way he handled an obscenity case. Sweeney liked to regard himself as a champion of civil liberties. It was a minor conceit. So when the state police and a prosecutor appeared before him with three eight-hundred-foot reels of what they termed 'hard-core pornography', Judge Sweeney's civil rights instincts were touched. The prosecutor wanted to charge the projectionist, and as he was describing the seized material, the judge intervened on behalf of fair play.

'Not in my court,' he bellowed. 'Your branding these pieces of evidence as "hard-core" is not sufficient to return an indictment. Not in *this* court. No! No! No! I will be the sole judge of that. Not you.' He chastised the prosecutor. 'Now, let's take a look at them.'

The first reel ran forty-five minutes. Judge Sweeney darkened the courtroom and sat through the entire film – all forty-five minutes of no-holds-barred sex. 'All right! All right!' he said. 'You're charging this defendant with showing all three: am I correct? Let's see the next one.'

The state trooper glanced at the prosecutor, who nodded, and the next reel was threaded.

Another forty-five-minute celluloid orgy flooded the courtroom. They had to lock the doors when the courtroom began filling up with viewers from the rest of the building.

'Put on the last one,' he said stoically.

With three minutes left on the last film, Judge Sweeney broke the silence in the courtroom. 'I've seen enough!' he rasped. 'Put the lights on. Lights!' he roared, pounding the gavel. 'This is pornography of the hardest core. Pure filth! Take him away.'

He peered out over his glasses. 'Well, Mr Galvin, I'm glad to see you could make it.'

On his desk were the voluminous pleadings, *Rosen v. St*

Catherine Laboure Hospital, et al. He moved them around his desk as if they would contaminate his hands.

'You know,' said the judge, sitting now in the massive leather chair, which, in his case, added dimension to his presence, 'when a plaintiff insists upon his right of trial by jury, he solicits the good offices of the Court and the jury. Looking for justice is like looking for a job: do you get the drift, Mr Galvin?'

'I'm afraid not, Your Honour.'

'You are supposed to be on time. If a prospective employer sets an appointment for nine thirty, you don't show up at eleven. Or do you, Mr Galvin?'

'It's only five minutes, Your Honour,' said Galvin, trying to hold his temper. 'It's only ten thirty-five.' He glanced at his watch, cribbing five minutes.

Galvin could feel his teeth grinding. The sanctimonious bastard, he thought, had forgotten what it was like in the pit, hustling to make a buck, trying to be in three places at once, scratching a living. A million last-minute things. Galvin was sweating. He fought to remain silent.

'Mr Galvin, this case will take at least a week to try. I have a responsibility to those jurors out there. *They* can't show up two hours late. *They* aren't making any money on this case. I will tolerate no further tardiness. You will be ready to begin at ten each day. Is that clear?'

'Understood,' said Galvin.

'That goes for the defence too,' said Sweeney in a show of impartiality.

'The defence will always be ready at ten, Your Honour,' said Concannon. This was Galvin's initial contact with his adversary. Galvin didn't like him.

'Now,' said Sweeney, straightening his robe, folding his hands on his lap and tilting the chair back as far as it would go, looking almost innocent, 'what's this case all about?'

'It's a medical-malpractice case,' Galvin began.

'I can see that!' snarled Sweeney, slamming back to earth. 'Good God, man, I can read! Now, you know what I mean. Have you boys tried to resolve your differences and save the Commonwealth the time and expense involved in a long trial?'

'It's an unusual case, Your Honour –' offered Galvin.

'I think both sides owe a duty to the Court to negotiate. Sharpen the pencil. Give a little. Take a little. Have you boys tried to do that? Maybe I can be of some help.'

'As I said, Your Honour, this is an unusual case –'

'All the more reason to negotiate. Compromise. Try to settle. If it's all that unusual and complicated, how the hell is a jury going to assess it? Unless men like you two sit down at the conference table and iron out the wrinkles, I don't think it's fair to send it to twelve ordinary citizens. Do you? They won't have the foggiest idea of what's involved.

'Now, I don't mind a little horse trading, if I can be of some assistance. Let's talk money. What will your client take to walk out of here right now, Mr Galvin? I mean, right at this very moment?'

'Well, Judge, my client can't walk. I couldn't even ask her, because she can't talk.'

'Don't argue the case,' said the judge. 'I am trying to be helpful here and you are giving me problems.'

'I have to consider my client,' said Galvin. 'She's going to be a vegetable for the rest of her life. That's a long time. Look, Judge, I made an offer to settle. I asked for six hundred thousand dollars. I would retreat another twenty-five thousand. But that's it.'

'You don't want much,' said the judge. Then, turning to Concannon: 'What do you say to that, Ed?'

'Judge, we offered the plaintiff three hundred thousand,' said Concannon. 'Bishop Brophey extended this offer personally. It was rejected. When it was rejected, we had no alternative but to withdraw the offer and prepare for trial. So since then, we have incurred added expenses for doctors, expert witnesses, trial-preparation costs. Our people had to cancel three weeks of appointments to stand by for this trial.

'You know, the defendant doctors and the administrator of St Catherine Laboure Hospital did not want the case settled at any price.'

The judge was nodding his head – a silent amen to Concannon's dilemma.

'They fail to see any negligence on their part. And I agree with them. Not a scintilla. They insist on trial and vindication. Of course, they do not understand the vagaries of the jury system as you and I do – the natural sympathy that would be evoked for the Rosen girl. So I took it upon myself to persuade the claim department at Consolidated Life and Casualty Company, who carry the liability on St Catherine Laboure, and Minnesota Mutual, insurer of the operating surgeon and anaesthesiologist, to renew the offer of one hundred fifty thousand each. I did this considering the imponderables hidden in any case, plus the time and expense that will accrue to the Commonwealth.'

'Very generous,' said the judge. 'Very generous.' Then, turning to Galvin, 'I think you should reconsider. One in the hand is worth two in the bush. Three goes into three hundred thousand rather easily.'

'I'm not interested,' said Galvin. 'Con Life and Double M will give you an apple for an orchard any day, Judge. I gave them a figure. I'm not going to start bidding against myself.'

'You may hate yourself when the jury comes back,' said the judge. 'I think Ed's offer is fair. You should take it and run like a thief.'

'I'm no thief,' said Galvin. 'And I'm not running.'

The judge's face turned to stone. The banter was over. 'I take it,' he said coldly, 'that Mr Concannon's offer is rejected.'

'Rejected,' said Galvin.

'Send in the bailiff. We will empanel a jury. I will not attempt to get the two sides together again. This case will be tried to completion.'

'Thank you, Your Honour,' said Concannon smiling.

'Okay with me, Judge,' said Galvin with a false lightness that stuck in his throat.

15

As the trial began, Galvin tried to keep from crumbling. His hands shook, and he lacked authority. Concannon, on the other hand, sat back confidently in his chair, eyes half closed and fully poised.

They were picking a jury – a dangerous art of hunches and emanations. There is no science in the study of faces. And yet some lawyers are good at it and others are not. They cannot tell you why, although they try. It's an innate sense, a gift.

Prospective jurors are chosen at random. Selected from the voter lists of the county. That is all they have in common: they live in the county and they have voted.

There are always a disproportionate number of blue-collar workers in the jury box: bus drivers, utility workers, telephone linemen, postal workers. They can afford to be away from work. They are even eager to get away. There are also a lot of housewives. Middle-aged women with children off in school who enjoy real soap opera in the courtroom.

But with all that, there are a fair share of civic-minded executives and college professors and accountants who serve as the 'collective conscience' of the community.

Galvin studied the jury sheet listing the names, addresses and occupations of the prospective panel members. He stared at their faces and their manner, trying to read character in a slouch or a swagger.

Mary McCauley: Hyde Park. She looked hard, thought Galvin. An Irish-Catholic mother with a grudge against the world. Scratch Mary McCauley.

John Brennan: Back Bay. A bus driver. He looked nice. One of life's boxers with cauliflower ears. Hold on to Brennan,

138

thought Galvin.

Lawrence O'Leary: South Boston. Retired Salesman. A large man with a big, bulbous nose and an Irish suntan. He looked like a guy who might give Catherine Laboure away. Keep O'Leary.

Concannon leaned over and asked for the investigative reports. 'Just the last two,' he whispered: 'Brennan and O'Leary.'

'Nothing on Brennan,' said Wilson. 'But O'Leary's made five claims for personal injury in the past two years.'

'We should strike O'Leary,' said Kaplan.

'No,' said Concannon. 'Challenge Brennan. Bus drivers tend to be a little soft. Protective. Help too many old ladies onto the bus. O'Leary's okay, though. He's a scoundrel. He knows what it's like to steal. He'll bounce the other way on this. He'll suddenly get religion. Scratch Brennan and keep O'Leary.'

There was no limit on the number of challenges for cause: an obvious bias; conflict of interests. An inability to sit and judge fairly for any discernible reason warrants removal.

After two hours of voir-dire questioning, with one peremptory challenge apiece remaining, twelve jurors were seated. Galvin would have preferred an all-male jury. Women, he believed, were stingy when it came to money awards. They were too conscious of the cost of things. They paid for the groceries and bought the children's shoes. But he couldn't challenge them for gender alone. And so he had to go with eight men and four women.

Concannon nodded. No smile. Just an affirmation that he accepted the jury.

'The defence is content, Your Honour,' he said.

Galvin was running through his notes and lists, trying to find the outline of his opening statement. His hair was flying in four different directions at the same time. He looked up, surprised, when he heard Concannon.

'Oh,' he said. 'Yes. Me too. Content.'

Judge Sweeney was leafing through some papers – motions and dockets – when Donna St Laurent came into the court-room. Galvin was feeling queasy as it was, what with the start of the trial and the pressure of the opening, but when she took her place at Concannon's table, his stomach lurched. He had known that she would go there. He was prepared for it. But that didn't help. He was still hurt.

The court stenographer, Elizabeth Ann McLaughlin, lifted her right hand as if she were about to strike the opening chord on a piano.

Judge Sweeney looked up from the papers, and from his elevated perch looked down at Galvin.

'Proceed, Counsellor.'

In twenty-odd years, Galvin had prepared and delivered more than two hundred opening statements. Some had been eloquent. Most had been competent. If he had a style, he was just himself, direct and to the point. He talked to juries the way he'd talk to a neighbour over the backyard fence. Some lawyers approached the jury with verve and a flourish. You could almost hear the background music. Then there were the aw-shucks, folksy lawyers who came on like Will Rogers or Sam Ervin. Just good ol' boys. Country lawyers in this slick land of city lawyers. There were the technocrats. Smooth. Steel-edged men who approached the law like precision machines.

Galvin had never consciously attempted to develop a style. In some cases, he would strike out boldly, attempting to overcome the opposition. Other times he back-tracked, under-sold, seemed timid as he stretched for sympathy.

But whatever tack he took, it seemed to come out of the case. If the evidence was strong, he charged relentlessly. If it was weak, he appealed for sympathy. It was work.

This case was different. This was the most important case. It required delicate balance.

And he was tight. He cleared his throat and wandered over to the jury box, touching the rail, fondling it gently as if he were touching the hand of an old friend. He knew as he stood there, looking into their open faces, that he might be addressing a jury for the last time.

'Ladies and gentlemen of the jury,' he began. 'What I am about to say is not evidence. It is merely an outline of the facts that will be presented to you.

'Both defence counsel and I have a chance to address you at the beginning of the trial so that you will be prepared to handle the evidence with greater facility as it unfolds before you.'

Going first, he had a valuable advantage. He became the host. It lent authority to his presentation. First impressions – especially if favourable – could be lasting. 'Let me introduce the representatives of the various parties.'

The judge, he told them, was Eldridge Sweeney. The defendants were Drs Towler and Crowley and Nurse Nevins. 'Corporate defendant, St Catherine Laboure,' he said, 'is being represented by Mr J. Edward Concannon, assisted by Mr Wilson Gaynor and Mr Sidney Kaplan' – and he paused and looked at Donna, then back at the jury – 'and by Miss Donna St Laurent.

'All from the law firm of Rutledge, Guthrie, Cabot and Moore. I might add that this law firm and these lawyers also represent Dr Towler, Dr Crowley and Miss Nevins. My name is Galvin. I represent the plaintiff, Deborah Ruth Rosen.'

Concannon was furious. He was doubly annoyed at his associates for smiling and nodding at Galvin's recognition, letting themselves be upstaged this way. He could have interrupted, throwing in a few objections, but Concannon was determined to be patient. Such tactics could backfire. The jury might not understand. They might think it rude and disconcerting. After all, what was Galvin doing but being polite, making courteous salutations?

'On behalf of His Honour and the defence attorneys and

141

myself,' Galvin continued, 'let me welcome you. This is a great inconvenience to you. But this is an important case. You do not choose to be here, and your lives have been interrupted. But there are high civic duties which demand the attention of good and fair citizens such as yourselves.

'True, you have left your homes and families and jobs and all those things which make life worthwhile. But the important thing is that you are here and you are about to perform the highest civic function any citizen can be called upon to perform in our free society – to render justice to your fellow man.'

The jurors were always attentive in the early stages. They were curious about the calibre of the lawyer and the quality of the case. Galvin wandered up and down, past the jury box. It was an old lawyer's trick. Hypnotic. Forcing their attention upon him, and then casting a spell before they even knew what was happening.

'This isn't just an ordinary case. For those of you who have sat on juries in the past, you're probably tired of hearing about back sprains and borderline disputes. This is a medical-malpractice case. This is a case in which the plaintiff, Deborah Ruth Rosen' – and Galvin stood square against the centre of the jury box, both hands on the rail, staring hard up and down at their faces – 'is as alive as this piece of wood.'

He looked down as if he had seen it for the first time and slapped his hand against the rail of the jury box. The dull sound echoed through the courtroom.

His voice dropped.

'She cannot talk. She cannot walk. She can't even sit up. She will never again smell a flower or run in the rain. She'll never hold her own children. Or tell them a story. Never. She'll never smile. Or cry. She'll never again taste a butterscotch sundae. Not ever. Because Deborah Ruth Rosen is a vegetable.'

The effect was stunning. If there had been silence before,

now even the breathing stopped. Galvin had taken their breath away. He waited. Letting it sink in. Letting it go deep.

'A vegetable!'

If it was theatrical, it didn't matter. It worked. There were those in the courtroom who saw the fine hand that went into creating the effect. But it didn't matter. He had them all looking at his hand resting on the rail, as if he were touching his absent client. They were looking at the piece of wood and imagining a young mother who would never walk or talk or taste a butterscotch sundae. Never.

'Deborah Ruth Rosen cannot be here. She is in a nursing home with tubes stuck into her arms and stomach and rectum. I'm sorry, that's not a pretty image, but that's the truth. Deborah Ruth Rosen cannot feed herself, so she must have bags of liquid food emptied into her veins. She cannot even void, so she must have catheters plunged into her body to drain the wastes.

'No, Deborah Ruth Rosen cannot be here, so I am here for her. She cannot speak, so I speak for her. She cannot tell you of the anguish and the cost. She cannot tell you what her fate is like. So I am here on her behalf to ask you to decide this claim of professional negligence against the corporate defendant, Catherine Labouré Hospital, and the others.'

He walked back to his desk and pretended to look through the blue-backed papers on it. He was demonstrating to the jury his care and precision. He would not tell them anything unless he checked it first with the printed notes and the material on his desk, the gesture implied. And if the jurors wanted to assume that he was fighting off a deep emotion, they were free to do that. It was, in fact, true. He didn't want to sob before the jury. They would count that cheap.

When he resumed, Galvin's voice had the brittle edge of business in it.

'The evidence will show that on May fourteenth, almost four years ago, Deborah Ruth Rosen was twenty-eight years old. She was married and the mother of two children. She was expecting a third. She was a hardworking mother. It was a hardworking family. Like you, like me. No one gave them anything. They worked for what they had.

'The evidence will show that Deborah Ruth had a few health problems. She had diabetes mellitus. She had had a heart murmur as an infant. Nothing too bad. She had had a little difficulty with her second baby, but nothing too serious. She saw her local family doctor when she suspected that she was going to have another baby. Dr Sheldon Rabb. You will hear him testify that he had the diabetes under control. And he will testify that as a precaution, he referred her to Dr Rexford Towler for a medical consultation. The evidence will further show that Dr Towler thereafter agreed to take over the patient's medical course and to follow her along and to deliver her third child. A patient–physician relationship was thus established.

'Once this patient-physician relationship came into being, certain mutual rights and obligations were created. The patient agreed to follow her doctor's orders and prescriptions, and the evidence will show that she did, and the doctor, of course, expected to be paid. And in fact he did bill the patient, and was paid in full.

'The patient, in return, expected the doctor to exercise reasonable skill and diligence in treating her, especially during delivery and aftercare. It is a natural and recognized procedure. A contract was established. Very much like a contract you sign when you buy your house or your car. You pay a set amount and expect something of value in return. You have a right to expect value. You have a right to expect the car won't fall apart as you drive it out of the showroom. And when you hire a doctor, a person has a right to expect a certain amount of expert care.

'And so Deborah Ruth Rosen presented herself to Dr Towler, and she was a vibrant, laughing, bubbly girl. She liked to go canoeing on the Charles. Imagine, canoeing!'

Galvin looked at the jurors. 'Some of you did that as a kid. We all did.' The jurors nodded. 'Those were great days. Salad days.

'She played some weekend tennis while she cared for two infants. Two boys. Four and two. You know what a handful little boys are at that age.' And the women jurors nodded.

Concannon was burning. Galvin was arguing his case in the opening! He seethed, working the muscles of his jaw, his lips two thin lines. Judge Sweeney, peering out over his thick-lensed glasses, which hung on the edge of his nose, failed to get the signal.

'In between the morning coffee and the afternoon shopping, she managed to squeeze in a little golf with her husband. No Babe Didrikson. Just a hacker, like the rest of us. But she enjoyed life. She loved to swim and to ski and to walk the Appalachian Trail in the early spring. She had a zest for living, and she was only twenty-eight, with her whole life ahead of her. Her whole wonderful life!'

He paused again and looked over his notes. 'And the evidence will show,' he said, still looking down at his notes, and then looking up at the jury, 'that she managed to cram twenty-five hours into each day, because she worked part time as a bookkeeper for a brokerage firm. Her husband, after all, was just starting out in an executive-training programme for a bank, and you men and women here know that banks and investment corporations aren't too princely when it comes to starting salaries.'

A few jurors smiled and nodded agreement.

'Well, this was the world of Deborah Ruth on May fourteenth. Alive. Well. Hoping for a girl to go along with her two sons. And then, sometime during the night, she started to get those signs which indicated she was about to bring a new child into the world. Pains every five minutes. Nothing alarming. Nothing unusual. The most natural pain in the

145

world. From time immemorial, women have welcomed these pains. It's nature's warning system.

'She called the hospital and was told to come in for admission and that everything would be fine. Everything would be available and it would be routine.

'The evidence will show that she called from Scituate, about thirty miles south of Boston. She was with a former college friend. Oh, yes, Deborah Ruth was a college girl. Mount Holyoke, class of 'sixty-seven, majored in education. When her children were a little more grown, she would resume teaching. Help out with the family budget.

'Now, remember the time. The time element is crucial in this case. Initial pains at four in the morning. She arrived at Catherine Laboure about an hour later. She had just finished a heavy early-morning meal and had just gone to bed when the pains began – and that's important. You know how pregnant women are: they can eat at four in the morning. You're feeding two. You're constantly famished, especially if you don't smoke. And Deborah Ruth Rosen didn't smoke. So Deborah Ruth had a full meal at four in the morning and then the pains began and she drove with her friend to Catherine Laboure Hospital. One hour after a huge meal. London broil with salad and baked potato. That's crucial.'

He paused again. Did they get it? Did they understand? It was always frustrating when you were a lawyer not to know whether or not they followed what you were saying. The jury just sat there – silent, impassive. So many staring faces. Absorbing. Absorbing. It would have been nice to ask if they understood and have them explain it back. But it didn't work that way. The nightmare was that after a complicated premise, they might come back with some off-the-wall question, like 'Was she pregnant?'

'The maternity team was ready and waiting for her. Dr Towler was there. He headed the team. The captain of the ship. Dr Daniel Crowley was there to administer the anaesthetic and to remain with the patient throughout her delivery. To monitor the vital signs: the blood pressure, the pulse, the rate of breathing. To watch her complexion . . .'

They could fool you. Juries could fool you. Sometimes they looked so intelligent, sitting there for days on end, and then they would send back a question from the jury room that showed they didn't understand the case at all. It was like some beautiful women he had known. Silent and mysterious. Eyes full of wisdom. But they hadn't the least notion of what life was all about. Dear God, he reflected inwardly, let them understand. Let one of them know what it's all about and explain it to the rest.

'It was Dr Crowley's job to take an admitting history, or if not take it, to check carefully one that had been taken. He was going to administer the anaesthetic and so he had to know the history. And this is very important. The history would dictate the type of anaesthesia he would use during delivery. It was his responsibility. Dr Crowley was chief of the Anaesthesia Service and on the staff of the defendant hospital. In fact, he was actually employed by it, thus acting in his own capacity and by way of an old legal maxim called respondeat superior . . .

'I don't want to bore you with Latin; I'm not too good at it anyway. But the phrase "respondeat superior" means that he acted for and on behalf of his principal, in this case the hospital – just like a Gulf Oil deliveryman. If the delivery-man negligently spills oil on your property, then Gulf Oil is responsible for the damage . . .'

Kaplan whispered to Concannon. 'He's getting away with murder, Mr Concannon. Shouldn't we stop him?'

'I'd rather have the judge do it,' whispered Concannon. 'Just be patient. Hold on awhile.'

'Dr Crowley also engaged as his first assistant Carolyn Nevins, a nurse anaesthetist, who was directly under his supervision and control and who was also in the employ of the defendant hospital.

'Also in the delivery room – and we will refer to this as the operating suite – was the scrub nurse, Miss Janet Stephens. It was her job to assist all the doctors. There was Barbara Cosgrove. She's referred to as the floating nurse. She provides overriding supervision for the nurses and, as the title implies, goes where she's needed. There was also an obstetrical nurse, Mary Rooney. They were all in the employ of the defendant hospital on the morning of May fourteenth when Deborah Ruth began her labour. She came into port, so to speak, a little buffeted, a little worn, but she was safe, or so she thought, in the harbour. She would ride out the storm. It would soon be over.'

Galvin knew it was time to back off a bit. He had gone to the forensic edge, and surprisingly, they had let him. He knew that if he pushed too much further the judge would come down on him hard. And so, as he watched Concannon begin to fidget and Sweeney looking over at the defence table, perhaps to catch a missed signal, Galvin gathered in what he was seeing and reverted to a strictly factual narrative.

'The evidence will show that the delivery was proceeding routinely. Her vital signs were all normal. The anaesthesia, which was nitrous oxide – and we'll have a qualified anaesthesiologist here to describe this type of anaesthesia and how much was given – was being administered by Dr Crowley. Miss Nevins, the nurse anaesthetist, was making notations in her chart, which is a running graphic commentary on just what is being done to the patient and how she is responding. This is extremely important. This is vital.

'Let me tell how it was. It was like the dirigible *Hindenburg*. I remember seeing it as a boy back in the thirties, coming in from the Atlantic – watched it glide over South Boston, then disappear out towards the west, over the Blue Hills, headed for Lakewood, New Jersey. Things were going fine. It was sleek. It was silvery. It was beautiful. Four hours later it began to ease into its quiet mooring.

'Then disaster! Cardiac arrest. The patient's heart stopped. Just like that.' He snapped his fingers. 'In the twinkling of an eye.'

'But it doesn't have to be like the *Hindenburg*,' he went on, leaning into the jury box. 'When a heart ceases to beat, a person doesn't have to perish. This was a modern hospital. The largest Catholic hospital in the world. The largest and best equipped. When it happened – when cardiac arrest occurred – the emergency, as in most hospitals from Shanghai to Sioux City, is known as a Code Blue. That's flashed throughout the hospital. Everyone reacts. There's a disaster unit. They should be able to resuscitate a heart. This was the strong heart of a twenty-eight-year-old girl. They had just four minutes to do it. After that, the brain dies. It's like crushing an eggshell. Once you crush the eggshell, or let the brain die, like Humpty Dumpty, you can't just put it back together again. Once nerve tissues die, they die forever.

'But there's that four-minute safety margin. They had four minutes and the best of facilities at Catherine Laboure Hospital. Four minutes! Nature's parachute. A man can run a mile in four minutes.

'But what happened? What happened was that they put Deborah Ruth Rosen under anaesthesia to deliver her baby, and she went into a coma. She emerged inside the prison she now inhabits. The prison of her own body, from which she can only blink at the world.

'And so we will show negligence. By competent medical testimony we will demonstrate that the medical personnel, the defendant doctors and nurse, had a standard of care to measure up to, and that a patient such as Deborah Ruth Rosen, with her presenting symptoms and medical history, should have been given a spinal, or caudal, anaesthesia. One in the low back.

'But contrary to that, she was given a general anaesthetic by Dr Crowley, Dr Towler, the operating surgeon, and Nurse

Nevins should have known better.'

Galvin paused. It was hard to tell whether or not he was through. But the jurors waited for him.

'I cannot tell you exactly what happened in the next few moments,' he continued, looking up from his notes and resting his hands on the table. 'My client cannot tell me. But we can see the results. The results are lying ten miles from here in a chronic-care facility with tubes stuck into every limb on her body. That's the result! If someone can give me a better explanation, I'll accept it, but so far, from the evidence, it looks to me like the results of negligence. Negligence! Gross negligence that we intend to prove. Thank you.'

There was a long silence when he sat down. He was through – there was no doubt of that. But no one wanted to make the next sound.

16

He had underestimated Galvin. He was angry and humiliated as he stood in the corridor after the judge called a short recess. Concannon was surrounded by aides and assistants who were downgrading and nitpicking Galvin's opening. But Concannon knew better. He knew that his premonition of danger was correct. The old pilot's sixth sense, the intuition, was accurate. Galvin was dangerous.

'You really laid it into him,' said Gaynor. 'You really took a piece out of him.'

Concannon didn't say anything, but he felt foolish. These assistants were young and eager, and he didn't want to dampen their enthusiasm. Or loyalty. And there was also some portion of his pride which refused to admit it, even to himself, despite all the evidence to the contrary.

But Concannon knew better. He knew that he had blundered when he got up to protest after Galvin finished. It was the surprise. But he just couldn't let Galvin go unanswered. Not after that opening. He had to say something.

'Your Honour,' he began, calling himself to the attention of the jury, which was fixed elsewhere. The opening remarks of Galvin were still on their minds. They were all surprised to hear Concannon's voice breaking the stillness. 'Your Honour, I sat back patiently and allowed counsel for the plaintiff to go far beyond the bounds of propriety in his opening statement. Counsel in fact argued his case. He knows, and I am certain that the Court is aware, just where those boundaries lie. I could have objected several times to his colloquies. Several times. But I refrained. I didn't want to interrupt learned counsel. I wanted to be completely fair . . .'

'So now you don't want to be fair,' muttered Galvin, loud enough for a few jurors to hear, but low enough to prevent Elizabeth Ann McLaughlin from writing it into the record.

'However,' continued Concannon, not trusting himself to recognize Galvin's impertinence for fear of unleashing an overkill, 'I cannot let the record stand. In justice to my clients, I object to the opening statement, which was not designed to apprise the jury of any factual details, but contrived to prejudice the jury. I think the opening statement was grossly improper. I most strenuously object and trust the Court will not condone these theatrics in the future. I would like that reflected in the record.'

'Your objection is noted,' said Judge Sweeney, 'and, I might add, well taken.' Turning to Galvin: 'Now, Mr Plaintiff's Attorney . . .'

'My name is Galvin, Your Honour.'

'. . . I must warn you at the outset to keep your remarks within the proper framework. Just outline the facts for the jury. No colloquy. And don't argue with the Court. Now we will take a ten-minute recess, and then, Mr Concannon, you may proceed with your opening statement.'

'I will waive my opening, Your Honour,' said Concannon, standing and bowing towards the jury, as if making a grand gesture to decency.

The judge nodded. approvingly. 'When we return from recess, counsel for the plaintiff may call his first witness.'

'Well,' said Donna, 'you couldn't just let it pass.'

He didn't answer her, but for the first time in a long time, Concannon would have liked a cigarette. He almost envied the nervous young assistants who felt free to smoke in the corridors during recess. He was not entitled to any weakness. I sounded flat, mean-spirited, garrulous, he said to himself. It was the wrong note after Galvin's opening. I sounded like a man objecting to a plain truth.

152

'You had to object,' said Donna. 'You have to establish a record.'

'You're thinking of the appeal,' he said.

'We have to protect the record. Not that our opponent is going to win. But if we're going upstairs after the verdict, we need to give something the Appeals Court can hang their hat on.'

'He was good,' said Concannon. 'I was surprised at how good he was. He doesn't have that kind of reputation.'

'This is his most important case,' said Donna.

'Still, you would think a man would show some signs of that kind of ability. You would think he'd have *some* kind of track record. Even a quiet reputation. But something.'

'He's in over his head,' said Donna. 'You know his predicament. Everything is riding on this one case. If he blows this, he's got nothing left. When you're in over your head, sometimes you get up for it.'

'He was good,' said Concannon. 'We mustn't get overconfident. We must guard against overconfidence. We have to bear down.'

Kaplan came back from the courthouse coffee shop with a tray of coffee containers – a bright young lawyer in a custom-tailored suit carrying a tray of coffee and doughnuts through the corridors of miscreants and hustlers.

But there wasn't time. The recess was over. He handed the tray to one of the attendants, who passed out its contents to the other court officers.

Galvin never left the courtroom during the break. For one thing, he didn't want to run into Donna and say something stupid. And there were notes he had to find. Nothing was in its proper place. He wanted to call Moe, but he would wait for the lunch recess.

Galvin called his first witness.

'I would like to call defendant Dr G. Rexford Towler.'

153

Tall, proud, with striking silver hair, Dr Towler was an impressive sight as he walked purposefully past the jury and sat down in the witness chair. He had the air of a man who had other, more urgent appointments to keep.

'You were Deborah Ruth Rosen's physician, were you not?' began Galvin.

'She was referred to me,' replied Towler. 'Her regular physician was Dr Sheldon Rabb.'

'But when she was referred to you, she became your patient, did she not? You were then her physician, were you not?'

'She was sent to me primarily on a consult,' Towler parried.

Concannon should have briefed him better. He was arguing the small points. Quibbling. It always looked as if you were trying to hide something when you quibbled.

Galvin pressed his point. 'So, then, you eventually became her doctor?'

'Well . . .'

'Well, isn't that a fair statement?'

'Yes,' said Dr Towler. He dried his hands on his handkerchief. 'I was her doctor.'

'When did she first come to see you?'

'It was when she was just going into her third trimester. She was six months pregnant. It was her third child and she had had difficulty with a previous delivery, and so Dr Rabb referred her to me. He felt that her condition was too difficult for him to manage medically, so he asked me to assist and to take over her prenatal care and impending delivery.'

Galvin smiled. 'I appreciate that, Doctor, but His Honour has asked me, and I'm sure that it pertains to all of us, in the interest of time and expense, merely to be factual. In other words, not to go beyond the bounds of the question. My question was very simple. I asked you when she first came to you, and that would have called for a simple answer, wouldn't it, Doctor? Merely a matter of time?'

'Your Honour,' Concannon said, rising from the counsel

154

table, 'the question of when may be interpretive. It could be a matter of what point in time or in what state or condition. I think the doctor was attempting to give a fuller explanation.'

'I will allow his answer to stand,' ruled the judge. 'You asked the question, Mr Counsellor for the Plaintiff. You just didn't like the answer. If you don't like the answer, you can't withdraw the question. Proceed.'

Galvin shrugged.

'Dr Towler, you were Deborah Ruth's physician in your specialty of obstetrical gynaecology on May fourteenth, four years ago, were you not? And I ask for a yes or no answer if the Court please.'

'Yes, I was.'

'And you saw her at regular intervals from February fifteenth to May fourteenth, did you not?'

'I did.'

'Four times, to be exact.'

'That's correct.'

'And you undertook, for a stipulated fee, to deliver her third child at Catherine Laboure Hospital, did you not?'

'Yes.'

'And as her physician, undertaking to deliver her child, you gave her physical examinations, inquired into her past and present medical history and gave her medical advice during these office visits, did you not?'

'Yes.'

'Now, Doctor, you were well aware of the fact that Deborah Ruth Rosen was diabetic, had a heart murmur and had had difficulty with her previous delivery, were you not? Please answer yes or no, if you would kindly.'

'Yes, I was.'

'And knowing this, you also knew that her case during delivery dictated extra caution, more so than with a healthy woman without these medical complications, did you not?'

'At St Catherine Laboure, Mr Galvin, every delivery

dictates extra caution. We are always on guard.'

'I am certain of that, Doctor, but wouldn't it be natural to take these other factors into consideration?'

'Naturally.'

'You wouldn't ignore them?'

'No. Of course not.'

'Okay. So now, on the morning of May fourteenth, when Deborah Ruth called the hospital on the telephone, you or someone on your behalf asked her how often the pains were coming: isn't that correct?'

'Yes. I believe it's on the record.'

'Correct, Doctor. It says that the pains were coming every five minutes. And you knew that because you asked her that question on the telephone, and when she told you, you marked it on the record: isn't that correct?'

'Yes.'

'That's the procedure, isn't it? A patient gives you information and you mark it down on the chart?'

'If it's pertinent.' He did not look at Galvin, but off in the distance, as if he would not waste his time even in a look.

'And you record it so that you will have a running record of history and treatment: isn't that correct?'

'That's right.'

Concannon stood. 'I fail to see the materiality in this line of questioning,' he said.

'I assume that Mr Counsel is laying some sort of foundation,' said the judge.

'That's correct, Your Honour. That record is crucial to our case. I am laying a foundation to determine the procedure and validity of the hospital record.'

'Very well. Proceed.'

'Now, Doctor, we were speaking about the chart. The hospital record. If another doctor were to come onto the scene, he would merely have to look at the chart and he would see that she was given such and such a treatment, such and such a drug, and so forth . . .'

'Your Honour,' said Concannon, 'now counsel is testifying. If he wants to elicit information or lay a foundation, please let him use the witness. Unless he wants to take the stand.'

'Sustained. Counsel will not answer his own questions. Please use the witness.'

'Sorry, Your Honour; it's just that they make me nervous. All those smart lawyers at one table and me all alone.'

'Objection,' said Concannon wearily.

'Sustained. I don't want to admonish you again, Counsellor. You know better. Do you have any further questions for this witness?'

'I've just scratched the surface,' said Galvin. 'Now, Doctor, what's the purpose of keeping this running record?'

'It is to make certain that the treatment is continuous. If another doctor comes along, he will see what treatment and drugs have been administered. It's a safeguard.'

'Thank you. Now, what time was it that Deborah Ruth called you?'

'As I recall, it was about four, four fifteen in the morning. I'd just finished a difficult caesarean, and fortunately I was in the hospital when my service –'

'Thank you, Doctor, but just the time.'

'About four.'

'Where did she call from?'

'I have no idea.'

'Well, wouldn't that be important to know?' asked Galvin. 'Wouldn't you want to know how long it would take her to get to the hospital?'

'Well, yes. But if she were in New York City or Toronto or someplace remote, I would assume she would have mentioned it.'

'But you didn't know where she was at the time she called: is that correct?'

'I assumed that she was in the vicinity.'

'I didn't ask what you assumed, Doctor. I asked what you *knew*. You didn't *know* where she was: isn't that right?'

'Well, yes –'

'She could have been five minutes away from the hospital or five hours away: isn't that true?'

'She would have said something –'

'We don't know what she would or would not have said in the midst of labour pains, Doctor. I am asking you for a simple yes or no answer. You did not know whether she was five minutes or five hours away from the hospital: isn't that true, Dr Towler?'

'Yes,' he said weakly.

'As a matter of fact, there is an admitting note which says that she arrived at the hospital at four fifty-eight A.M.: isn't that correct?'

'I believe so.'

'So that's about an hour after she called you?'

Dr Towler's neck began to redden. 'If you say so.'

'No, Doctor, let's not take my word for it. I'll show you the record and you look at what it says and then you tell me if that's correct.'

Galvin picked up the chart and started to walk in front of the jury towards the witness.

'Just hold it,' growled Judge Sweeney. 'I didn't say you could approach the witness. You know the rules, Counsellor. This isn't your first case.'

'You're right, Your Honour. Forgive me. May I approach the witness?'

'You may,' the judge said, with a lordly flourish of his arm.

'Dr Towler, I now show you page three of the hospital record, which I would like marked in evidence.'

'Plaintiff's Exhibit one?' asked the stenographer.

'P-one,' said the judge, noting the first exhibit on a large sheet of yellow paper. *P-1 – hospital record of Deborah Ruth Rosen.*

158

'I now show you page three and I ask you to read the line I am indicating with my finger. Please, just read that aloud to the jury.'

Dr Towler paused – just a flicker of hesitation. Then he read: ' "Patient arrived at four fifty-eight A.M. looking apprehensive, complaining of severe abdominal distress." Is that the part?'

'Yes, Doctor, thank you. You read well. Now, you were present when she came into the hospital, were you not?' Galvin asked.

'I was.'

'By the way, Dr Towler, this information on page three of the chart: is that your handwriting?'

'No, it is not.'

'Do you know whose handwriting it is?'

'That would be the admitting nurse. Natalie Campanelli. She took the admitting history.'

'How can you tell, Doctor?'

'Her initials are at the bottom there. See? N.C.'

'Yes. Thank you, Doctor. By the way, where is Miss Campanelli today, if you know?'

'I have no idea,' he replied. 'She was a young student nurse four years ago. She left St Catherine a few months after the incident. I believe she got married. I couldn't tell you whether she is still nursing patients or nursing triplets.'

A few of the jurors laughed. Galvin bent over his notes and then asked the next question facing the jury. 'Tell me, Dr Towler: whose duty was it, medically, to advise the patient about the type of anaesthetic that was to be administered?'

'The anaesthesiologist,' said Dr Towler. 'Dr Crowley told her he would use nitrous oxide and advised her of the effects and that it was the best anaesthetic to utilize under the circumstances.'

'You heard him say that? You heard those exact words spoken to Deborah Ruth Rosen?'

'I did.'

'And you agreed? You were in accord with his medical judgment?'

'I was.'

'Nitrous oxide is a very powerful anaesthetic agent, is it not?'

'Dr Crowley would be better qualified to answer that, but generally speaking, I can say that it's a powerful anaesthetic.'

'It induces coma, does it not?'

'Well, it gives you a great level of relaxation.'

'But in fact what it does is induce coma: isn't that correct, Doctor?'

'Technically, that's true. Controlled.'

'Not controlled for Deborah Ruth. She never recovered from her coma –'

'Objection,' shouted Concannon angrily.

'Sustained.'

'All right, Doctor, let's get back to this controlled coma, for a moment,' said Galvin. 'Nitrous oxide works pretty fast, does it not? Say, within two or three minutes?'

'I believe it does.'

'As a surgical gynaecologist, you make deliveries ten, twelve times a week: is that correct?'

'More like twenty to twenty-five.'

'Fine. Twenty to twenty-five times a week. Four or five times a day. So you get to see nitrous oxide in use quite a bit. You know all about its side effects and any possible warnings concerning its use, isn't that true?'

'I keep abreast of the literature. I know what contra-indications to look for.'

'So you know all about the indications and, as you say, the contraindications of various types of anaesthetics: correct?'

'It's my job.'

'And you try to give the agent which will give you the maximum relaxation or coma so that you can avoid the patient going into shock?'

'And experiencing pain.'

'And, Dr Towler, nitrous oxide is induced by placing an anaesthetic mask over the patient's face, holding it tight and having the patient inhale until you have achieved the proper degree of relaxation or coma: correct?'

'Generally speaking, that's true.'

'And one of the things that you doctors try to avoid is having a patient take anything by mouth, liquid or food, just before an operation: isn't that true? For optimum results, patients are restricted from eating for eight to nine hours in elective surgery: isn't that true?'

'We can't always control events, Mr Galvin. We can't always choose the hour when a baby is going to arrive. Usually nature is provident and brings them at three in the morning. On a snowy Saturday night in most cases.'

A few jurors chuckled. Galvin's temper flared.

'Deborah Ruth Rosen is a vegetable! She never recovered from her coma: isn't that correct, Doctor?'

It was a jolt. Galvin leaned hard on his table and asked the question through his clenched teeth. 'The last time you saw her was when?' he asked.

Concannon was on his feet, trying to rescue his client. 'Two questions there, Your Honour. Can counsel limit himself to one at a time.'

'One question at a time,' agreed Galvin. 'When was the last time you saw Deborah Ruth Rosen, Doctor?'

'A month after the delivery,' he said.

'Could she talk?'

'No.'

'Could she walk?'

'No.'

'She was alive, wasn't she?'

'Yes,' replied the doctor.

'By that I mean, she was technically alive. But she couldn't move, could she?'

'No.'

'She couldn't sit up?'

'No.'

'And they fed her by sticking tubes through her nostrils and down her throat and into her stomach; and they punctured her arms so they could inject sugar and liquids into her veins: that's true too, isn't it, Doctor?'

'Yes.'

'A vegetable, wouldn't you say, Doctor? Isn't that the term of art? Isn't she medically considered a vegetable?'

'Yes.'

'But when she came to you in the early morning hours on May fourteenth, she could walk and talk and was a rational human being; is there any doubt in your mind about that, Doctor?'

'No.'

Galvin put the stiletto away. He spoke softly now. 'So something happened to Deborah Ruth and she suffered brain damage: is that correct?'

'On the operating table,' said the doctor nervously. He was shaken by the outburst. He recovered. 'She suffered cardiac arrest, which resulted in brain damage.'

'Cardiac arrest,' said Galvin. 'That's what's listed on the hospital record.'

'That's right, Mr Galvin. It is one of the most feared risks in any procedure. It can happen in a dentist's chair when you're getting a tooth pulled.'

'Now, Dr Towler, you made numerous entries on the hospital record, did you not?'

'I did.'

'And it was your duty to review the record to see that it was complete and accurate, was it not?'

'The doctor of the patient can only vouch for his own entries,' said Dr Towler, looking uneasily at Concannon, who avoided throwing a signal. 'These should be as complete and accurate as possible. The nurses' notes, their observations, the observations of consultants, the X-rays, EKGs, lab studies, orders for medication are all conducted by a lot of different departments in the hospital. We assume that each does his or her job. But we can't attest to their specific accuracy. We're only human.'

'Yes, Doctor, but in the interest of your patient, as you follow her along day by day, you refer to the record. You rely on it. The entries made by the night nurse as to temperature, pulse, respiration. Fluid intake. You must rely on that to determine your patient's condition, do you not?'

'Yes, of course.'

'It's a running commentary on the patient's condition, is it not? Day by day? Hour by hour?'

'Yes,' said Dr Towler. 'That's a fair summation.'

'Now, in your review of the hospital record, at the time you were treating Deborah Ruth four years ago, and when your attorneys were preparing the defence of this case, you saw nothing unusual in the entries made in that record: is that correct, Doctor?'

'Yes. That's correct.'

'And is it not true that from the time you made your initial observations and reviewed the hospital record four years ago until your recent review four years later, the record was complete and accurate then as it is today?'

'I don't follow you.'

Concannon half rose out of his chair to object, and there were enough grounds for a sustained objection, including one of clarity, but he was curious. He wanted to see what Galvin was up to.

'Well, Doctor, what I'm getting at is that the record is intact, isn't it? It is the same record today as the one made four years ago?'

'Of course.'

'I mean, none of the entries have been changed or altered?

163

There were no deletions or additions?'

'Certainly not!' he replied indignantly.

'No changes?'

'No!' bellowed Dr Towler in the first authentic display of emotion Galvin had seen in him.

'You wouldn't authorize any change in any portion of the hospital record, would you, Doctor?'

'The hospital record speaks for itself, Mr Galvin. It is there on the table, exactly the same as it was four years ago when it was made. There have been no changes – none. I don't know how to be more emphatic or to make it any more clear. No changes!'

'That's pretty clear, Doctor. Just making certain.'

And then they broke for lunch.

17

'What'd he say?' asked Moe.

'What do you think he said?' replied Galvin. 'He denied it. Most emphatically. Unequivocally. Indignantly.'

'But you asked him, right?' said Moe.

'Of course,' said Galvin.

'Specifically, you asked about the chart, right?'

'I asked what you told me to ask. You told me to ask about the chart and I asked. And he denied it. He said no one could tamper with that chart. Is that clear?'

'Wait a minute. You asked if the chart was exactly the same, didn't you? Exactly?'

'Right. Exactly the same,' said Galvin. 'I put it to him. "Is this the same chart that was prepared four years ago?" and he said that it was indeed. Was that good?'

'Oh, boy!' said Moe, who was clapping his hands and stalking around his office. He had just returned from New York City on the shuttle and rushed to his office to make certain that Galvin had got his message and asked the proper questions.

'And you know I hate airplanes,' he said, underlining the urgency of the mission.

And then he felt the flutter again. It was like a pair of wings that flared for a moment in his chest. He had been up all night with the flutter, but he'd dismissed it as excitement and anxiety. The subway. The plane. The success of his mission in New York. He was excited about finding the girl and he was building up to tell Galvin the good news.

The flutter passed, and Galvin looked at him.

'You look pale, Moe.'

'It's nothing,' he said. 'It's my natural colouring, pale.'

Moe's secretary, Sarah, knocked and brought in a bag of lunch. She dropped the change on the desk to signal her displeasure at fetching lunch. Why should she – a legal secretary – trot all over town to get her boss and his friend lunch? She had read enough feminist literature to know better.

'I wanted roast beef,' said Galvin, disappointed, finding a ham-and-cheese inside the waxed paper. 'I specifically asked for roast beef on rye.'

'Okay. So you got ham-and-cheese. It won't kill you. She thinks all you goyim want ham-and-cheese, no matter what you ask for.'

'You should get rid of that girl, Moe.'

'How can I get rid of her? She's crazy. No one else would hire her. She says being a lunch gofer is not her idea of a career. You know what she brought me for lunch last week? Pastrami salad. Can you believe that? A pastrami salad!'

'I hate ham-and-cheese,' said Galvin. 'Especially with butter. Who puts butter on ham-and-cheese?'

'She always gets ham-and-cheese with butter. She thinks all you goyim want butter on your ham-and-cheese.'

Galvin tried to scrape the butter off the white bread. 'And why tea?' he asked. 'Why did she bring me tea when I asked for coffee? I hate tea!'

'She hates coffee,' said Moe.

'You should fire her, Moe. You should definitely get rid of her.'

'And break in a new girl? Forget it. Listen, Galvin, she's been here for two years. When she first came, I thought she was stupid. She couldn't do anything right. Couldn't file. Couldn't type. Couldn't even answer a telephone. Then, one Friday afternoon, when everything is coming apart and I'm up to my eyeballs in cases and whatnot, and I haven't even eaten yet and

166

I'm ready to go totally deaf, she looks up from her typewriter and she says, "What do you want for lunch?" So now she owns me. She's got a good heart, Galvin. I've always been a sucker for a good heart. That's why I never fired you.'

'But Moe, supposing, just for argument's sake, you should have a yen for a roast beef sandwich. A real powerful yen. You know what I mean? Nothing else will do?'

'Sure,' said Moe. 'It's simple. Just ask her for a ham-and-cheese on white with a little butter.'

Moe held the coffee cup filled with whisky close to his face. He wanted to feel the ice – the cold rising out of the cup. He didn't want to feel the flutter, like an angel of death in his chest.

'What happened with Mary Rooney?' said Galvin. 'Hey! What's wrong? You look terrible.'

Moe smiled. 'No one looks good at my age,' he said. 'You don't look so hot either.'

'It's Sweeney,' said Galvin. 'It was a real mistake going up before him. He's doing everything but polishing Concannon's brass. He'll do that soon, too.'

Moe sipped the whisky and the tightness went away. He felt strong again.

'So what happened with Mary Rooney? Was she a help?'

'Yes and no,' said Moe. 'She was a hard person to persuade. She's not a very trusting person. Lawyers are not her favourite people. It took some doing, but I finally got through to her.'

'So? Will she testify?'

'She's not your witness, Galvin. First of all, she'd be a bad witness. Too overwrought. Second, she's not the key.'

'But she was there when it happened.'

'Don't go off so half cocked. When *what* happened? She was there when the cardiac arrest happened. But that's not the negligence. That's not where they screwed up.'

'When, then? When did they screw up?'

'Mary Rooney lives in New York City –'

'I know. I know. I sent you there.'

'She lives near another former nurse at St Catherine Laboure Hospital.'

'Really?'

'Do you know Mrs Rocco Stampanatto?'

'Never heard of her.'

'First, let me make certain: Dr Towler said for sure that the record was the same?' said Moe.

'Christ, yes, Moe, but who is this Stampanatto dame?'

'First tell me what Dr Towler said when you asked about the record.'

'He said no one tampered with the record. He said it was the same today as it was four years ago. He said that they keep very careful check on it.'

'Let me look at your copy,' said Moe.

Galvin fumbled in his briefcase and came up with the hospital chart. Moe studied the chart while Galvin sat on the edge of his chair, eating a ham-and-cheese sandwich that he did not want.

'Amazing!' said Moe.

'What?' said Galvin.

'I wouldn't have believed it.'

'Believed what?' said Galvin.

'You know, Galvin, when you first came to me and told me the story about Bishop Brophey and how he tried to bribe you off this case, I thought you were full of shit. Then I believed you, but I couldn't understand why these people would go to so much trouble to stop a case that they had locked up . . .'

'Goddammit, Moe, what did you find out and who is this Stampanatto?'

'Then when you asked me to go to New York, I knew that there was a lot more to this than met the eye. A lot more . . .'

'Don't do this to me, Moe.'

'I think those bastards were trying to steal it,' said Moe. 'The three hundred thousand dollars would have been cheap. You were right to hold out.'

'I knew it,' said Galvin. 'I knew it. There's a mistake on the charts.'

'There's no mistake,' said Moe.

'No mistake?'

'No mistake . . . The bastards lied.'

At first, it felt like an electrical storm inside his head. It was not alarming. Not at first. At least it wasn't the breathless flutter in his chest. Just a spasm inside his head that didn't even hurt.

He saw Galvin looking at him and he tried to say something to him; he wanted to reassure him because Galvin looked so worried. But nothing seemed to work. It all happened so fast. And he was preoccupied with that terrific upheaval inside his head.

'What's wrong, Moe? Moe? Moe!'

But by then it was too late. The stroke had knocked out all his circuitry. It was like a high-tension wire sparking and running wild inside his head.

He didn't hear Galvin calling. He wasn't even aware of falling and hitting his head on the desk.

The paramedics arrived quickly, but they wasted a lot of time on the cut on his scalp. By the time they got Moe to St Catherine Laboure Hospital, he was paralysed and unconscious. The doctor said that he would not even be conscious for a day or two, and even then there was no telling what brain damage he had suffered.

Concannon was on his feet, moving for a dismissal of the case

169

in the absence of any plaintiff, when Galvin walked into the courtroom.

'You are late, Counsellor,' said the judge from his perch.

'But I'm here now, Judge,' said Galvin holding his temper in check. 'I am here now.'

18

The afternoon session passed quietly as Concannon patched the doctor's testimony, stitching the holes and doubts poked there by Galvin.

'It is medically true, is it not, Doctor, that there are inevitable risks and dangers in the use of any type of anaesthesia?'

'Yes,' replied Dr Towler. 'That's true. There is no foolproof anaesthetic.'

'And you took every precaution with Deborah Ruth, as you would with any such case, did you not?'

They were jack-in-the-box questions in which the answer popped up at you. Self-serving, but necessary.

'And isn't it medically true, Doctor, that there will always be a certain number of anaesthesia casualties – an irreducible minimum?'

'Unhappily true. Unfortunate, but unavoidable. Some fraction of one percent succumb no matter what. With nitrous oxide it is low.'

They sounded like generals, the doctors, measuring the battlefield cost against the advance of science. It sounded cold-blooded in the courtroom. Two people in a thousand would not survive nitrous oxide as opposed to five with, say, halothane. It was an equation.

There was no hospital smell at St Catherine Laboure Hospital. This was consciously so. The hospital had been conceived by Bishop Brophey's predecessor as a monument to life, rather than a temple of suffering. The smell of medicine was scrubbed, soaked, perfumed away.

171

Everything about the hospital was bright and optimistic. The nurses were perky, and the interns and doctors were young and eager. The people who worked at St Catherine's thought of it as a great white passenger liner riding at anchor athwart the Charles River – a thing of matchless beauty and grace. The spirit was one inspired by St Catherine Labouré, who fought disease in the streets of Paris in 1849. They would not tolerate rubella or racism or religious radicalism within its confines; so said the motto. It mattered not whether a man believed in God or was black or had Blue Cross; it mattered only that a man was down.

St Catherine's rose twenty-five floors above the banks of the Charles. From its upper windows there was a splendid view of the crew races, and Beacon Hill and Cambridge. But one could also see Mt Auburn Cemetery.

It was all of that – the spirit, the achievement, the hope – which the Bishop had sought to protect when he had gone to see Galvin. Now, on the evening of the first day of battle, he drew Concannon aside in the staff dining room, where the defence team had repaired after court.

'You're worried,' said the Bishop out of earshot of the others. They stood at the windows, equals at the height of their professions. They were men who understood the great stakes involved.

'No,' said Concannon. 'Why do you say that?'

'I don't know. I just had a feeling that you were worried. Isn't the case going well?'

'It's going just fine. What makes you think I'm worried?'

'I don't know. I thought it would be over. I was hoping that it would be ended by now.'

'It's only the first day,' said Concannon. 'You weren't in court.'

The Bishop didn't think it appropriate to show up in court – taking sides in something that could get ugly. Taking sides in

172

something in which he might even lose. How would it look? He always had to have the ability to be on every side of an issue. Even when he was being sued. They stood side by side looking down at the river.

'It's not my place,' said the Bishop. 'I don't want to go to court. Isn't it working out?'

'It's the first day,' reassured Concannon. 'The field is still full of smoke, but I'd say we were still in command of the field.' Concannon liked to season his conversation with wartime metaphors.

'We're going to win, Your Excellency. There's no doubt of that.'

'It's not that,' said the Bishop, turning now to face Concannon. 'Winning isn't really that important.'

'What is?'

'We have to be *right*,' said the Bishop. Then, glancing at his watch, he said, 'I'm sorry, Mr Concannon, but I have to go. I have appointments. Good luck tomorrow.'

Bishop Brophey smiled courteously and left, still troubled. He worried, and he didn't want to know . . .

It was after 7 P.M. when the full flotilla of the defense sailed into the penthouse conference room of the hospital. The men were taking comfort in the after-dinner cigars. There was a general murmur around the table when Concannon rapped for attention. Doctors, nurses, insurance men, lawyers and Church representatives all turned towards the man at the end of the table.

'You know,' said Concannon easily, 'the first case I ever tried was a medical case. I had old Dr Wolfgang Von Richling-hausen on the stand.'

'Von Richlinghausen?' asked Dr Towler, toying with his pipe.

'The same,' replied Concannon.

'He was a fraud and a pirate!' Dr Towler said with a snort.

'Was he ever! A real harpooner. He even looked like Captain Ahab, with his craggy face and eyes that blazed like coals. Something out of the Old Testament. Scared the *hell* out of a young lawyer like me. I was a neophyte then. He could sink a defendant's case faster than any medical expert I ever saw. Just had to look over at the jury; they'd think God was testifying.'

Donna St Laurent had never seen this side of Concannon. She noticed the easing of tension around the room. Telling stories around the campfire – even the centrally heated, oak-panelled campfire of the conference room at St Catherine Laboure Hospital – warmed a body in the night air. She felt a pang of something for Concannon. And it was only partly admiration.

'He'd always hit you below the waterline,' Concannon went on. 'Of course, he made his living in the courtroom. Same as me. An expert's expert. You couldn't ever budge him. He was like Stonewall Jackson on the witness stand.

'Old Wolfgang was an expert on everything. Cancer. Multiple sclerosis, scleroderma, myasthenia gravis. Any crypto-genic disease you could name. Even neurosyphilis. Had always treated several cases of whatever disorder was at issue. Von Richlinghausen always knew the cause. Medical science didn't know, but to Wolfgang it was simple. It was due to a slip and fall at Jordan Marsh or being hit in the rear by a taxicab.'

Concannon leaned back in his chair and grinned.

'But the time of which I'm speaking was my first case. I was defending for the Transit Authority, and old Wolfgang was up there on the stand. It was his testimony that a carcinoma of a woman's left breast was causally related to her being pushed forward against a bus seat.'

There were groans and chuckles around the table.

'Well,' continued Concannon, 'I knew that Wolfgang had gone to a third-rate medical school, so I started in on him.

174

"Doctor," I said, "do you happen to know what nerve roots mediate the achilles reflex?"

' "No," says old Wolfgang. "I do not."

'Very dignified. Ice. So, I followed that up. "Well, Doctor, if I can refresh your memory, isn't it the first and second sacral nerve roots that innervate the lateral and medial gastrocnemius, the plantaris and the soleus muscles, thus causing the foot to go down in the plantar flexion when the ankle tendon is tapped by a reflex hammer?"

' "I don't know," says Wolfgang.'

There was a hearty buoyancy to the group. They were caught up in the spirit of the joke, anticipating the funny parts.

' "Well, Doctor," I said, "as a medical practitioner, aren't you supposed to know anatomy and physiology?"

'So Von Richlinghausen fixes me with a terrible stare; he looks right through me, like an X-ray; then he turns to the jury and, his voice dripping with contempt, says, "My dear boy, anatomy and physiology are known only by God and the first-year medical student. I am neither!" '

They were still laughing when a nurse brought in coffee.

'I take it by that parable that you are telling us not to get too precious with the jury,' said Dr Towler, who stirred his coffee until it was cold. He looked at the coffee and then at Concannon. He was a man who always left himself an alternative; he would ask his unpleasant questions to the coffee. 'You think we may be too . . . well, precious?'

'You put your finger on it, Doctor,' said Concannon. 'It is possible to be too correct. We are all human. You may be eminent doctors and leading scientists, but you are still human. The people on the jury have to relate to you. You cannot come on like God, unless you are Wolfgang Von Richlinghausen.'

'It's hard to know what attitude to adopt with a jury – even for the best of us,' said Dr Towler, dipping his spoon into and out of the empty cup.

'Impossible,' agreed Concannon. 'Just try to remember that they're human and you're human. They'll respond to the human thing.'

There was a decanter of liqueur, and Donna poured herself a small glass. She sipped it while Concannon organized the defence. He rose and walked over to a blackboard at the side of the room.

'What is the insurer's position at this time?' he asked Arthur Aloisi, the claims manager for Consolidated Life and Casualty. 'Would you renew the offer of three hundred thousand dollars tomorrow morning?' Concannon asked.

Aloisi paused, as if he hadn't considered it before. Aloisi never answered a question quickly. 'No,' he said slowly, pushing back his chair and standing now. 'Once the offer was withdrawn, it was permanently withdrawn. I spoke with the home office about this after today's court session, and we all agreed. At this point, we believe that it is a question of vindication.'

Aloisi leaned forward, placing his hands squarely on the table. 'One of the reasons we tendered the offer to Mr Galvin in the first place was to avoid the publicity and embarrassment of a trial. We did not wish to expose the doctors and the hospital and the profession itself to any undue notoriety. That's all forfeited now. If we backed away now, it would look as if we had something to hide. It would defeat the whole purpose of the first offer.'

He was a cautious man, Aloisi. It was in the nature of the work, but also in the nature of the man. The caution covered all aspects of his life – from choosing a wife who was not too beautiful, and therefore less likely to run around, to calculating on an actuarial table the approximate date of his death, all factors considered, with a plus-or-minus margin of error of five years. He knew that he would in all probability never see his

176

youngest child graduate from college. He made plans around that knowledge. When he got involved in the *Rosen* case, he had argued against any offer of settlement. Not because he dismissed the costs and bother, but more because he was offended by Galvin's chaos. When he insisted that it was a question of vindication, he also wanted some vindication for his own carefully plotted and thought-out life-style. He wanted to punish Galvin.

'The highest award ever paid in this state for malpractice has been four hundred thousand,' he went on. 'It's not likely that a man like Frank Galvin will be able to persuade a jury to award more than that in this case. His expert, by the way, is a bit of a quack. He may get to the jury, but we are not worried about a runaway verdict.'

'We appreciate the confidence,' said Dr Towler.

'Not at all,' replied Aloisi. 'I am a lawyer myself, you know, and I believe we have to draw a line somewhere and protect you fellows from the parasites. Someone has to put an end to these malpractice cases. You know, insurance companies all over the country will be watching this one. This will be a landmark case. And we have everything going for us. We have the best doctors in the nation. We have a world-renowned hospital. We have an unimpeachable set of circumstances. There is no doubt that there was never an iota of negligence.'

Monsignor O'Boyle led the applause as Aloisi sat down.

Concannon wandered back and forth in front of the blackboard, reviewing testimony, outlining further aspects of the case.

'You know, there's always one cheap way that the plaintiff can get over the rail,' he said. 'By getting over the rail, I mean have the case decided by the jury. It's a legal term. We try to stop a case from reaching a jury by having it thrown out on a motion at some earlier stage of the case.'

'The husband,' said Donna.

'Right,' said Concannon. 'The husband. If we get him on our side, they'll toss it out. Right after the event, Dr Towler spoke with the husband. By the way, he now lives in New York City and is remarried. He has no abiding interest in the case. The Rosen girl is confined at the Holy Ghost Chronic Care Hospital in Jamaica Plain. He hasn't visited her once.'

'How do you know?' asked Donna.

'We've checked the visitors' registration book,' said Concannon. 'In four years, he hasn't been there once. He wasn't even the one who hired Galvin. It was the conservator, Karen Ross, and she sure isn't a surprise witness.'

Concannon played with a piece of chalk while he paced in front of the blackboard. 'Now, Mr Rosen has not even met with our friend Mr Galvin, so we do not believe that he is a secret, surprise witness. But we have to be prepared. We are working on the theory that Galvin's whole strategy is to reach the jury through his expert. But if his expert doesn't hold up, then what? Then Mr Galvin may get desperate and produce Mr Rosen, who would swear that Dr Towler confessed right after the incident. Mr Rosen would place his hand on the Bible and swear that Dr Towler broke down and admitted that the whole thing was a big mistake and his fault.'

'But that's not true,' said Dr Towler hotly. 'That's a monstrous lie!'

'Of course it is,' Concannon added quickly. 'But we have to prepare for that *possibility*. It is one of the more desperate tactics used by some lawyers in cases of this sort. Let me explain how it works.

'After the incident, Mr Rosen *did* come to the hospital and Dr Towler *did* speak to him. It was the normal commiseration of one human being with another. We have the exact words . . .'

Concannon held out his hand and Kaplan handed him a sheet of paper: 'The exact words were: *"Mr Rosen, I don't know what to say. This is a terrible tragedy. She was a lovely girl.*

What can I say? We did everything known to medical science. But unfortunately, the brain was damaged. She's in a coma. I'm very sorry."

'The key here is the regret. He said, according to his own statement to me, *"I'm very sorry." '*

'But that was just the normal, human expression of sympathy,' protested Dr Towler. 'That wasn't an admission of guilt.'

'I know,' said Concannon. 'The jury will know. But there are cases in which a malpractice suit has been won without a medical expert. Someone gets on the stand and swears that the doctor said, "It's all my fault; I'm sorry."

'We all know that a doctor would never say that. But there are times when a jury can be naïve enough to believe it. They can find for the plaintiff on that alone. It won't happen in this case, so I don't want you to worry. But it's something we have to guard against.'

'I don't understand,' said Dr Towler. 'How is it possible to just take someone's word?'

'Well, confessions make up all the evidence there is in a lot of cases. In the thirties, they used to railroad political prisoners and troublemakers like that. Just get some cop to say the guy admitted everything. The defendant would deny it, but it would go to the jury. See, in that case, there is evidence on both sides. One guy says he said it and another denies it. There is evidence both ways, so the judge gives it to the jury to decide. It's a question of fact. The jury decides which story they believe.'

Dr Towler accepted another cup of coffee from the nurse, who went silently around the table.

'In the sixties, the Supreme Court started tightening up the safeguards,' continued Concannon, waving off the nurse. 'There were too many phony confessions. There were the *Miranda* and *Escobedo* decisions, in which the Supreme Court

179

put out some pretty tough guidelines for confessions. They had to be voluntary and the prisoner had to be advised of his rights. Including a right to counsel. A lot of admissions went out the window. Lawyers weren't going to let clients make admissions.' He got up and walked around, gesturing as he spoke.

'But that was in criminal cases. There are no such safeguards in civil cases. The reason is that the authorities are out of it in civil cases. You don't have policemen who are suspected of beating confessions out of suspects. You have two separate and equal parties suing each other. One says one thing and another says another thing. Whom are you going to believe? The courts found the easy way out. Leave it to the jury.'

'But why would I confess to Mr Rosen? Why would I go against my own interest?' asked Dr Towler.

'That's an interesting point of law. The law recognizes a confession against interest as even more valid *because* it goes against the interest of the party involved. Whether or not he ever made such a statement is another matter.'

He could see the gloom developing in the medical-personnel room. 'Let's not worry prematurely. I don't believe that he is staking the whole case on his medical expert. If the expert folds, which is unlikely, then he may try to round up Rosen. But I don't think so.'

'What *about* the expert?' asked Dr Crowley.

'The so-called expert is Dr Lionel B. Thompson from Mineola, Long Island. We have a report' – and he held out his hand and Kaplan placed a folder there. 'City College of New York, Class of 'Twenty-six. Bachelor of Science. New York College of Medicine and Husbandry, Class of 'Thirty. He graduated nineteenth in a class of twenty. He practised in Jamaica, British West Indies, for years, then served a stint as a VA doctor and recently got a courtesy appointment to the anaesthesiology staff at East Hampton Hospital for Women.

That was in 1975. He is kicking eighty and has no honours or degrees of any particular distinction. He is not board certified, nor is he listed in the *New York Medical Directory*. Apart from East Hampton, he has no other hospital affiliation.'

'How do we know so much about this guy?' asked Dr Crowley, relighting a dead cigar. The ashes spilled down the front of his jacket. 'How can we even be certain that he is the plaintiff's expert?'

'Oh, he's the expert, all right. We have our professional secrets, Doctor.'

'Of course,' said Dr Crowley. It was a comfort to know that an intelligence system was in their service.

'Now, getting back to Dr Thompson. He is no Wolfgang Von Richlinghausen. I guess we can be grateful for that. He is not a member of the American Medical Association, or the New York Medical Society, or the American Board of Anaesthesiology. He does claim membership in some local county medical society, which, it is our understanding, will take anyone in off the street for a twenty-five-dollar membership fee.

'In addition, he claims to be dean emeritus of some organization known as the Legal-Medical Society, based again in New York. We're checking on that right now. In the last five years he has testified in twelve malpractice cases and in a total of forty-four court cases.'

'A hired gun,' said Dr Towler, looking around for approval of his glib metaphor.

'A dangerous man,' said Concannon quickly. 'That means we have to be careful. It means that he has been up on the witness stand before and he knows what to expect. I never underestimate the calibre of the guns ranged against me.

'Let's look at what we can expect from Dr Thompson. There are three tacks he can take. First, he'll testify that good medical practice dictates that once a cardiac arrest develops, a delay longer than three to four minutes in resuscitating the heart constitutes negligence per se.

'We can attack that. That theory is not medically or legally sustainable. We have our own experts: Dr Kesloff from University General and Dr Kemper from Boston Presbyterian – two of the most distinguished anaesthesiologists in the world. Diplomates of the American Board and Fellows of the American College of Anaesthesiology.'

'How will you rebut?' asked Monsignor O'Boyle.

'Science does not even know the origin of the heartbeat, Monsignor.' Concannon paused to explain the strategy. He always assumed that he was dealing with inferior minds, although he went to great lengths to disguise it. 'It is controlled by the vagus and accelerator nerves, but they only regulate the heartbeat. The vagus slows the heart down while the accelerator speeds it up. Cut the vagus nerve and the heart speeds up. Cut the accelerator and it slows down. Cut them both and not too much happens. The heart continues to beat.

'Our medical experts will testify that the heart is a mysterious and autonomous organ. That's why you can do transplants. We'll be able to show that Dr Towler and Dr Crowley followed every conceivable medical procedure in the fastest possible time to try to restore the heartbeat. But it just wouldn't kick over. No negligence.'

'Number two?' asked O'Boyle, who sensed the insult in Concannon's tone and was attempting his own counterpoint. The battle went unnoticed by the others.

'His second premise will probably be that due to Mrs Rosen's delicate condition, a general anaesthetic was not indicated. He'll say that the anaesthetic should have been caudal – in the spine. Again, not sustainable. A spinal is not as thorough as a general. There's a great risk of surgical shock, especially in Mrs Rosen, who had a low haemoglobin and diabetes mellitus. In fact, in obstetrical anaesthesia, shock from a spinal is the second most common cause of death.'

'How so?' asked O'Boyle.

'Shock is caused by a drop in blood pressure. Blood pressure is maintained by contractions of blood vessels. It's like water flowing through a garden hose. If I step on one end of the hose, the water pressure increases. It sprays out faster. Okay? So all this is controlled by the sympathetic nervous system. Spinal anaesthesia blocks the contractions. The blood pools and doesn't return to the heart. The blood pressure drops. Then loss of oxygen to the brain and to the vital nerve centres in the brain stem which control respiration and regulate the heart. Then, cardiac arrest. You can also cut off blood flow to the uterus and damage the foetus.'

'Very good, *Doctor* Concannon,' said Dr Towler. 'Now tell us what's the third possibility.'

'I like to be prepared,' said Concannon, a bit embarrassed. But he remained in command. 'The third possibility is faulty equipment,' he said staunchly. 'Too much nitrous oxide. Not enough oxygen. That's conjecture, and we won't allow him to chase that particular hypothesis. The equipment was tested right after the event by the manufacturer and an independent research company. The machine and the mixture were perfect. We will be prepared with the experts and the results of the tests.'

'What else will they throw at us?' asked Nurse Nevins, twisting her hands together as if under a tap.

'They will throw Deborah Ruth Rosen at us,' said Concannon. 'They may even bring her into court. He'll attempt to wheel her in front of the jury, and attendants will testify to her day-to-day condition. They may even recite a day in the life of Deborah Ruth Rosen, and it will be hard to find a dry eye in the courtroom. Including my own, ladies and gentlemen. Including my own. It is not possible to try this case and not be moved by the plight of this unfortunate girl. Which

183

is not to say that the plaintiff's case has any merit. It is just to remind you to fight on firm ground. We do not contest the tragedy. We contest the blame.'

It was still early when they left the meeting. Donna and Concannon stood together for a moment in the parking lot.

'You're doing a good job in this case, Donna,' he said, touching her arm. 'When this case is over, perhaps we can fly down to Nantucket for a day or two.'

Donna smiled. 'Perhaps we can.'

19

The nurse grinned. She said there was an 'Oriental person' in the downstairs lobby insisting on seeing Mr Galvin. 'Said something about how she was going to put *you* in the hospital.' The grin became a giggle.

'Stay here,' he told Miriam and Rhonda Katz. They had been waiting on the corridor bench outside the intensive-care unit at St Catherine Laboure Hospital. Another battery of specialists had gone in to examine Moe. 'I'll be right back.'

She looked sad sitting in the lobby of the ocean-liner hospital. She looked sad and dumpy. Galvin had never noticed it before, or if he had, he didn't pay any attention, but Lois Chen was very short and getting dumpy. It was as if her features were being crushed by gravity. A surrender to nature, collapsing into a broad nose and a thick face.

'You son-of-a-bitch,' she began in a low voice as he approached, rising out of the couch. 'You lousy bastard rat-fuck –'

'Who's watching Sam?' he asked.

'You rotten mother-fucking son-of-a-bitch . . .'

'You said that already,' he said, grabbing her under the arm and leading her out into the parking lot.

When they got outside, she seemed to capitulate. She leaned in against him, in a familiar fashion, and she quietly began to weep. It was not crying. It was weeping. Soft, heartbroken tears that ate like acid through his defences against guilt.

'I love you,' she said.

'I know,' he replied.

But he could not reciprocate. He could not quite tell her that he loved her.

'You prick!' she started up again.

'I know that too.'

'Is it something I've done?' she asked.

'It's nothing,' he said.

'Don't hand me that. It's something.'

It was dark in the parking lot and there was a breeze off the Charles, and he headed into it like a sailor.

'If I tell you I am so caught up in my own problems right now, that will sound selfish and terrible.'

'So what is it?' she asked, walking beside him.

'I am so caught up in my own problems right now that I am selfish and terrible.'

'And I am one of your problems?'

He smiled. 'No. You and Sam are the single unpolluted joy in my life.'

'What's going on, Galvin? Tell me that much. Tell me what's going on.'

'Professional menopause,' he said. 'I am having hot flushes in my career and I don't know if I want to be me anymore.'

She stopped. 'Be serious, Frank.'

She never called him Frank. Not even when she wanted to annoy him. It was a jolt. He didn't know what it meant, except that things were serious.

'Okay, Chen, but first tell me, who's watching Sam?'

'I left him with his grandparents. He's holding court in my father's restaurant, wearing a Mandarin gown and getting stuffed with all the delicacies of the East. Marco Polo never had it so good.'

He laughed. 'He's getting spoiled.'

'No worse than his father. He thinks he's the centre of the universe. The trouble is, no one can resist the appeal of honourable futility.'

'What are you talking about?' asked Galvin.

'The look he gets in his eyes when he knows that something

is about to happen that he cannot avoid, but he's determined to go through with it anyway. Dumb integrity. You know?'

'I know,' said Galvin.

They walked past the parking lot, out towards the water. They sat on a bench, holding hands. He always held her hands passionately.

'Do you want to call it off?' she asked meekly – a plea for reassurance.

'No,' he said. 'I do not want to call it off. When we first met, then I wanted to call it off. All during that early time when I was falling into your trap, then I wanted to break it off. I could see it all coming, you know. The first time I looked into your eyes, I saw infinity.'

'So what do you want?'

'I want you there for me. Even when I'm not there, I want you there waiting for me.'

'You don't want much,' she said.

'People tell me that. The judge told me that today. Maybe I do want too much. It's our national disease: greed. Everybody wants more than what's coming to him these days.'

She got up and kissed him on his cheek.

'I'll be home,' she said. 'Waiting.'

And then she walked away.

'I love you,' Galvin called after her.

Donna St Laurent watched it all from her car, annoyed with herself for feeling slightly hurt at Galvin's last words. She watched Galvin walk back across the parking lot and into the hospital. Well, she would wait all night if necessary. She was determined to find out what Galvin had up his sleeve. It wasn't just the expert from Long Island. She was sure there was something else.

'Did you bring back coffee?' asked Miriam Katz, Moe's wife. She had been camped outside the intensive-care unit all night.

The coffee shop was on the first floor and she didn't want to leave her post.

It occurred to Galvin that he spent a lot of time waiting for outcomes. Verdicts. Sentences. Disclosures. Out of the corner of his eye, Galvin could see Moe's wife glaring at him, blaming him for what had happened. And he had even forgotten her cup of coffee.

Moe's daughter, Rhonda, who had once had a suffocating crush on Galvin, sat at the end of the couch. She had come last.

'What happened, Galvin?'

'You mean with Moe?'

'What's your case got to do with my father, and why was he chasing down to New York for you?'

'Moe was doing me a favour,' he said. 'I needed some help in New York. I couldn't be in two places at the same time, and he agreed to help me. It wasn't anything hard or strenuous. We were working on a case, Rhonda. Just like the old days.'

'You know he hates planes.'

'It was really important.'

'This important?' she said, swinging an arm to sweep in all the medical high technology of intensive care.

'How could I know?'

'You couldn't know,' she said.

A young doctor came out and saw them and approached. 'You're Galvin, aren't you?' he said.

'Yes,' said Galvin.

'The guy who's suing the hospital.'

'Hey! Come on, fella. This is Mr Katz's family.'

'I'm Dr Brooks,' he said to Miriam and Rhonda. 'If you'll just follow me into the consultation room, I'll fill you in.'

As Galvin began to trail along, the doctor held out a hand. 'Just the immediate family,' he said. 'Lawyers can wait outside.'

Galvin was pissed, but if he got into a brawl at St Catherine

Laboure Hospital with one of the cardiac residents, it would look bad in the newspapers. He would lose his case and his licence and his freedom. So, all things considered, he decided not to leap on Dr Brooks's back and pound his head in.

When Miriam and Rhonda finally emerged from the two swinging white doors, they were smiling.

'Daddy's going to be fine,' said Rhonda.

'What did the good doctor say, exactly?'

'Well, he said that with a stroke it's hard to tell all the damage right away, but that it appears that Daddy had a very minor episode.'

'Just to scare the hell out of everyone,' laughed Galvin, relieved.

'It will take a few days, but he seems to have all his mental faculties. No paralysis, which he said was the greatest danger.'

'Thank God,' said Galvin.

They were walking to the car when Rhonda asked, 'Who's the girl Daddy brought back from New York?'

'What?' said Galvin.

'The girl he brought back from New York. He said she had something to do with the case you were both working on.'

'He brought back a girl from New York?' asked Galvin again.

'Don't you know about her?' asked Mrs Katz.

'Oh, sure,' said Galvin. 'Where is she?'

'She's at our home,' Rhonda said, 'where Daddy left her. He walks in with a girl and leaves her and goes and has a stroke. You think there's something funny going on?'

'I thought you knew about her,' said Miriam.

'What's her name – Mary Rooney?' asked Galvin.

'Something like that,' said Mrs Katz. 'It's an Irish name, anyway.'

'Stampanatto,' said Rhonda. 'Her name's Stampanatto, and she used to work at this hospital.'

'Stampanatto?' said Galvin. 'That's Irish?'

'It's not?' said Mrs Katz. 'It's definitely not Jewish.'

'Let's go,' said Galvin, swinging the car door open for them and flipping the key in the ignition.

'Where are we going?' said Miriam, settling back in the seat.

'Moe won't be able to see anyone tonight. I want to talk to Miss Stampanatto.'

'It's Mrs,' said Moe's wife. 'The first thing I checked was that she was married so I knew Moe wasn't fooling around with a young chippie.'

As Galvin's car swung out of the parking lot and into the late-evening traffic, another car started up across the street. Donna St Laurent waited for a quick count of ten, then eased her car into the traffic behind them.

20

Peggy was at her desk. She handed him a pile of phone messages and greeted him in her fashion.

'Boy, you look like hell.'

His face was puffy from lack of sleep. His white shirt was stained at the collar, and his suit was rumpled. It was the same one he had worn yesterday.

The first call he made was to St Catherine Laboure Hospital, where they told him that Moe's condition was stable. Then he called the Parker House and spoke to Dr Thompson.

'Just having my breakfast,' said the doctor, sounding chipper. 'Pancakes and a slug of Scotch.'

'Hey!' said Galvin. 'Take it easy; you're on the stand today. Or are you?'

'Listen, my young friend, when you reach my age you need a glass of Scotch to start your heart up in the morning,' Dr Thompson replied. 'It's just what the doctor ordered.'

'What about the other thing? Is that okay?'

'What other thing?'

'You know. The pressure. The Long Island Cement and Asphalt Association. You said that your colleagues would put you in the mixer and you'd wind up as part of the Cross Island Parkway.'

'That doesn't matter anymore. They've made the mistake of getting me good and angry. I'll be up on that witness stand come hell or high water.'

'Thanks, L.B. You don't know what this means to me.'

As he hurried to court, Galvin suddenly felt misgivings. They would smell whisky on Dr Thompson's breath and he would be dismissed as an old rummy. No. No one would smell anything. It would be all right. Please, God!

There was a line in the lobby outside of Courtroom 903. Word had somehow got around that today would be the day when the stars would fall on Galvin. The distinguished J. Edward Concannon would squash the gnat today. That was the morning bet when Galvin rose to resume his case.

'Proceed,' ordered the judge.

'I'd like to recall Dr Towler to the stand,' requested Galvin.

'Objection,' said Concannon, leaping to his feet. 'Mr Galvin concluded with this witness yesterday.'

'It is a little irregular,' began Judge Sweeney.

'Your Honour, in the interest of justice I implore you to allow me a little leeway,' said Galvin.

'All right, Counsellor, but let's not get started in a whole mishmash of cancelling the rules. We all play by the same rules in this ball park.'

'Just rounding second,' said Galvin dryly.

Concannon smiled and sat down. 'What's going on?' whispered Wilson. 'I don't get it.'

'I believe that Mr Galvin has lost his expert,' he said softly, leaning into Wilson's ear, 'and maybe even his cause. He's going to try and get Towler to crack and admit that he made an error. In that conversation to the husband.'

Concannon pulled away and straightened his jacket. How do I defend against this? he asked himself like a chess master who sees a piece moved on the board.

There were two witnesses to that conversation, he wrote on his legal yellow pad. *Get Crowley and Nevins to affirm conversation with Mr Rosen.*

He folded the note and handed it to Wilson, satisfied that he was defended in depth.

'Dr Towler,' began Galvin, 'yesterday I asked you if you inquired as to where Deborah Ruth Rosen had been prior to coming to the hospital. And you said that you hadn't. Isn't that correct?'

'Yes.'

'Now, Doctor ... May I approach the witness, Your Honour?'

'Yes, of course,' said the judge, visibly annoyed.

'Now, Doctor, would you look at the admitting sheet again, page three of the hospital record, the one you said was in Nurse Campanelli's handwriting, and would you tell me if I am reading correctly: "When did patient last eat?" '

'You have read correctly,' said Towler.

'Is that an important question?'

'Yes. Of course.'

'Why? Why is that an important question?'

'Well, ideally, you want a patient's stomach empty before surgery. So they don't eat or drink for six hours prior to induction. That's, of course, when we have a choice. That's for elective surgery, in which you have plenty of advance notice. But many times you get an emergency situation – accidents, a fulminating event – things like that in which you don't have that kind of choice or time.'

'So you wouldn't give a patient a general anaesthesia on a full stomach, would you?'

'No.'

'Not if she ate a full meal – say, steak and potatoes – an hour before surgery or delivery?'

'No. A local anaesthetic, or a spinal,' he replied. 'That is, of course, if we were apprised of the fact.'

'Of course, Doctor. We were just speaking hypothetically. I understand that. Now, let me follow this another step. One more step down the road of this hypothetical. Okay?'

'Okay.'

'If I understand you correctly, and I am just an ignorant layman, the reason you would give a spinal to a person who just ate would be to avoid the possibility of that person throwing up into the anaesthesia mask.'

'Well, I suppose –'

'And then that hypothetical person would drown, literally drown, in her own vomit: isn't that correct?'

'That's an oversimplification,' said Dr Towler.

'Well, I know you'd like to complicate it for us if you could, but isn't that essentially correct, Doctor?'

'It's not that black or white. Your explanation is too simple. There are individual circumstances which the doctor and the anaesthetist must assess. There are risks to weigh against benefits. There are questions of judgement, and the patient's physical condition. You cannot ignore the patient's physical condition –'

'Your Honour, I ask you to instruct the witness,' said Galvin. 'I asked for a simple yes or no answer on that question.'

'Objection,' said Concannon, rising. 'Your Honour, the plaintiff's attorney deliberately cut Dr Towler off in the middle of his answer. He should be allowed to complete his answer. The Court and this jury should be allowed the benefit of his full answer.'

'Absolutely,' ruled Sweeney. 'Doctor, you can't give a simple yes or no answer to a question that complicated, can you? I mean, I know just from the practice of law and the many years I've spent on this bench that there are questions which demand fuller explanations –'

'Your Honour!' yelled Galvin. 'That's unfair. That's not a ruling – that's two paragraphs.'

'I warn you Mr Galvin, you are standing on the brink of contempt,' said Sweeney between clenched teeth. 'This Court, not you, will make the rulings here. If you have an objection to my ruling, plead your objection. I'll rule on it. If you feel aggrieved, you may take an exception. But do not test this Court's patience with your temper. Now, Dr Towler, I'm sure we would all like to hear your explanation. At least almost all of us would.'

'Please note my objection and exception,' said Galvin. 'And so the record will be perfectly clear, will Your Honour please direct the stenographer to read back my last question to Dr Towler so that we do not mistake my exact line of questioning?'

'Not necessary,' snapped Judge Sweeney. 'Go ahead, Dr Towler.'

'Let me once again renew my objection and exception to Your Honour's denial of my request.'

'Noted. Proceed, Doctor.'

'Okay. Hold it. I'm sorry, I mean I have a motion,' said Galvin. 'I withdraw the question.'

'Withdraw the question?'

'Right. I withdraw the question. That means that there is no question now pending before Dr Towler. So if I may proceed, I'll rephrase it.'

'Cute. Very cute,' said the judge. 'Go ahead.'

'Dr Towler, if a patient consumed a full meal *one* hour before induction of anaesthesia, and you were apprised of that fact, the anaesthesia of choice would be spinal: isn't that correct?'

'I believe I already answered that.'

'Indulge me, Doctor. Would you repeat your answer?'

'A caudal, or spinal, anaesthesia would be indicated,' he said.

'And if a patient consumed a full meal one hour prior to induction of general anaesthesia, there would be a high risk factor that the inhalation of a vaporous anaesthesia, such as nitrous oxide, would induce vomiting during the initial stages: isn't that medically correct, Doctor? Just yes or no, please.'

'Yes.'

'And if a patient told you that she ate nine hours before presenting herself to you, with her history of diabetes mellitus, heart involvement, low haemoglobin, then you say that a general anaesthesia would be the method of choice: isn't that

195

correct?'

'I assume that we have left the hypothetical person and we are now talking about Deborah Ruth Rosen?' said Dr Towler.

'We always were, Doctor. We always were. Now, in regard to the last question, could you please answer that?'

'Yes, that's correct.'

'A general gives more relaxation, deeper anaesthesia from pain, and would facilitate an easier delivery: isn't that medically correct, Doctor?'

'Essentially. There are some exceptions, but that's essentially correct.'

'And you would not be too concerned about the patient regurgitating large quantities of undigested food into the trachea – or, as we lay people say, the windpipe – thus clogging the breathing ability?'

'Digestion is not an automatic thing,' replied the doctor. 'Just because someone hasn't eaten for a while doesn't mean that they have an empty stomach. Time is not the only factor. Undigested food can remain in the stomach for many hours. Especially if someone is apprehensive or in pain. These are factors that inhibit gastric juices.'

'But you were not concerned with Deborah Ruth because you were told that she had eaten nine hours before she showed up and her stomach would have been empty in nine hours. Correct?'

'Yes. Even though we are always cautious, it was an important factor that she had eaten nine hours prior to delivery.'

'Let me picture this. Why wouldn't it be better to intubate a patient, Doctor? I'm just a layman, but if you put a tube in the windpipe, wouldn't that bypass the problem – you know, ensure an open passage regardless?'

'There are no guarantees. There's no perfect solution to avoid the risk of aspiration in any mode of anaesthesia – local, spinal or general. When you place an endotracheal tube into

196

the patient's trachea, this in itself could produce aspiration of mucus, gastric juices, other secretions. Naturally, if we knew that she had a full stomach, we would have taken extra precautions. I would have administered a topical anaesthetic into the trachea, sprayed the mouth and pharynx with a nebulizer and then intubated her.'

'And if you had knowledge that Deborah Ruth had a full stomach, then it would have been good medical practice to give her a spinal rather than a general anaesthetic. Isn't that medically correct?'

'We had no such knowledge,' he replied, stiffening.

'Well, let's just go back to the hypothetical, Doctor. Just for the sake of answering the question, assume my facts.'

'Yes. On that assumption, a spinal would have been preferred over a general.'

Galvin paused for a moment and looked over his notes. Concannon looked puzzled. His move to cover the possibility of the husband seemed wasted.

'Now, tell me, Doctor,' said Galvin softly, so that everyone had to strain to hear, 'did you or Dr Crowley or Nurse Nevins or Miss Campanelli, the admitting nurse – did any of you inquire about when Deborah Ruth had had her last meal?'

'Yes. Of course. Nurse Campanelli made the actual inquiry.'

'And you were there?'

'Not actually. But the information was transmitted to me.'

'By whom?'

'By Nurse Campanelli.'

'Did Nurse Campanelli also transmit this to Dr Crowley?'

'Yes.'

'Now, where is this in the hospital record, Doctor? Where is it recorded, that fact of when Deborah Ruth last ate? Would you read it for the jury?'

'Right here. *Nine* hours.'

'Now, where did this information come from?'

'From the patient, Deborah Ruth Rosen.'

'Doctor, what would you say is the cutoff point for safety in giving a general anaesthesia?'

Concannon rose slowly. 'Your Honour, I must object. This has all been covered many times. Counsel is repeating the same questions and getting the same answer. Dr Towler has stated many times that he would not give a general anaesthetic if a patient had just eaten. We stipulate that. But the facts show that Deborah Ruth Rosen ate nine hours before delivery.'

'Your Honour, it is exactly these facts which are in dispute. Counsel for the defence can stipulate all he wants, but I want to prove my case.'

'I will permit a little more travel on this particular road, Mr Counsel, but you must either come to some conclusion or make an offer of proof.'

'Just a few more questions, Your Honour.'

'Proceed.'

'Doctor, if a person ate a full meal six hours before delivery, would that be safe to administer a general anaesthetic?'

'Six hours is marginal. But I feel that it's safe.'

'So if someone came to you and said that they had eaten six hours before, you would give them a general anaesthetic?'

'That would depend. I would be very cautious. I might give a spinal. Six hours is one of the grey areas.'

'How about seven hours?'

'Seven hours is definitely the preferred time interval for a general anaesthetic. Again, there is no hard-and-fast rule. Even with a spinal a person can regurgitate. Chunks of food can get into the bronchial tree. The tongue can even clog the trachea.'

Galvin looked at the yellow pad, then dismissed the witness. 'Thank you, Doctor. That will be all.' And turning to Concannon, he said, 'Your witness.'

'No questions,' said Concannon, half lifted out of his chair. 'However, I reserve the right to recall Dr Towler as part of my ase in chief.'

'Granted,' said the judge. 'Doctor, thank you for your
estimony.'

Galvin checked his notes. He didn't look at Dr Towler as the
handsome figure stepped down off the witness stand and
nodded slightly to the jurors as he walked by.

'I'd like to call Dr Daniel J. Crowley to the stand.'

Jeremy Callahan held the Bible right under Dr Crowley's left
hand as the doctor raised his right. There was an unlit cigar in
that hand, and he quickly stuffed it into his jacket pocket. 'Do
you solemnly swear to tell the truth, the whole truth and
nothing but the truth, so help you God?'

'I do.'

'Just a few questions, Dr Crowley. Just a few.'

'Ask all you want,' said the doctor, pulling the cigar out
again. He would have chomped it between his teeth, but to
Concannon's relief, he remembered where he was. It was said
that Crowley would have cut a hole in his mask and smoked in
the operating room, but for the oxygen problem. He claimed it
helped his nerves.

'Very generous of you, Doctor . . . You were the chief of the
Anaesthesiology Department at Catherine Laboure Hospital
when Deborah Ruth Rosen was admitted four years ago, were
you not?'

'I was.'

'And you still head up that department, do you not?'

'I do.'

'And you administered anaesthesia to Deborah Ruth four
years ago at the time of her delivery, did you not?'

'Yes.'

'Did you meet Deborah Ruth when she arrived at the
hospital at about five in the morning?'

'A little later in the pre-op room.'

'You just happened to be at the hospital?'

'Dr Towler and I had just completed a difficult caesarean

together. We often work late. Doctors aren't like lawyers,' h
said with a small smile.

'That's why we're here, Doctor. Now, let me ask you
Doctor: you were here yesterday and today when Dr Towle
testified. Did you hear his entire testimony?'

'Yes, I did.'

'As chief of the Department of Anaesthesiology you ar
aware of the many indications and contraindications of variou
types of anaesthesia and their mode of induction, are you not?'

'It's my job,' he replied.

'And I assume that you keep abreast of the latest medica
literature on these indications and contraindications, do yo
not, Doctor?'

'I do.'

'Are you familiar with Dr Sidney Garelitz' textboo
Fundamentals of Anaesthesiology?' Galvin handed a copy of th
book to the clerk, who passed it to Dr Crowley.

'I'm familiar with it,' said Crowley, leafing through th
book. 'I wouldn't say that it was the bible on the subject
There are more informed studies.'

'Would you call it authoritative?' asked Galvin, taking i
back and thumbing through it, looking for a particular page.

'As a general treatise, I would concede that much. Ther
may be certain portions that I differ with. Some of these area
are not black or white. It calls for judgement. Anaesthesia o
choice. Things like that.'

'Do you agree with this statement on page four – oh – six
Chapter Thirteen: "Contraindications to general anaesthesia
Ideally a patient should refrain from taking nourishment o
liquid up to nine hours prior to induction of genera
anaesthesia, particularly with halothane, nitrous oxide, cyclo
propane or ether"?'

Dr Crowley took the text back from Galvin and read th
passage. He had the cigar clamped in his mouth, then
remembered and put it away.

'That's sound. No one could quibble with that. Good advice.'

'Now, do you agree with the statement on page four-eighteen: "If a patient has taken substantial nourishment within one hour of inducement of anaesthesia, a general anaesthesia should be avoided, because of the grave risk to the patient that he will aspirate food products unnoticed into the inhalation mask, which could compromise pulmonary ventilation"? Do you agree with that statement, Doctor?'

'No quarrel. That's also sound advice.'

'You were present when Nurse Campanelli asked certain questions of Deborah Ruth Rosen when she was being admitted to the hospital, were you not?'

'No. I saw her later with Dr Towler in the pre-op room.'

'Did you inquire when Deborah Ruth last ate before coming to the hospital?'

'No. Miss Campanelli inquired, and I noted Deborah Ruth's responses on the chart. I glanced at the admitting chart prior to inducing anaesthesia.'

'You are under oath, Doctor.'

'I understand that.'

'So it is your testimony, Dr Crowley, that Deborah Ruth Rosen told Nurse Campanelli that she ate nine hours before arriving at the hospital?'

'That's what the chart said.'

'And based on this information, you decided that a general anaesthesia was indicated, and nitrous oxide was the anaesthesia of choice for Deborah Ruth Rosen? Is that right?'

'Right.'

'And in fact, you did induce Deborah Ruth Rosen with general anaesthesia?'

'My nurse, Miss Carolyn Nevins, actually secured the inhalation mask and turned on the nitrous oxide. I watched her, checked the patient's vital signs and recorded her level of consciousness.'

201

'And you were present when the cardiac arrest occurred?'

'I was.'

'Where was everyone at that time? I mean, physically. Can you point out the physical situation.'

'I was on the right of the patient's head. Dr Towler was at the base of the delivery table performing an episiotomy, which is an incision in the vaginal wall to facilitate delivery. Nurse Stephens was towards the patient's head on her left. Miss Nevins was near the patient's foot, watching the valves and dials on the anaesthesia machine. Have I left anyone out?'

'Mary Rooney?'

'Oh, yes. Nurse Rooney was at the patient's head.'

'Could you tell us, Doctor, at what point in time did the blood cease to flow at the site of the incision?'

'It was six twelve A.M.,' he replied.

'How can you tell that? There's no notation in the chart.'

'Dr Towler called over to me from the site of the incision, and as an anaesthesiologist I am always conscious of time. You have to be aware of how long a patient has been under, and so on. So I am always looking at clocks and cross-relating. When the episode occurred, I was conscious of the time. That's my best recollection. It was six twelve in the morning.'

'How soon after that did you obtain a heartbeat, Doctor?'

'A little over four minutes later,' he said. 'I would guess about four minutes fifteen seconds, pinning it down as close as I can.'

'So you are saying, Doctor, that Deborah Ruth Rosen's brain was only deprived of oxygenated blood for about four minutes: is that what you're saying?'

'Give or take ten or twenty seconds.'

'And yet there's no question in your mind that she sustained severe brain damage: isn't that correct?'

'She sustained brain damage.'

'Not just brain damage, Doctor: she has ninety-eight percent of her brain gone! Isn't *that* true, Doctor?'

'It's a good percentage.'

'There's no doubt about that in your mind, is there, Dr Crowley?'

'No. She suffered severe brain damage.'

'No doubt about it.'

'None.'

'Now, in order to incur that kind of brain damage, the brain would have to have been deprived of oxygenated blood for longer than four minutes: isn't that medically correct?'

'No, not necessarily.'

'No?'

'I've discussed this case with many of my colleagues; anaesthesiologists from all over the world; and they agree that brain damage can set in as soon as two minutes after cessation of cardiac activity, especially in children or in elderly people who have arteriosclerosis and whose blood supply is diminished to begin with. In cases of anaemia or of low haemoglobin content, such as was the case with Mrs Rosen, the blood's ability to carry oxygen was diminished, and so the brain survival time is diminished, presenting the same effect as cerebral arteriosclerosis. The so-called four-minute rule to which you refer is very flexible. Deborah Ruth Rosen had a haemoglobin of nine point 0, almost bordering on anaemia.'

Galvin was shaken. He had not expected that response. He had violated the cardinal rule of cross-examination: never ask a question unless you know the answer. Moe had taught him that lesson early.

'Well, in any event, Dr Crowley, you will concede that there was a delay in obtaining the heartbeat of some four minutes fifteen seconds, as you put it, which in Deborah Ruth's case was enough to cause severe brain damage: isn't that true?'

'I suppose –'

But the answer was interrupted by Concannon, who had watched the ambush develop. He wanted to punctuate the moment with an interruption.

'May it please the Court, Your Honour,' said Concannon. 'There are two premises contained in that question. The second assumes the first. And one could argue that both premises are false. There was no delay in instituting cardiac resuscitation. These doctors worked quickly and efficiently, as this witness has testified. He has heard from the lips of his own witness that the heartbeat was restored within the four minutes he originally brought up.'

'You're right,' said Judge Sweeney, who turned to Galvin. 'Mr Attorney . . .'

'Galvin, Judge,' he muttered; 'the name's Galvin.'

'What's that?' said Sweeney. 'I didn't hear that. Don't you mumble in my courtroom.'

'I said that my name is Galvin, Your Honour. It's not Mr Attorney. It's Galvin! G-A-L-V-I-N.'

'Mr Attorney, you will follow the rules of the game –'

'This is no game,' shouted Galvin, feeling embattled and angry. 'This is the only chance my client has. And –'

'Enough! Ask your next question, Counsellor, or dismiss the witness.'

Concannon had accomplished his purpose. Galvin remained ruffled and the judge was antagonized, and the jurors witnessed a strange lunge and counterlunge, understanding only that the judge didn't like Galvin. And Sweeney was provoked. He would lean again on Galvin. And again.

'Well, Dr Crowley,' began Galvin, trying to recover, 'do you consider four minutes a delay in restoring a heartbeat?'

'Absolutely not,' he replied. 'The instant I said I could not get a pulse, Dr Towler informed us that there was no bleeding at the incisional site. He sounded the Code Blue immediately. He plunged right in to perform cardiac compression. That kept the heart pumping blood to the lungs. Mechanically. Everyone was right there, doing their job. The nurses readied the pacemaker. The crash team was right there. We took heroic measures. Heroic measures! –'

'Doctor, please,' interrupted Galvin. 'I –'

'Please! Please Mr Galvin,' said Concannon. 'Be fair! You cut the doctor off right in the middle of what he was saying. You say you want the truth; well, let him finish. Or don't you want the truth?'

Galvin was deflated. Concannon was making him look small and astringent.

'Please continue, Doctor. By all means. I thought you were through.'

'All I wanted to say was that the people in that operating theatre were all dedicated professionals. When a crisis struck, all of us behaved as dedicated professionals. It was heroic. I don't mean to be self-congratulatory. I mean it as fact. We, all of us, pitched in. But the heart – well, it was like a car on a cold winter morning. You pump and you pump and you deliver the gas and the juice and the electricity and it just won't start. People get discouraged. But we didn't quit. We were professionals. Finally, it kicked over. No one could have done more. Tried harder. No one. I would be proud to scrub with these people any day, any place.'

Silence dropped like a curtain on the speech. Galvin stood back, impressed. Concannon sat at the defence table clinically weighing the emotional effect for his side. A powerful blow.

Galvin had tried to avoid this very thing.

Finally, Judge Sweeney looked down at Galvin and said smugly, 'Do you have any more questions, Counsellor?' His tone suggested 'foolish questions.'

'Just one,' said Galvin. Then, turning to Dr Crowley: 'I just want to clear up one more point, if you don't mind, Doctor.'

'Go ahead,' he said, smiling, as if he had a choice and were being generous.

'Nurse Nevins induced the anaesthesia under your direction and control: is that right?'

'Yes.' Dr Crowley's guard was down. He had scored heavily and was adopting the attitude of a generous victor. He was tolerating Galvin's redundancy.

'And you read a medical history related by Deborah Ruth Rosen when she arrived at the hospital?'

'Correct.'

'And she said that she had eaten nine hours before she arrived at the hospital?'

'Also correct.'

'And you reviewed the notation on the admission chart to that effect prior to induction: is that correct?'

'Yes,' said Dr Crowley.

'And based upon this information, which was important to you, you gave her nitrous oxide by general anaesthesia?'

'Correct again.'

'And it would have been bad medical practice to give her a general if she told you that she had eaten a substantial meal one hour prior to admission: isn't that so, Doctor?'

'Four or five in the morning would have been an odd time to eat a full meal,' said Dr Crowley.

'That's an interesting point, Doctor. But that wasn't my question. I didn't ask the logic of the question. I asked you the question.'

Concannon whiffed danger. 'Objection, Your Honour. Mr Galvin persists in throwing allegations into his questions. Next he'll be asking the doctor if he was drunk when he induced anaesthesia. The witness is being harassed!'

'Your Honour,' said a weary Galvin, 'this is cross-examination of an adverse and hostile witness. I must be allowed the basic latitude of posing hypothetical sets of facts before the witness to elicit his opinion about good or bad medical practice. The jury will decide the facts –'

'Don't tell me the law, Galvin,' said the judge. 'I know the law. I instruct on the law. I was trying cases before you were born. Now let *me* ask this witness a question or two.'

Galvin stood against the jury rail, his face flushed, perspiring heavily as the judge took over the interrogation of

Dr Crowley.

'Is there any evidence in the hospital record or in the conversation that you had with Mrs Rosen or that Nurse Campanelli had that she ate at any time other than nine hours prior to her admission?'

'None, Your Honour.'

'Then you have no business asking that question,' said Sweeney to Galvin. Turning back to the witness stand, he said, 'Thank you, Dr Crowley. You have been more than patient. You may step down.'

'Your Honour, with all due respect, I was not finished with the witness,' said Galvin. 'If you are going to try my case for me, Judge, most respectfully, I'd appreciate it if you wouldn't lose it.'

'We will take morning recess,' said the judge, barely in control of his anger. 'I will see both counsel in chambers.'

21

They swept down the corridor, boiling to get behind closed doors and tear into each other. Galvin and Sweeney were snorting with impatience as they entered the judge's chambers. Concannon adopted a stance of wounded spectator.

'Christ, Judge,' flared Galvin as the door closed, 'what the hell are you trying to do to my little girl?'

'Don't use your damn profanity in my chambers,' shouted Sweeney. 'I can toss a few extra charges to the bar association. I'll hang your shingle on my wall as a trophy.'

Something snapped inside Galvin. He might have been prepared to placate the judge when they came back to chambers. He might have endured a stream of rebukes and offered a polite apology. It had even been possible that he would say that he was sorry for something he hadn't done. But no more.

Behave, his mother had said. Behave yourself and all things would come your way. Behave in school. Behave in church. The world likes a well-behaved little boy. But somehow he had never been broken. There was always some spark of anger ready to flare into the fire of rebellion. At the most crucial times, he could never quite be docile. He could never behave.

'You aren't going to frighten me,' said Galvin coldly. He even sounded cold and frightening to himself. He felt the calm that overtook him before every fight: an icy, cold-blooded, I-don't-give-a-shit-about-the-consequences serenity that permitted any behaviour. Anything at all. 'I'm not going to be intimidated – not by you. Not by the white knight here. Not by anyone. I am an attorney on trial before the bar representing my client. My client! That means if I let you kill me, you kill her too.'

'Listen to me, you miserable little –' began Sweeney.

'No,' said Galvin. 'You listen. All I ever wanted in this case was a fair shake. An even chance. People told me that Sweeney is a defendant's judge. Concannon won't be able to do any wrong. He could make speeches, whatever. But I said, Fuck it, I'll take my chances. I'll take my chances that he'll be fair.'

'Look, Galvin, I was a lawyer too,' began Sweeney, trying to placate the man who was dangerously on edge.

'Don't give me that. I don't want to hear that "I-was-trying-cases-before-you-were-born" bullshit! You couldn't hack it as a lawyer and that's why they stuck you on the bench. You carried a bag for the big guys and now you screw plaintiffs out of their day in court. You can't see over those little squint glasses of yours. So don't give me that crap about you know how it is because you were there once yourself.'

Concannon sat on his hands.

'Are you finished?' asked Sweeney. His voice was a furious whisper. 'Because I don't want to interrupt you if you're not finished.'

'Goddamned right I'm finished,' fired Galvin. 'I'm going to ask for a mistrial and I am going to request that you disqualify yourself from sitting on this case. And then I am going to take a transcript of this case to the State Judicial Conference and ask that they impeach your ass.'

'You're not getting any mistrial in this case,' said Sweeney. 'I know the cheap stunt you're trying to pull now and it won't work. You're trying to provoke me into declaring a mistrial. The game's not going your way so you want to replay the first half. Well, it won't happen. And just between us three fellows, I advise you, Mr Galvin, to look up the contempt statutes and get yourself a good lawyer. Right now this *Rosen* case is going to completion. Got that? Completion. I will charge the jury and they will render a verdict and life will go on. But your legal life will come to an end. I'll see to that. I can do that. I have that power. And I will do it if it's the last thing I ever do.

'Now get out of here before I call the bailiff and have you strapped into a straitjacket!'

When the jury reconvened, Judge Sweeney's face did not reveal a trace of what had taken place in chambers. He even smiled as he turned to the front of the court and said softly, 'Mr Galvin, you may proceed; do you have any further questions of Dr Crowley?'

'No further questions,' said Galvin, still burning.

'No? All right. Would you please call your next witness, Mr Galvin.' The cobra smiled again.

'Dr Lionel Thompson,' he said, turning.

He was a tall, thin man, hunched at the shoulders so that he walked with a kind of stoop, as if he were always fighting a wind. He had the kindly air of a family doctor, with five pens sticking out of his tweed-jacket pocket. He would have inspired an instant of confidence in strangers, except for the fact that his skin was black and this was Boston.

When Galvin elicited Dr Thompson's credentials, they sounded impressive. Dean emeritus of the Law-Surgical Society, visiting anaesthesiologist and so on. And Galvin was quick to make it known that he had solicited the doctor's services and that Thompson was being paid for his appearance. A good attorney always takes the sting out of cross-examination by bringing out the worst on direct examination.

And so Thompson testified that he was a paid consultant on a case in litigation and that he had reviewed the record and had developed his own theory of the case.

When it was Concannon's turn to cross-examine Dr

Thompson on his credentials, he made the doctor wait uncomfortably in front of the jury while he studied a ream of notes.

'Dr Thompson, so that we may acquaint the jury with your exact role in this case, let me ask you. You never treated Deborah Ruth Rosen: isn't that correct?'

'That's true,' replied the doctor.

'Neither before nor after the unfortunate episode?'

'That's right, Mr Concannon. I was engaged to render an expert opinion.'

'Engaged? Did you say engaged? I am not familiar with that term as it applies to medicine. It has always had a *theatrical* connotation to me.'

'I suppose "engage" is a bit indelicate,' replied Dr Thompson politely. 'Mr Galvin asked me to review the record and facts of the case and I said that I would, and then I agreed to testify.'

'For a price, correct?'

'For a sum agreed upon.'

'Well, that's a quid pro quo, isn't it? That's a price, is it not? You're being paid to sit there.'

'Just as you are being paid to stand there,' replied the doctor, demonstrating his sting.

'Are you board certified in anaesthesiology?'

'No. I practise anaesthesiology. I am a doctor of medicine with a subspecialty in anaesthesiology. It's quite common. Many anaesthesiologists are not board certified, but they practice anaesthesiology in New York State.'

'Yes, Doctor, but this is Massachusetts. Do you happen to know anything about the certification procedure in Massachusetts?'

'No, I'm not familiar with the licensing statute in Massachusetts. But the administration of anaesthesia is the same anywhere. It's a science and its technology has no geography. I'm familiar with New York law, which demands high standards. I assume Massachusetts comes up to New York.'

'When you say that you are a doctor of medicine, does that mean that you are board certified in any specialty of medicine? For example, you are not certified in internal medicine are you?'

'No.'

'Neurology?'

'Nope.'

'Cardiology?'

'I'm afraid not.'

'Orthopaedics?'

'I can save you trouble. You don't have to recite the whole AMA job index. I'm just an MD.'

'You are not even a qualified surgeon, are you, Doctor, even though you list that fancy title on your résumé – dean emeritus of the Law-Surgical Society?'

'I have done minor surgery.'

'Hernias and haemorrhoids – that sort of thing, Doctor?'

'I have assisted in all types of surgery. Broken bones. I rotate on call at the hospital and have to perform many emergency procedures.'

'Yes, but even a dermatologist has to do that on occasion, isn't that true, Doctor? But he must call a surgeon if one is available: isn't that correct?'

'That's right, Mr Concannon.'

Galvin stayed out of it. For one thing, Thompson could handle himself. And for another, Concannon was starting to sound like a bully.

'How many beds in East Hampton Hospital for Women, Doctor?'

'It's a small hospital – eighty-five beds.'

'Do you know Dr Towler, by the way?'

'I know *of* him.'

'You know, of course, that Dr Towler, who is board certified in surgical obstetrics and who has been certified as a Fellow of the International College of Surgeons, a Diplomate of the American Board of Obstetrics and Gynaecology . . . . I'm sorry, Doctor, but you know all this, right?'

'If I don't, you'll let me know.'

There was a laugh in the jury box, and more than a few outside.

'It's not exactly a professional handicap to be past president of the American Society of Obstetricians and Gynaecologists, or to have been a full professor teaching surgical obstetrics at the University of Massachusetts Medical School: you wouldn't call that a career drawback, would you?'

'I'd be the last.'

'I should think not. And the fact that he's chief of the Obstetrical Department of St Catherine Laboure Hospital – a hospital with sixteen hundred beds, by the way: that's not something to be ashamed of, is it?'

'Not to me.'

'Would you concede that Dr Towler, who was a full professor, teaching general practitioners such as yourself – would you say that he's better qualified than yourself to judge medical competence?'

'The number of beds and the number of credentials doesn't always tell the whole story,' said Dr Thompson. 'In 1912 the *Titanic* was the largest ship afloat –'

'Your Honour, I ask that the remarks of the witness be stricken as unresponsive. My opponent made a point of trying to confine Dr Towler to a yes or no answer. I respectfully ask the Court that this witness be similarly instructed.'

'Dr Thompson seemed right on the money to me,' said Galvin, defending his witness. 'And I respectfully remind the Court that Dr Towler was allowed wide latitude.'

'Stricken,' said Judge Sweeney. 'The jury will disregard the

213

reply. The witness is instructed to answer the question. Let's keep the colourful flights of fancy to ourselves.'

'Sorry, Your Honour,' said Dr Thompson. 'Just trying to get at the truth.'

Everyone in the courtroom grinned at the remark. From his elevated bench Sweeney was quick to pick it up. It was a little disconcerting.

Concannon noticed a glass of water perched on the edge of the witness stand. 'You're familiar with the facts of this case, Doctor: correct?'

'I've studied the charts and depositions, yes.'

'So you know that we are dealing with obstetrics, and I assume you are familiar with the anatomy and physiology of the female pelvic region?'

'I am familiar.'

Concannon reached under the defence table and picked up a small leather suitcase, and while he questioned Dr Thompson, he removed an anatomical model of a woman's torso.

'So you would be able to tell where the episiotomy was performed just when the onset of the episode occurred?'

'Of course.'

'With His Honour's permission, I would like to hand you this anatomical model and ask you to explain to the court where you would commence the incision and how it would have proceeded.'

'Go ahead,' said Sweeney.

'You know, Dr Thompson, that in handling the female pelvic region, especially doing an episiotomy – cutting the vaginal orifice is a very delicate procedure requiring utmost caution, careful steady hands.'

'I'm well aware.'

With his back to the jury, blocking their view, Concannon passed the model to the doctor, and as Thompson reached for it, Concannon dropped it. Thompson lunged, juggled it and

ent the glass of water tumbling off the stand as the model
ipped and crashed onto the floor, sending pieces flying. A
idney here, a vagina there, a thighbone rolling across the floor
n front of the jury.

The court officers quickly cleaned up the mess. Thompson
at back, furious at the sneaky ploy. Galvin had seen it coming,
ut couldn't believe that Concannon, the great J. Edward
Concannon, was capable of such a stunt.

A few jurors laughed. But one or two saw and understood
what had really happened.

'Thank God it was only plastic,' quipped Concannon. 'Now,
Doctor, you testify against a lot of other doctors, don't you?
'ou're available, as they say: isn't that right?'

'When I see something wrong, like there is in this case, I
efuse to be silent,' he said. 'When something stinks so bad
at it's almost criminal, then I am available, as they say!'

Thompson was hanging in there. He refused to go down.
Concannon sensed a need for a break in the action.

'One moment, if Your Honour please,' said Concannon, and
e leaned over the defence table and consulted with his
olleagues. 'Where's Miss St Laurent?' he asked Gaynor.

'Haven't seen her since last night at the hospital conference,'
e replied.

'Me neither,' said Kaplan.

'Damn,' said Concannon. He didn't know if she had found
nything, but he had clearly sent her on a mission. He didn't
ke surprises, and today he was being surprised. He was
urprised at the sturdy endurance of this old doctor with so few
redentials and so much credibility. And he was surprised to
nd that Thompson was getting the better of him.

He turned away from the table and faced Sweeney. 'Your
Honour I will agree that the doctor is qualified as a general
ractitioner who practises anaesthesiology. I do this to save the
me of the Court and the jury.'

215

And so Galvin had his expert.

Dammit, where *is* she? wondered Concannon, glaring at th
defence table.

Galvin resumed his direct examination of Dr Thompson.

'Did you go to Jamaica Plain last February, Doctor, an
examine Deborah Ruth Rosen at the Holy Ghost Chronic Car
Hospital, at my request?'

'I did.'

'Would you describe your observations?'

'Objection! Objection!' blurted Concannon. 'I object to th
witness testifying to his observations. He is not the treatin
physician, nor has he ever been consulted concerning th
plaintiff's medical care. He is not a factual witness. His onl
purpose is that of a hired expert. His testimony should b
limited to the hospital records and he should only be permitte
to give an opinion based on a hypothetical question. There ar
numerous precedents in the common law, and I will be happ
to provide Your Honour with the citations.'

'Not necessary,' said Judge Sweeney. 'That's sound blac
letter law. It's been the rule of this jurisdiction for tw
hundred years. Goes back to *Williams v. The City of Quincy*
I'm sure you're familiar with that, Mr Galvin.'

'Just because a rule of law is old doesn't mean it's right,' sai
Galvin.

'Well, we must operate within the framework of the la
whether we like it or not,' said the judge, smiling. 'Maybe fiv
bases would make baseball a livelier game. But I'm not abou
to change the rules in the middle of the game.'

'Wisdom shouldn't be rejected simply because it comes late
replied Galvin.

On the surface, the argument sounded almost cordial.

'Personally,' Sweeney said, 'I don't think it's the best rul
but it is the established precedent. The witness will confine hi
testimony to an opinion based upon a hypothetical questio

and his review of the hospital records. Please proceed, Mr Galvin.'

'With all due respect, I believe that the Court is in error and I would like to note my exception.'

'Noted. Proceed.'

'Dr Thompson, from your review of the hospital records, particularly the Catherine Laboure record of May fourteenth, what, in your opinion, happened to Deborah Ruth Rosen?'

'During delivery, her heart stopped. Medically, this is known as cardiac arrest. It is one of the most feared risks in any type of surgery . . .'

He explained the crucial time factor and the deterioration of the brain that begins instantly when it is deprived of oxygen.

'Dr Thompson,' began Galvin, 'the treating doctors, Drs Towler and Crowley, have testified that they restored the heartbeat within about four minutes. From your review of the record, do you have an opinion about whether or not it was restored within that period of time?'

'My opinion is that it was not,' he replied. 'Too much brain damage. Almost total disintegration. Cardiac activity wasn't restored for at least seven minutes to eight minutes, and that's a conservative estimate. If the heartbeat had been restored when they said, the patient would have been left with only a few very mild neurological deficits – a hyperactive patellar reflex, or a slight slurring of speech. Hardly noticeable.'

'And you are of the same opinion, knowing that the patient had a history of heart murmur as a child, had controlled diabetes mellitus, a difficult delivery of a previous child, had a haemoglobin of nine point oh when she was admitted to the hospital on the morning of May fourteenth?'

'Certainly.'

The judge leaned over the bench and peered down into the witness box. 'Dr Thompson, are you stating that the mere fact that the doctors couldn't restore a heartbeat until the brain

217

damage set in constituted bad medical practice? Is that what you're testifying to?'

'Well –' said Dr Thompson, who was surprised by the question coming from over his shoulder.

'Your Honour!' Galvin bellowed. He didn't mean it to come out that loud, but it did and he could not help it. 'I would like to get around to this line of inquiry in my own way.'

'You're not suggesting that the Court has no right to ask questions or make inquiries of any witness at any time, are you, Counsellor?'

'No, Judge. I would just like to lay a proper foundation as to the standard of medical care, and you have infringed upon my right to pose certain questions.'

'I don't like beating around the bush,' snapped the judge. 'And Mr Witness, I direct you to answer the question. It calls for a yes or no.'

'To answer the question in the context and manner you pose it, I would have to say no,' said Dr Thompson.

'In other words, you are saying that there was no negligence based upon my question?'

'Given the limits of the question, that's correct, Your Honour,' replied Thompson.

'Thank you, Doctor. Any more questions, Mr Galvin?'

'Oh, maybe one or two more,' said Galvin, with an airy wave of a hand. 'If Your Honour will indulge me.'

'Proceed.'

'Dr Thompson, would the administration of general anaesthesia, namely nitrous oxide, to Deborah Ruth Rosen, as was done in this case, be good or bad medical practice if she had eaten a large meal one hour before delivery?'

'Objection!' yelled Concannon. He was not the master of poise he should have been at this stage of the game. 'Once again, Your Honour, plaintiff's attorney is injecting unfounded allegations into evidence. There is no foundation, no basis in fact, for his premise. No one has suggested anywhere, anytime, that Deborah Ruth Rosen had anything to eat less than nine hours before delivery.'

'The question premised that she ate one hour before delivery?' asked the judge.

'Right,' said Concannon. 'There's no evidence of that. No suggestion. Nothing. Just Mr Galvin's wild supposition.'

'There is no evidence of a meal one hour before delivery,' said the judge.

'Your Honour,' said Galvin, as the courtroom fell into a deep hush, 'that is exactly what I intend to prove.'

22

The judge backed off.

'All right, Counsellor,' he said. 'I will let you have your question de bene – that is, provisionally – since you say that you have such evidence. But if you have no such evidence, then I will sustain defence counsel's motion to strike the question and the answer.'

'Thank you, Your Honour,' said Galvin.

At the defence table, Gaynor and Kaplan both stopped scribbling as Concannon sat down. Their hero and mentor was overreacting, starting to perspire; his voice had lost its calm authority.

'Goddammit, I want you to go out and find that woman,' he whispered to Kaplan.

'Who?' asked the young attorney.

'St Laurent!' said Concannon almost loud enough to be heard in the courtroom. 'Find her!'

'Now, Dr Thompson,' said Galvin, standing where Concannon usually stood, in front of the last juror in the first row, 'do you understand the question?'

'Could you repeat it, please?' he asked.

'The question was "Would the use of a general anaesthetic, namely nitrous oxide, which was used with Deborah Ruth Rosen, be good or bad medical practice if she had just eaten a large meal an hour before delivery?" '

'It would be bad,' said Dr Thompson. 'It would be terrible. Gross malpractice.'

'Why is that, Doctor?'

'There's an old law of everyday hard knocks. It's called Murphy's Law. It says that if something can go wrong, it usually does. No one gives a general anaesthetic one hour after a patient has eaten a big meal.' The black man sounded convincing, decisive. 'This was a big modern hospital. They should have given her a spinal. If she regurgitated with a spinal, they would have seen it and controlled it. But they had an inhalation mask over her face and she drowned. The cardiac arrest wouldn't have happened if it hadn't been for that.'

'Thank you, Dr Thompson. Your witness, Mr Concannon.'

Concannon looked at Dr Thompson and he saw old Wolfgang Von Richlinghausen staring back at him.

'Just a question or two, Dr Thompson.' He studied some notes at the counsel table, then walked slowly towards the far end of the jury box.

'Well, Doctor, if you say the heartbeat wasn't restored until seven to eight minutes, you are in effect saying that no oxygenated blood was getting to the brain during that period of time? Do I understand you correctly?'

'You do, Mr Concannon,' he replied in a courteous but strong affirmation.

'Now, Dr Thompson, you are well aware that Dr Towler was performing cardiac compression during the period of time that the heart was in a standstill?'

'I heard him testify to that.'

'And, from your experience and study you are well aware that Dr Towler was pumping oxygenated blood to the brain by mechanical compression, simulating contraction and dilatation of the heart.'

'That's just the point,' offered Thompson.

'What's the point,' said Concannon, warily.

'No oxygenated blood was getting to the brain.'

'What?'

'You see, Mr Concannon,' Thompson looked at the jury, 'Mrs Rosen's blood was borderline to begin with. Her haemoglobin was dipping to anaemic levels. So to begin with, the blood going to the brain had only fifty percent oxygen.

Also, what everyone overlooked was that Mrs Rosen had a large haematoma on her thigh. It's documented in the hospital record but everyone overlooked it. She had had an injury with resultant blood loss. She had an inadequate number of red blood corpuscles. In fact, we had one haematocrit reading and that showed the cellular content was down to twenty-seven percent. So two things were happening: one, the oxygen content of the blood was down and, two, the cells to carry the oxygen were down. Mrs Rosen should have been given a transfusion of packed red blood cells prior to induction of anaesthesia. This wasn't done . . . Oh, yes, this was another element of negligence. A medical student would have known this –'

'Move to strike!' snapped Concannon.

'No, please, Mr Concannon,' said Thompson in his unruffled manner; 'please be fair.'

Concannon looked at Judge Sweeney and said cavalierly, 'By all means, Mr Witness. Please continue.'

'Thank you . . . Well, what Dr Towler was pumping to the brain was unoxygenated blood. For all the oxygen she was getting, he might just as well have been pumping water. The brain tissues were still dying. You can see the end result.'

Concannon turned his back to Thompson and walked in front of the jury. 'Are you finished, Doctor?' he said with the proper degree of sarcasm.

'I'm sorry, Mr Concannon. I didn't hear your last question. You turned your back on me and I couldn't catch it.'

Concannon whirled quickly. His voice loud and caustic. 'I said, "Are you finished?" *Are* you finished?'

'Yes.' Dr Thompson said quietly, politely. 'I am finished.'

Judge Sweeney's lunch hour went from twelve to two. He reasoned that it gave opposing counsel more time to negotiate, jurors more time to deliberate, and it allowed him some couch time, without which he was in serious danger of falling off the bench as the afternoon session droned on.

Galvin usually grabbed a quick sandwich, a date bar and a carton of milk at the courthouse lunch counter. But on this particular lunch hour, despite the press of a dozen imperative tasks, he took a walk. He needed the nourishment of a moment in the sun on a perfect New England day, when the scent of the ocean blew in from the outer islands. He walked down State Street: past the New England Life and Casualty Building, a granite-and-glass temple which housed the offices of Rutledge, Guthrie, Cabot & Moore; past the old State House, with its golden unicorn bowing down to the cement slab marking the spot of the Boston Massacre. He walked past Faneuil Hall, the old meeting house which was now a shrine to liberty, to the market district with its flower stalls and steak pubs and bright boutiques. They all looked young, the lunch-hour crowds who took it all for granted and strolled among the antiques – real and fresh-hewn – as if there were no other destinations in the day. They laid a possessive, familiar hand over that time and that place, as if it were their man or their woman. And Galvin felt left out.

He paused at the waterfront and inhaled the smells and sights of the sea. The yachts at Rowe's Wharf, with their pennants snapping in the wind, bobbed and creaked with the rise and flow of the tide. Gulls cried noisily, veering, hovering, constantly riding the thermals, occasionally diving into the brackish waters.

Across the Bay was the Quincy shoreline. He could see the last vestiges of Squantum Airfield, where Amelia Earhart learned to fly. One day in 1935, he had sat on his father's shoulder and watched Wiley Post take off in the *Winnie Mae* from there. Post's red-and-white monoplane circled the field, saluted the crowd and then flew on to rendezvous with Will Rogers and Point Barrow and destiny. The field was pockmarked with industrial buildings now.

He looked at his watch. It was 1.15 P.M. He had ten minutes

before he had to pick up his next witness.

There was a quiet buzz inside the dining room at Rutledge, Guthrie, Cabot & Moore, atop the New England Life and Casualty Building, where Galvin had recently passed on foot. There was an artificial buoyancy to the defence team, a pumped-up conviviality. Concannon didn't like it. He was brooding over his lamb chop.

Kaplan came in and took his place at the table. 'Where is she?' asked Concannon.

'I don't know, sir. She's not at home. One of the secretaries said she went out with Mr Rutledge and hasn't come back yet.'

What the hell did that mean? No time for that now. Whom could Galvin produce to testify that Deborah Ruth Rosen had eaten an hour before delivery? Her college sisters? The person who brought her to the hospital?

That wouldn't work. Even if she had eaten an hour before delivery, the doctors hadn't *known* about it. She hadn't told anyone. She'd told them nine hours. How were they supposed to know if she ate a big meal an hour before she came to the hospital? They weren't omniscient. They weren't God.

He didn't talk or lecture as he ate, as he usually did. And no one disturbed him. The conversation had been stopped at the start when Gaynor noted that Galvin was certainly losing this case, his star witness having conceded that there hadn't been any negligence. The boast rang too hollow.

Concannon thought of Gettysburg and old 'Pete' Longstreet sitting on a fence post watching the disastrous charge of Pickett when along came an English colonel, an observer, who totally misunderstood the battle. 'Marvellous,' he had complimented General Longstreet, as he watched Pickett's men march in parade-ground formation to their doom. 'Perfectly marvellous. It will be a great victory.'

'You don't understand, Colonel,' said the general, who saw the outcome as the engagement began. 'We are just about to se the war.'

Like the English colonel, Gaynor saw only the pageantry
nd pomp. He didn't understand the subtler moods of a battle.
here were moments when the tide shifted, when the earth
oved and victory became defeat. Concannon's seismic
nsors were all in the red. He didn't answer Gaynor, but
veryone at the table understood that something troubling had
appened in court, something Concannon didn't like.

Call your next witness,' intoned Sweeney.

'Mrs Rocco Stampanatto,' said Galvin.

From a spot near the back door a girl in her late twenties,
oderately dressed in a light blue knit suit, stood and made
er way to the aisle. As she walked forward, there was the
rious buzz of people who wondered who she was. At first, no
e recognized her. And then Carolyn Nevins said, 'Oh, my
od!' She motioned to one of the lawyers, who poked Dr
owler. When he turned towards her, Nurse Nevins, pointing
wards the witness, mouthed the name 'Natalie Campanelli.'

Dr Towler put on his glasses. Then he dug his fingers into
r Crowley's arm. 'Dan, don't panic, but it's the Campanelli
rl.'

'Oh, Christ!' cursed Crowley, the colour draining from his
ce as the former admitting nurse stepped up to take the oath.

'Take it easy,' said Dr Towler. 'Just take it easy. Don't fall
part on me now.'

Concannon noticed the flurry of concern among his clients,
ut decided to ignore it. He had his own problems. He eyed
e witness.

'Would you tell the court your name,' said Galvin.

'Mrs Rocco Stampanatto,' she said.

'And what is your first name?'

'Natalie.'

'And your maiden name?'

'Campanelli,' she said, and there was some flicker of

recognition among the jurors. They had heard the nam
during this trial, but they couldn't say just how.

'Where do you live, Mrs Stampanatto?'

'At Three Twenty-one West Eighty-seventh Street
Manhattan, New York,' she said.

'What is your present occupation?'

'Housewife.'

'They say that you aren't supposed to ask a woman her a
or guess it, but how old are you, Mrs Stampanatto?'

'Twenty-seven.'

'And how long have you lived at your present address?'

'Three years.'

'By the way, what work does your husband do?'

'He's with Con Edison,' she said. 'He's an electric
engineer.'

'Before you lived in New York, where did you live?'

'East Boston, Massachusetts.'

'How long did you live there?'

'All my life. I was born there.'

'Where did you go to school?'

'East Boston High and St Catherine Laboure School o
Nursing.'

Concannon looked around. He couldn't understand th
agitation of his clients. He kept taking notes. He knew that sh
was the admitting nurse, but he didn't understand what wa
about to happen. It sneaked up on him, slowly. Gradually
And it was too late by the time he guessed.

'You were the admitting nurse when Deborah Ruth Rose
came to the hospital, were you not?'

'I was.'

'By the way, Mrs Stampanatto, did I ask you to appear her
voluntarily?'

'Yes, you did.'

'And did you agree to do so?'

'I did.'

'Where are you staying in Boston?'

'At the home of Mr and Mrs Moe Katz.'

'He's a colleague of mine, is he not?'

'He is.'

'And it was Mr Katz who first asked you to come back to Boston: is that true?'

'Yes. That's true.'

'When did you leave your job as a nurse at St Catherine Laboure Hospital?'

'Three and a half years ago. Almost four.'

'Why did you leave?'

'I got married. My husband took a job in New York.'

'Any children?'

'Three.'

'In three years?'

'In three years.' She smiled.

'Have you heard any of the testimony in this case?'

'No. I have not.'

'Have I offered to pay you for appearing here?'

'Only my plane fare.'

'Now, four years ago, on the night – or early morning, to be exact – of May fourteenth, 1976, what was your occupation?'

'I was a registered nurse.'

'Certified in Massachusetts?'

'Yes.'

'What hospital were you affiliated with?'

'St Catherine Laboure in Boston.'

'Were you on duty on the night in question?'

'I was.'

'What were your hours?'

'I was working the midnight to eight A.M. slot.'

'What were your duties?'

'I was the admitting nurse.'

'You were present when Deborah Ruth Rosen came into the hospital?'

'I was.'

'Who else was there?'

'Just the admitting-room nurses and two orderlies.'

'Do you know Dr Rexford Towler and Dr Daniel Crowley

'Yes, I do.'

'Are those the two gentlemen who are seated in the fi
row?'

'Yes, sir.'

Towler had his arms folded tightly across his chest, a
Crowley was gripping the arms of his chair. Concannon kn
that something was drastically wrong. He handed a note
Gaynor: *Check Mrs Rocco Stampanatto of 321 W. 87th
Manhattan. Check husband. Complete investigation. Urge
Need report by 6 P.M. Call tonight.*

'Get one of our New York City investigators on this *no*
whispered Concannon. Gaynor left with the note.

'Now, Mrs Stampanatto,' said Galvin, who waited until t
commotion at the defence table subsided before continui
'you say that when Deborah Ruth Rosen arrived at t
hospital, you, some other admitting nurses and two orderl
were at the admitting desk: correct?'

'That's right.'

'Where were Dr Towler and Dr Crowley, if you know?'

'They were both in the delivery area.'

'Where is that in relation to the admitting room?'

'Adjacent to each other.'

'How do you know they were there?'

'I talked to Dr Towler on the intercom.'

'Who was the person who asked the admitting questions
Mrs Rosen?'

'I asked some.'

'Did you ask when she ate last?'

'I did.'

'And did you hear what Mrs Rosen said?'

'I did.'

228

Galvin turned and faced the jury.

'And what was Mrs Rosen's answer to the question of when she last ate?'

'She said that she ate a full meal one hour ago.'

'One hour ago?' asked Galvin.

'One hour,' she said.

She said it softly, but the answer ran like a shiver through the courtroom. And everyone froze. No one nodded. No one coughed. No one turned to a neighbour and poked him to register the drama. One hour! The implications were staggering.

One hour! Concannon was not certain he had heard it right. He felt an urge to ask the court stenographer to read it back. His clients were squirming. He looked hard at Natalie Stampanatto. She seemed calm in the eye of all this. The investigators were already in action. They would come up with something. It would be her word against the doctors'. And again he had a sick feeling.

Galvin was almost strutting, trying to get the number 'one' in as many times as he could. If he could, he would have stood there for a while yelling. 'One! One! One! One!'

'Did you write the numeral "one" down on the hospital record?'

'I did.'

'Standing for one hour?'

'Yes.'

'A single hour.'

'Yes,' she said. 'One.'

And then he did the boldest thing he had ever done in all his life.

'Your witness,' he said to Concannon.

Concannon felt a rush of colour to his cheeks.

'Uh, Your Honour, it's been such a long day and I have so many questions to ask this witness, it will run into the evening. If we could begin with this witness tomorrow on cross-examination it would be appreciated.'

'Granted,' said the judge. 'Court is recessed until ten A.[
The jurors are again cautioned not to discuss this case wit
friends or relatives, husbands and wives. Especially not wive
Do not read anything about this in the newspapers, and if
comes up on television tonight, I urge you to turn it of
Adjourned.'

On the way out of the courthouse, Galvin passed Donna [
Laurent and Roger Rutledge. They had slipped into and out o
the courtroom together, just in time to catch Natal
Stampanatto's testimony. Besides Galvin, they were the onl
people in the courtroom who were not surprised.

23

Concannon had the evening paper on his desk when the call came in. The headline at the bottom of the second front read:

HOSPITAL NOT NEGLIGENT
PLAINTIFF'S EXPERT ASSERTS

The *Boston Sun* reporter wrote that Galvin's case had been torn apart by his own expert, 'Dr L.B. Thomas of Jamaica, New York.' Concannon took no comfort from the story, since he knew that it had been filed before Mrs Stampanatto's appearance on the stand. The morning-paper reporters, on the other hand, had all been camped outside his office, bristling with defiant questions. But he had marched past them into his office to wait for the call.

'Jack Taylor,' said the operator, 'calling collect from New York City.'

They were all assembled in the conference room at Concannon's offices. It was the same cast as the previous night, save two. Donna St Laurent and Roger Rutledge were absent.

They were silent as Concannon muttered a few 'uh-huh's' into the phone. The news was not good, they could tell.

'Not even a parking ticket,' said Concannon after he hung up. 'She's apparently a model parent and a model citizen. Teaches Christian Doctrine, for God's sake. She's even a Red Cross volunteer.' The disgust in his voice brought a gloomy sigh from the others in the room. Concannon realized he had to pull them all together. 'Let's get down to work,' he said. 'Dr Crowley, please do not take offence, but I must ask you. Is there any chance that you have not told me everything?'

'This is as much a surprise to us as it was to you,' said D[
Towler, who took charge of the medical team. His empty pip[
lay on the table as he searched his pockets for his tobacc[
pouch. 'We cannot understand this. Why would she tell such [
story?'

'Do you think she was promised a share in the cas[
settlement?' asked Nurse Nevins.

'No,' said Concannon. 'People who teach Christian Doctrin[
and volunteer for the Red Cross do not throw away thei[
immortal soul for a bag of gold. No, she looks to me lik[
someone who believes in what she is doing . . . Now, I mus[
assume that the girl is lying. Why? I have no idea. If we ha[
more time, we could dig around and find out what her motiv[
could be. She may be a crank who sees this as a chance to strik[
a blow for people in nursing homes. Who knows? Whateve[
the reason, she's a strong witness and she will carry the case t[
the jury.'

'Damn!' said Dr Towler, puffing on the empty pipe.

'I'm sorry, but there's no way around it. She's a witness wh[
gives Galvin enough of a case to warrant a decision by the jury
I was going to ask for a directed verdict, and I think I woul[
have got it. But I don't think I'll get it now.'

'Maybe we should just settle,' said Dr Crowley, sweatin[
and laughing inappropriately.

'Let's not panic yet,' said Concannon. 'She's a witness, bu[
she's not the only witness. She's not even the best witness. W[
still have quite a few cards left to play. I am going to put bot[
you doctors back on the stand. You are going to rebut her. I ar[
going to ask you what Nurse Campanelli reported when yo[
asked her on the pre-op-room intercom when Mrs Rosen las[
ate, and you are going to repeat *nine* hours. It will be her wor[
against yours. One against two. One lapsed nurse against tw[
of the most distinguished doctors in the field. I don't think w[
have too much to worry about. Any sensible juror is going t[

eigh the value of the two sides and decide to believe you
entlemen.'

They all looked relieved.

'I just want to ask once more, and I'm sorry to repeat
myself, but there isn't anything else that you haven't told me,
there?'

The two doctors looked at each other and then at Concannon
and shook their heads. 'I don't like surprises,' said Concannon.

In his own office, Galvin was halfway through the bottle of
Jameson's before he drank himself to sleep. The phone kept
ringing, but he didn't answer it. It might have been someone,
he thought, chuckling. He drank until he felt on the brink of
passing out and then he stumbled to the couch and slept. It
was as if he had been purified by his ordeal and he didn't want
to contaminate himself. He had professionally scrubbed off
every other consideration, like a doctor, and he wanted to
remain germ-free for court the next day. Only he didn't wash
with soap and water. He used the antiseptic of alcohol.

And the phone rang all night long.

The Bishop rubbed his eyes and turned away. Rutledge looked
over at Donna, and she shrugged. The silence was awesome.
He knew that it was intentional – the Bishop's study was
designed to allow easier access to God – but Donna did not see
how anyone could work in such an atmosphere.

'You're certain about her?' said the Bishop without looking
round.

'The woman in New York is a former nurse at the hospital,'
said Donna. 'Her name is Mary Rooney. She was very sure.
She is a devout woman and thought that someone should
protect the diocese.'

'She's right,' said the Bishop decisively. Then turning to
Rutledge: 'I want you to pull out.'

Rutledge looked over at Donna, who rolled her eyes. Then

he cleared his throat and said, 'That will be awkward, Yo[ur]
Excellency.'

'Why?' said the Bishop.

'Well, for one thing, we brought Concannon into the case [in]
the first place. How can we just leave him stranded like th[at?]
We have to tell him what we know.'

'The woman spoke to us in confidence,' said the Bish[op.]
'We will respect that confidentiality.'

'But how can we not warn Mr Concannon?' said Don[na,]
glancing over at Rutledge for support. He shrugged.

'She asked for protection, didn't she?' said the Bishop. 'S[he]
expects protection. The Church cannot accept a tempor[ary]
advantage at the risk of losing trust.'

'But Concannon –'

'No more argument,' said the Bishop. 'I do not want eith[er]
of you at the defence table. We are pulling out. You are [no]
attorney. You represent the Church. Let Mr Concannon fig[ht]
the case with whatever ammunition he has. If he wins, [he]
wins. We will not interfere, one way or the other.'

'But –' Donna began.

'That's final,' said the Bishop, getting up and leaving the[m]
alone.

She was waiting in the parking lot. Concannon was surpris[ed]
and annoyed. 'I'm sure there's an explanation,' he said as th[ey]
stood talking over the roof of his Mercedes.

'I'm tired,' said Donna. 'Could we go somewhere and talk?'

The firm kept an executive apartment within walki[ng]
distance. It was, as such things must be, built arou[nd]
discretion. The doorman was reliable. Concannon had the k[ey]
and was certain that the apartment was not being used. [He]
made a point of knowing who used it and to what end.

As they rode up in the elevator, Donna leaned against th[e]
rail. She felt ragged, uncertain, pressed on every side. Sh[e]
could tell Concannon everything and betray the Bishop. [Or]

he could let nature take its course and remain silent, thus
etraying Concannon. Either way, someone was going to get
urt. Either way, someone was going to blame her.

She needed someone to talk to. She would have preferred
Galvin. He might not know what to do, but at least he would
ave a sense of humour about it.

'We missed you in court today,' said Concannon, struggling
o remain patient.

'I need a drink,' she said.

When he was on his third bourbon and she was on her
econd martini, she began to relax. 'Why is it,' she said, 'there
re no female associates in your firm?'

'Did you forget about the trial?' he asked. 'Did you oversleep
r get lost at the hairdresser?'

She kicked off her shoes and curled up on the couch and
eached over and touched Concannon's arm. 'Give me a
ninute, please, Edward. I haven't had an easy day.'

She closed her eyes and stretched. She was feeling lonely,
nd dangerously amorous. She brushed back a strand of hair,
nd then her hand brushed against her breast.

Concannon turned away. 'Look, goddammit, the only thing
ny of us should have on our minds is this case. Now, what
ave you found out about Galvin?'

'Oh, Edward, don't be such a prig. Get me a drink and I'll
ell you a secret.' She smiled and held out her glass for a refill.

Concannon leaped off the couch. 'I don't have time for this,'
e said, glaring at her. 'I'm not Galvin.'

'What are you talking about?' she said, reddening. 'What do
ou think I'm doing here?'

'I mean that I'm not interested in a roll in the hay. Not in the
niddle of this case. Put your shoes back on and tell me what
ou have on Mr Galvin.'

'Nothing,' she said putting her shoes back on.

Recall Mrs Rocco Stampanatto!' the bailiff cried.

The word had got out on the grapevine, only this time wasn't so definite. No one knew exactly what was going on Judge Sweeney's session, but it was electric. The courtroo was even more crowded today than it had been yesterda with a current of excitement running through the spectat section.

This guy Galvin was putting up one hell of a fight again Concannon. Going up against the champ. Taking a few sh and getting up and delivering a few himself. He just would stay down. That was how the old-timers saw it: the underd was making it a hell of a battle. Now there were two rooti sections.

Natalie Stampanatto blushed under all the attention. T old-timers looked at her and judged her, weighing her abili to take a tough cross-examination as some would measure rooster's chance in a cockfight. She was a small woma already growing thick despite her youth. Three children three years had seen to that.

She'll cave in, said some of the veterans in the courtroo Concannon will break her and make her cry, and that will the end of her value as a witness. It would be like Senat Muskie when he cried and lost the Presidency – human, b not quite reliable.

Instinctively, she knew it, and she bit her cheek raw again it.

Concannon sensed his moment. The smell of blood had p extra colour in his cheeks, and he glowed with it. He sto there like a statue, watching her walk towards the witne stand. His dark blue suit was new and meticulously tailore His white-on-white shirt set off the sky-blue tie. His cuff link a replica of his Air Force fighter, caught the sun and sparkle The details were perfect.

In his manicured hands, Concannon held a copy of th previous day's transcript. He was reading Mrs Stampanatto testimony, letting her stew for a while on the witness stan until he was ready to begin.

Galvin tried to drown his tongue with the water pitcher. It felt like a great snake after last night's drinking, and he hoped it would stop throbbing before the water ran out.

'Mrs Stampanatto, are you aware of the penalties for perjury in the Commonwealth of Massachusetts?' Concannon spoke gently and smiled as if he were unsheathing a dagger. 'Do you happen to know the penalties for that particular crime in this state?'

'I know that it's wrong,' she said.

'We all know that it's wrong, Mrs Stampanatto. But that wasn't my question. I was wondering if you knew the price for lying. Under oath?'

'I know that it's wrong,' she said finally.

'Well, let me ask you this: do you know the difference between a misdemeanour and a felony?'

'I believe a misdemeanour is a minor violation.'

'That's right. A misdemeanour is a minor violation. Spitting on a sidewalk. A parking ticket. And a felony is a serious crime. A felony can send you to jail. Perjury is a felony. Do you understand what I'm driving at?'

'I understand,' she replied.

'So we are not dealing here with something minor. Something trivial. We are talking about a prison offence.'

'I understand,' she said.

'Now. Mrs Stampanatto, you weren't here when Dr Towler testified or when Dr Crowley testified: am I correct?'

'Yes. That's correct.'

'Both of these men took the same oath that you took. They stood there and held one hand on the Bible and raised the other to God and swore to tell the truth. And that's a sacred oath, is it not?'

'It is to me.'

'I know it is. I can tell that, and I am not just making a point for argument's sake, since you are what we call a hostile

237

witness. I can tell that you are a person who would take an oath seriously.

'So you would think very carefully and be extra cautious before telling His Honour and the court something that could be mistaken.'

'I hope so.'

'Well, it has to be more than a hope, Mrs Stampanatto. We try to be more precise than to hope.'

'It was just a figure of speech.'

'Of course. Now, Mrs Stampanatto, did you know Dr Towler and Dr Crowley when you worked at St Catherine Laboure Hospital?'

'Everyone who worked there knew them.'

'And how long did you know the doctors, professionally?'

'My entire stay at St Catherine's. Three years.'

'And when you worked there and knew these two gentlemen, what was your opinion of them?'

'I thought they were dedicated men.'

'Dedicated?'

'Yes. Dedicated doctors.'

'A noble profession. These men were healers. Men who drove themselves to the breaking point to save human lives: is that right?'

'That's right.'

'And that was the reputation they enjoyed at the hospital among the rest of the staff?'

'Objection,' said Galvin. 'It's speculative and hearsay at best.'

'No. I'll allow it,' said Sweeney.

'What?' cried Galvin, who could not believe that such a flagrantly objectionable question was permitted.

'I said that I would allow it,' said Sweeney firmly.

'Exception,' said Galvin in wonder.

'The question was what kind of reputation Drs Towler and Crowley enjoyed at the hospital.'

'Well respected,' she replied.

'Well respected,' said Concannon for emphasis. 'And both of these men, who were well respected according to your own testimony, both at the hospital and in the medical community, have staked their careers and reputations and freedom on stating that Mrs Rosen told you she had eaten nine hours before coming to the hospital. Are you aware of that?'

'I know,' she whispered.

'I'm sorry, the jury cannot hear you if you whisper,' said Concannon.

'I know!' she said loudly.

'You know,' he repeated, then absorbed himself in the transcript of her previous testimony. 'So it is your testimony that she ate a full meal at nine o'clock in the morning – one hour before coming to the hospital. Is that right?'

'That's right.'

'No doubt about it?'

'No doubt in my mind.'

'I wonder if I could have Miss McLaughlin read back the last two questions and answers,' said Concannon, walking back to the defence table.

Miss McLaughlin leafed through her stenographic tape while the courtroom waited.

'Question', she said. ' "So it is your testimony that she ate a full meal at nine o'clock in the morning – one hour before coming to the hospital. Is that right?' Answer: 'That's right.'' Question: "No doubt about it?" Answer: "No doubt in my mind." ''

Concannon let it sink in. He had stuck nine o'clock in there when she had earlier testified that Mrs Rosen said she ate at four. It was so subtle no one noticed. Not Mrs Stampanatto. Not Frank Galvin. Not the judge. Not anyone.

And when it was read back, they all caught the error.

'It was at four o'clock,' said Mrs Stampanatto softly. 'She told me she ate the meal at four o'clock – one hour before coming to the hospital.'

'Of course she did,' said Concannon. 'I was just showing how easy it is to make a mistake. The fact that I said nine o'clock when it was four o'clock was just a mistake. But you see how easy it is to make a mistake?'

'I wasn't listening now,' she said. 'That wasn't fair.'

'Oh,' said Concannon. 'You weren't listening? Were you listening then when Deborah Ruth Rosen showed up at the hospital in pain?'

Galvin groaned.

Concannon walked over to the defence table, where Kaplan handed him a blue-backed acrylic-covered folder that looked important and official. Concannon glanced at a page.

'Now that we have all had a chance to see how easy it is to make a mistake, unintentionally, do you wish to retract your testimony?' He was still leafing through the folder.

'I can't,' she said.

'You can't?' Concannon said. 'Of course you can. There's always time to admit a mistake. A possible error.'

'I can't,' she said, 'because it's the truth.'

'You do not wish to change it in any way? In no respect at all?'

'What I said, what I testified to, was the truth, Mr Concannon. I couldn't change it even if I wanted to.'

'Let me get this straight, Mrs Stampanatto: you would like His Honour, Judge Sweeney, and this jury of twelve – who represent the collective conscience of the community – to believe that Dr Towler and Dr Crowley have risked seven years in prison, have perjured themselves, for a few measly dollars? Because they could have settled this for enough money. They could have avoided all this. But they wanted vindication in an open court. They didn't want these charges to lie over their heads. Is that what you suggest, that they're not telling the truth?'

'I respect both of these doctors . . .' she began, and she was

240

on the verge of tears.

'Wait a minute! Hold it, Mrs Stampanatto, please. We are serious people here. These are serious issues and these are serious charges. Let us take the charges and the issues and the people seriously. The question can be answered by yes or no. Please answer it yes or no.'

'Dr Towler and Dr Crowley are not telling the truth,' she said, looking at Galvin for help. He turned away.

Concannon just looked at her for a moment. 'I would like to approach this witness,' he said.

'Go right ahead,' said the judge.

'Let's get to the bottom of this,' began Concannon. 'Let me show you a piece of evidence – P-one, as a matter of fact. It's the hospital admission chart for May fourteenth of Deborah Ruth Rosen. Do you recognize it?'

'I do.'

'And those initials, N.C., at the bottom of the page, are those yours?'

'They are.'

'And when you signed that, it was like the moment here when you took the Bible in your hand and raised the other to God, isn't it?'

'I don't understand,' she said.

'You took an oath, Mrs Stampanatto. When you put your initials to that page, you took an oath, swearing to the truth of what appeared on that page. Isn't that true?'

'I suppose,' she replied.

'No "I suppose," Mrs Stampanatto,' he blared. 'That's the purpose of the initials there, isn't it? It's an oath, isn't it? It's not there to see your nice handwriting, is it?'

'No,' she replied quietly.

'It is there so that when someone picks it up they will know who prepared it and who is responsible and who swore to the truth of the notations on that chart. Isn't that so, Mrs Stampanatto?'

241

'Yes, Mr Concannon. I guess you're right. It is a kind of an oath.'

'No "kind" about it. An oath. A witness before God because that oath is as good as the one you took here, isn't it? An oath is an oath, isn't it?'

'Yes, sir. That's right.'

'Okay. Now, on this page, in your handwriting, are the name of the patient and the address of the patient, along with initial blood pressure and respiration, pulse and Blue Cross number past history, chief complaint and so on. All the things you would have to know to admit her to the hospital, correct?'

'That's right, sir.'

'And that is your handwriting – also correct?'

'Also correct.'

'And you had done this many times?'

'A number of times,' she replied.

'How many?'

'Quite a few.'

'Ten, a hundred? A thousand? How many?'

'More than a hundred. Less than a thousand,' she said.

'Fine. So we know that you are a pro at this. And the patient would come in and you would ask a question and the patient would give you an answer and you would record what the patient told you: is that the way it worked?'

'More or less.'

'More or less? How much more and how much less? We have to be very precise here, Mrs Stampanatto. Is that the way it worked?'

'The procedure was that patients would come in and I would ask questions and they would answer and I would write down the answer.'

'Okay. That's the procedure. And all this information i correct?'

'I wouldn't know. I would only know what the patient told me.'

242

'Exactly. So if someone came in and said that she had had five children in the past, you wouldn't know whether or not that was true, would you?'

'I had no way of knowing.'

'And if she said that she had pains every ten minutes and the pains were every five minutes, you couldn't tell if that was true or not?'

'Right.'

'You wrote what she told you, right?'

'Right.'

'And if a patient said that she had eaten nine hours ago and she had really just eaten, you wouldn't know if that was true, right?'

'No,' she said.

'What?' said Concannon. 'I'm sorry, I didn't hear you. You said that you would have no way of knowing whether or not a patient ate nine hours ago or one hour ago: is that right?'

'That's right, Mr Concannon.'

'You had to rely on what the patient told you, right?'

'Right.'

'And if the patient lied or made a mistake, you would have no way of knowing?'

'Also true.'

'You just wrote what she told you, or what you thought you heard.'

'Yes. But she said one hour, Mr Concannon.'

'If Your Honour please!' implored Concannon, looking up at the bench.

'Yes,' said Sweeney. 'Just answer the questions as they're put to you. Strike the last answer.'

'I'm sorry.'

'Now, there is a notation on this chart, Mrs Stampanatto, which says that the patient last ate nine hours earlier. Did you see that?'

'Yes. I did.'

243

'I would like the jurors to take a look at this,' said Concannon, and he passed the chart to the foreman.

The courtroom waited while the chart worked up and down the two rows of jurors. Then it was handed back to him.

'Thank you,' he said. 'Now, did anyone else take this admitting history?'

'No one else.'

'So you wrote down the pulse and respiration and Mrs Rosen's address?'

'Yes, sir.'

'And you also wrote down that she ate nine hours before coming to the hospital – correct?'

'No,' she said firmly. 'I did not.'

'You didn't?'

'I did not.'

'But it's right here on the chart, over the place where you signed it and took that oath about the truth of what was recorded there. Let me show it to you.'

'I've seen it. But I didn't record nine hours.'

'That's your handwriting, isn't it?' said Concannon, who was jolted by this. He had been confidently sailing through his cross-examination, planting doubts that would sprout an acquittal. He was certain. Just enough doubt about how a person could hear 'nine' instead of 'one' or had put the wrong number on a page.

'You just told us that you took this history,' he said, sounding betrayed.

'That's not my handwriting,' she said.

They were going off like explosions. The questions and unexpected answers came back and blew up in his face. And Concannon hated nasty surprises.

'Whose handwriting is it, then?' he asked.

'I don't know,' she said. 'All I know is that I recorded one hour and someone changed it to nine.'

There was a rising murmur throughout the courtroom.

244

'This is incredible,' snapped Concannon. 'This is your record, which you made, for which you are responsible, and now you want us to believe some fairy tale about gremlins who come in and change your notes. What are we supposed to believe? Who made those phantom changes?'

'I am telling the truth.'

'Well, let's see if we can figure it out. Who was there, besides you and the two orderlies?'

'I'm not sure,' she said.

'You're not sure?'

'It was four years ago.'

'Well, you were pretty sure a few minutes ago about some of the details in that report. Do you just remember what you want to remember, or what Mr Galvin tells you to remember?'

'I just can't remember who was there,' she said.

'You remember fine when Mr Galvin interrogates you, and that's the same four years.'

'I can't remember who was present, that's all.'

'Maybe we can try to refresh your recollection. Does it refresh your mind if I say that Nancy Ryan and Muriel Burnett were on duty?'

'I seem to recall both being present. Yes.'

'But you didn't remember a moment ago: isn't that correct?'

'No, I didn't recall a moment ago.'

'By the way, how was Mrs Rosen dressed that night?'

'I don't recall.'

'Was she wearing slacks or a dress?'

'I don't remember.'

'Okay. Never mind that. What colour was whatever she was wearing?'

'What colour?'

'Yes. What colour?'

'I'm sorry,' she said, and her voice was beginning to tremble, and the courtroom buffs leaned in closer. 'I didn't notice the colour.'

'You don't know?'

'I don't know.'

'But you remember the difference between the "one" and the "nine" pretty good, don't you?'

'Yes, I do.'

'Doesn't that seem a little unusual? You don't remember who was there. You don't remember anything about the way the woman looked or what she was wearing. And yet you remember one small digit on the admission chart. Doesn't that stretch credibility?'

'No, sir.'

'How can you remember that so clearly and everything else is hazy?'

'Because I kept a copy.'

'What?' shouted Concannon.

'I kept a photocopy of the original.'

The jaws of the buffs and the veterans and the judge and the jurors and even the unflappable Miss McLaughlin all dropped.

'I have it right here in my handbag,' she said.

And Galvin leaned back in his chair and didn't even mind the snakes in his head.

24

It was the nastiest surprise of all. Concannon was staggered. He wandered back and forth in front of Mrs Stampanatto, trying to pull out of this nose dive.

'Would you like to see it?' she said, reaching into her handbag. 'I have it right here with me.'

'No! No!' said Concannon. 'I object to any photocopy. In the first place,' he added, addressing Sweeney, 'it violates the best-evidence rule. The best evidence is the record itself . . . which is already in evidence.'

'Not if it's been tampered with,' shouted Galvin, now on his feet and ready for combat. Concannon glanced at him and in a flash saw the innocent face of the wounded German pilot. He knew the man was dangerous! He knew it!

'Your Honour,' said Galvin, 'the hospital record which is now in evidence does not reflect the original. Not if it's been tampered with. And we contend that it *has* been tampered with.'

The judge was caught in the middle. He was uncomfortable. 'Do you have any further questions of this witness?' he asked Concannon.

'None,' replied Concannon, who turned towards his two clients, who looked away.

'You may examine your witness in redirect,' said the judge. It was all going according to Galvin's plan. He was amazed with himself. He had never before made such a plan and seen it through.

'Just one or two questions,' said Galvin. 'Is that a photocopy of the original hospital record you are holding?'

'It is.'

'May I look at it?' – and the clerk handed it to Galvin. It was marked P-2 for identification. 'I am now reading from your copy. It says "one hour PTA".'

'What does PTA mean?'

'Prior to Admission.'

'Was this what Mrs Rosen told you in response to the inquiry about her last meal?'

'Yes, it is.'

'And you wrote down what she told you?'

'Yes, I did.'

He showed it to Concannon, who scanned it and handed it back. He was beet red and unable to focus.

'I would now offer it in evidence,' said Galvin.

'I most strenuously object,' said Concannon. 'Again, it violates the best-evidence rule. It is only one sheet out of ninety-six pages. It has not been authenticated. It is self-serving –'

And then, in a voice ragged with fatigue, Judge Sweeney jumped ship. He had seen and heard enough.

'I will allow it,' he ruled.

Galvin felt a burst of exhilaration.

'Your Honour, I respectfully ask that it be passed to the jurors,' said Galvin.

'Objection,' said Concannon. 'For the same reasons. It has not been authenticated –'

'Overruled,' said Judge Sweeney, now sitting tall at the bench and delivering his rulings like the blows of a gavel. 'I will note your exception, Mr Concannon.'

'Mr Foreman, ladies and gentlemen of the jury,' said Galvin, 'this is a photocopy of page three of the original hospital record. It contains the notation that Mrs Rosen ate one hour prior to admission. Please examine it carefully. I will also pass around page three of the hospital record as it was produced here by the defence and ask the jurors to compare the two versions.'

'Objection,' said Concannon, without much conviction.

'Overruled,' said the judge. 'Exception noted.'

The jurors studied the two documents carefully. Concannon was trying to calm down. He turned around and saw Donna and Roger Rutledge in the third row of the courtroom. And he knew at that moment that he was all alone in the sky with this one. The judge was lost. Rutledge was lost. He could not rely on his clients. There was only himself. Out there alone against the blond pilot who was out to kill him.

Galvin stood slumped against the jury box. He was wearing the same suit that he had worn for three days. The legs were baggy. He needed a shave. The electric razor that he kept in the office was old and didn't get too close.

But he had never felt so good.

Galvin had played the longest shot of his life. His twenty years of trying cases in the bush, the pit work, getting bruised by the big boys – the Mike Kellermans, the Clint Darraghs – gave him insight into the superegos. Always, they had to have the last word. He was counting on that.

Galvin looked around the room, at the judge and the jury and Concannon, and decided to stop right there. That was the final bait. The scales were tilted slightly in his favour – enough to avoid a directed verdict, enough to get to the jury – but the evidence was not devastating. It was enough to ensure sympathy, but not a big win. He would take the chance that Mrs Stampanatto would bring the jury all the way home under cross-examination. *If* Concannon took the bait. If he didn't, if he decided then and there to rest his case, the verdict would be a timid one. He wanted more than moral vindication now.

Finally, Galvin turned to the judge and said, 'I have no further questions. Your witness, Counsellor.'

'Mr Concannon, any recross?' Judge Sweeney peered down at him.

Instinctively, Concannon leaped to his feet. He might be

wounded, but he would come back at the witness with all the firepower he had. He was certain that Galvin was behind it all, and he had to destroy the man.

'One last question, Mrs Stampanatto,' he began, turning his back on the witness, to rest his hand on the jury rail. 'Why is it that you made a photocopy of the so-called original?'

'Because,' she said quietly, 'I thought I would need it.'

'Why did you keep it all these years? Why did you come forward only now, for this case, simply at Mr Galvin's request?' He still had his back to the witness. He looked steadily at the jurors.

'Because,' she said, 'later that morning, after what happened to Mrs Rosen, Dr Towler summoned me up to his office and asked me to change the record. He asked me to put a loop at the top of the "one" and add an "s" to the word "hour" to make it plural. But I wouldn't do it.'

Concannon just stood there, frozen.

'Mr Concannon,' the judge said.

He shook his head. 'No further questions,' he said.

'Thank you, Mrs Stampanatto,' the judge said. 'You may step down.'

'The plaintiff rests,' said Galvin.

'You may proceed with your opening,' said the judge to Concannon.

The old pilot looked around him. All the young lawyers were anxious and worried. All the old pros scented blood. Donna St Laurent and Roger Rutledge had left.

'The defence rests,' said Concannon.

At lunch, Monsignor O'Boyle suggested a settlement. Galvin would take $450,000, he said. Concannon kept on eating. The young attorneys kept their heads in their plates. St Catherine was insured up to $500,000, argued O'Boyle. A settlement beyond that would eat into private assets. Galvin would take the $450,000. Go to $500,000 if necessary.

'It's too late,' said Concannon, wiping his mouth, picking up his briefcase and heading back to the courthouse. He checked himself in the mirror of the men's room, searching out lint the way he had once found enemy trucks on the landscape thirty-six years ago.

Courtroom 903 had room for ninety spectators. But at the afternoon session of *Rosen v. St Catherine Laboure, et al.,* one hundred and forty people jammed into the benches. Those associated with the case were there: Arthur Aloisi from Consolidated Life was joined by L. Walker Angoff, president of Minnesota Mutual. Monsignor O'Boyle. The legal echelons. But what was more notable to Concannon was the missing: Bishop Brophey, Donna St Laurent and Roger Rutledge.

Judge Sweeney was ready to hear final arguments. In civil cases, they were usually limited to twenty minutes, but Sweeney said he would tolerate reasonable extensions. After all, this was an important case. 'But let me remind you gentlemen that a closing argument should be like a woman's skirt: long enough to cover the subject, short enough to be interesting.'

'Your Honour,' Concannon said, standing. 'I would like to move for a directed verdict for the defendants. The plaintiff has failed to establish a case to any degree of reasonable medical certainty.'

The ruling came like thunder. There was in Judge Sweeney's voice the echo of something taught in law school long ago. He was being faithful to things he hadn't even known existed inside himself anymore.

'Denied,' he said. 'It will be up to the jury to decide, after

'Proceed with your summation, Mr Concannon.'

251

25

Concannon rose. The late-afternoon sun filtered through the arched windows of the courtroom, highlighting the patches of silver in his dark hair. He looked fresh, crisply tailored, eager for the final challenge.

'Your Honour, Mr Justice Sweeney; my opponent; Mr Foreman; ladies and gentlemen of the jury. It's an old saying that there are no souls saved after twenty minutes, so I will be brief. I have been trying cases for over thirty years, in both state and federal courts. May I, here and now, compliment you on the way you have performed as jurors. This has been a long and difficult case with complex issues, and you sat here throughout, not complaining, attentive, catching every word. You have been remarkable. In fact, you are one of the finest juries I have ever tried in front of in my thirty years of practice at the bar.'

He paused to assess the effect of his little rhetorical flourish. The jurors seemed pleased. 'Do you recall how this all came about?' he continued. 'Do you remember how it all started? It was a difficult medical case. Deborah Ruth Rose went to her family doctor, Sheldon Rabb, and told him about her problems, and it was more than he could handle. He had to seek help.

'And whom did he call on? He called upon the best in the field. Dr Rexford Towler. The best. You have only heard the surface of his record. He is an honoured and esteemed physician. That, even from the lips of the plaintiff's own witness. You heard Mrs Stampanatto say that both doctors, Dr Towler and Dr Crowley, were dedicated and well respected.'

Donna St Laurent had entered the courtroom with Roger

Rutledge. Both stood near the back wall.

'They could have turned the case down. They were busy men with tight schedules. It was a difficult medical case. Why should they risk failure? Because they are, in Mrs Stampanatto's words, dedicated men. So they took this difficult case, with all the risks and none of the glory. And why? They didn't do it for the fee. Mrs Rosen was not a wealthy woman. She couldn't afford to pay them the regular fee. They charged her a modest amount. A token fee.

'Then why did they do it? Because they are not summer soldiers. Sunshine patriots. Because if not they, then someone else would have to. And that someone else would not be the best.

'We lawyers lose cases. In every lawsuit there are a winner and a loser. There are thousands of lost cases. Would you penalize a lawyer for losing a case? Would you stigmatize him? Lawyers lose cases. Doctors lose patients. It's no one's fault. No one meant to lose the case or the patient.'

Concannon leaned in on the rail, talking sense, it seemed. Confiding. Opening his heart to the jurors.

'Think what it would mean if we lawyers only took the safe cases. The sure winners. Who would defend the long shots? Who would take a chance? And doctors. Think what it would mean if a doctor only took a guaranteed survivor. Think of that.

'"Sorry, that tumour looks bad. I only handle ninety-nine-percent recoveries." Think of that!

'Now, what happened to Deborah Ruth Rosen was deeply unfortunate. No one denies that. It was a tragedy. Dr Towler and Dr Crowley have suffered greatly, as they would suffer over the loss of any patient. These are sensitive men. Their profession is life, not death. They reach into the valley of death each day, each night, plucking thousands back from that place of no return; thousands who, if they could, would be here today and say, "Thank God for Dr Towler, thank God for Dr Crowley, I am living. I am here today with my wife, my children. Thank God." '

The jurors' eyes were riveted on Concannon. His presence was electric, his delivery incisive.

'Accidents do happen,' he said. 'Remember the line from *David Copperfield*: "Accidents will occur in the best-regulated families." The unforeseeable event, that no one could predict. For the unavoidable act of God, the plaintiff's attorney has subjected all of you; Dr Crowley and Dr Towler; Nurse Nevins; St Catherine Laboure – a hospital second to none, the finest in the world – to this ultimate harassment.'

Concannon raised his voice. It was tinged with the proper degree of anger. 'He has tried to make a dollar! Yes, a dollar! Imagine! Not for Deborah Ruth Rosen; not for Mr Rosen who has since remarried . . . and, incidentally, Mr Rosen never visited Deborah Ruth at the hospital. Never! . . . Not once in four years! . . . Where will the money go? It will go to attorney's fees and relatives. Deborah Ruth Rosen is not going to profit. She is past all human need. God help her. And I won't bring her back to punish these physicians. What good will it do? What's done is done.'

Galvin clenched his fists. He should have objected. Mr Rosen's nonappearance was not in evidence and had no bearing on the case. But Galvin held his fire.

Concannon knew that Mrs Stampanatto was the plaintiff's strongest witness. Thompson not so strong. He would centre his attack at the weakest point. First, Mrs Stampanatto had to be reckoned with.

'Now, the plaintiff's attorney presented two witnesses. You heard them. Mrs Rocco Stampanatto and a Lionel Thompson.

'As for Mrs Stampanatto, do you recall how she couldn't get my questions straight when I brought up the number "nine" and she had said earlier "four"? Four, nine, one. I suggest that what really happened to Mrs Stampanatto in the early morning of May fourteenth is that she had worked all night, was at the end of her shift. She was tired. Numbers came at her quickly. Birth was imminent. She was more concerned with getting Deborah Ruth Rosen upstairs than getting the medical history straight.

'Do you recall how we had my question read back by the court stenographer, Miss McLaughlin, so that there would be no mistake? It was Mrs Stampanatto's initials at the bottom of the hospital record – the real hospital record – that showed Deborah Ruth had not eaten for *nine* hours.

'And where was Mrs Stampanatto all these years, with her strange evidence? Why does she appear mysteriously with a so-called photocopy of the record – and at whose request? At the request of Mr Galvin, who has most to gain here. Doesn't it appear strange that she remembered certain events after the passage of four years' time and couldn't remember ordinary things, things that you and I would remember?

'And I tell you this, ladies and gentlemen of the jury, no one on God's earth can swear that those two good doctors did not rely on that record, taken by Mrs Stampanatto, when they delivered Deborah Ruth's baby.

'No, the plaintiff's attorney shopped around and came up with a self-professed expert, Lionel Thompson. You heard him. I tried to cross-examine him. The most difficult task in the world is to cross-examine someone without credentials. He'll say anything. A professional witness.'

Concannon paused again for several seconds and looked the foreman of the jury right in the eye.

' "I'm available." Those were Thompson's very words. And do you recall how he puffed out his chest when he said it?

'God help us. Anybody can talk in the light of an after-event. Hindsight is always twenty/twenty. Sure it's easy for this old courtroom pro to get up now, four years later, after spending hours in his comfortable study, smoking his pipe, scrutinizing the hospital record, a decanter of brandy at his side. Sure it's easy. But he wasn't under the gun. He didn't walk the tightrope between life and death, didn't face the crisis that confronted Dr Towler and Dr Crowley and the medical team that fateful morning.

'It comes right down to this basic issue. Does a doctor, every time he sees a patient, have to say to himself, "Now, let me see, I wonder if I will end up in a lawsuit"? And will St Catherine Laboure continue to provide a sanctuary, as it has for this past decade, for the sick and dying? Or will it be crushed in order to pay financial damages to anyone who comes along and brings suit for any cause whatsoever?'

In crisp, eloquent tones, he reminded the jurors of every aspect of the case before leading them to his final words.

'This has been a long, painful and lonely quest for personal redemption on behalf of these men and women in white. I grant that this case contains sadness, a tragedy for all of us, and it tugs at our emotions because it is painful and sorrowful, to which neither you nor I are strangers. But do not decide this case out of sympathy. If you decide it out of sympathy and not on the merits, then a grave injustice is done. We are all compassionate; we are all sympathetic to the plaintiff. Yet a wise man once said, "We must be just before we are generous."

'It is not going to be easy to return a verdict for the defendants in this case. It will take strength. But I know that all of you are equal to the task. And when you leave here, you can look each other in the eye years after your verdict, and you can say, "We did the just, the right thing."

'Now I take leave of you . . . I cannot believe, as we share these last moments together, that you will fly in the face of the evidence. I have complete faith that you good jurors will vindicate my clients and allow them to go back and practise medicine, as they were gifted by God to do. I thank you.'

It is rare that there is applause in a courtroom. The veterans have their own way of expressing admiration. And as he returned to his own chair, Concannon could hear and feel the murmur of admiration and approval – their gesture o applause.

Wilson Gaynor and Marvin Kaplan tried to shake his hand, but he waved them off. He sat at the defence table and folded his arms and tilted his head back. He was at ease. He might even have pulled it off.

Galvin felt a knot tightening in his stomach. He would have to fight back again. 'Mr Galvin,' said Judge Sweeney for the second time. He hadn't heard the first summons.

'Mr Foreman, ladies and gentlemen of the jury . . .' he began slowly. His voice was unsteady.

'I haven't the expertise of my opponent. I won't pretend that this is the first case I have ever tried, but this is the biggest case I have ever tried. I won't try to kid you. I might botch things up, say things I shouldn't, omit to say things I should. Right now I'm a little scared. If my voice cracks again, please bear with me. I'm not eloquent. Stay with me. Give my little girl a chance. This is all I ask.

'You know, Mr Concannon told you that you were one of the best juries he ever tried in front of in thirty years of practice. I've been at the bar, oh, for half that time, and I honestly can't say you are one of the best juries. Frankly, I was too busy to notice. Shuffling papers. Reading depositions. Worrying. I don't have his staff. It was just me alone. So I won't try to kid you, and you give me an even break – okay?'

Galvin paused. 'You know, perhaps to the defendants' lawyers this trial is some sort of a game, a game of chess, where a slight memory lapse brings disaster. You may recall how Concannon chided Mrs Stampanatto for slight imperfections of memory. Mr Concannon had the hospital record. Had studied it. Knew every page. Every line. And with all his knowledge, his ability for instant recall, Phi Beta Kappa, Harvard Law School, he tried to wring out concessions based on memory. Now, in discussing what happened on May fourteenth, I'm not going to take any witness to task – not even

257

Dr Towler or Dr Crowley – for some inconsequential difference in memory of things that took place four years ago.

'Suppose I asked you, Mr Foreman, how many light fixtures there are over your head at this moment. You might say two. Or you, madam' – Galvin nodded to a woman in the back row – 'you might say three, or you, sir' – he addressed a juror in the front row middle – 'you might say one.' A few jurors looked at the ceiling. 'Now, you've all been here for a solid week. Actually, there are no light fixtures over your heads at all.

'You had an opportunity to observe the entire courtroom on numerous occasions. But the light fixtures were not that important to you. They were inconsequential. But that doesn't mean that you weren't here, that you didn't observe, watch, listen . . . You see, the colour of Deborah Ruth Rosen's dress wasn't important to Mrs Stampanatto. But the admitting history, especially when she last had eaten, was.

'If I were to play this kind of memory game with you, and you were impressed by that sort of stuff, then no one – no one – neither you nor I nor Deborah Ruth Rosen – could ever get justice in any courtroom. And if we can't get justice in the courtroom, then we might just as well give up. If we can't get it here, there's no place in the world we can get it.

'Mrs Stampanatto is an ordinary person, like you and me. And ordinary people have frailties in observation and recall that you would expect from honest persons who testify after the passage of a great period of time. It's the opposite I would suspect: pat consistency, perfect recall – the recall exhibited by the defendants Dr Crowley and Dr Towler.'

Galvin put both hands on the jury rail and looked left to right. He had their attention. Slowly, the jury was beginning to respond. He waited for a few seconds. The tightness in his stomach was gone.

Here goes, he thought. Oh, God, I have to reach them. 'There is a time for living and there is a time for dying. And the early morning hours of May fourteenth, four years ago, th world that little Deborah Ruth Rosen knew died with her. And it was not her time to die.'

Twenty-four eyes followed him as he walked a few feet to the middle of the jury rail.

'There was a plea by Mr Concannon not to decide this case out of sympathy, out of charity, but on the merits. No one disagrees with that. If you bring in a verdict for Deborah Ruth because you feel sorry for what happened to her, for her poor children . . . deprived of a natural mother; if you feel you can't reject either Deborah Ruth or her children by an adverse verdict; if that's your reason, then although you may have reached a proper verdict, you have done so for the wrong reason. By the same token, if you find against Deborah Ruth and in favour of the doctors, the nurses and the hospital because you feel that it might be financially injurious to them to be held responsible, or if you are troubled about the reputation of Catherine Laboure in the community, your verdict might be justified by the evidence, but your reasons for reaching such a verdict would be wrong.

'I say this to you; I say it as frankly, and as loud and clear, as can: Decide Deborah Ruth Rosen's case only on the evidence, only on the merits. Nothing more, nothing less. No sympathy. If she hasn't proved her case, find against her.

'Now, this is not a complex case, as Mr Concannon suggested. Someone – either my witness, Mrs Stampanatto, or Dr Towler or Dr Crowley – is lying. There are no shades here, no nuances. It's black or white. The testimony is unalterably opposed. In this respect your job is easy.

'Who is telling the truth? Mrs Stampanatto – a nurse herself one time, the admitting nurse, mother of three children – or Dr Towler and Dr Crowley? If Mrs Stampanatto did indeed record the fact that Deborah Ruth Rosen had eaten a full meal one hour earlier and nevertheless she was given a general anaesthesia, negligence on the part of the hospital is clear. If you honestly think Mrs Stampanatto is not levelling with you, has something to gain by all this, an axe to grind, then you must find against Deborah Ruth. It's as simple as that.

'Now, if Mrs Stampanatto merely testified as she did, it would be Mrs Stampanatto's word against Dr Towler's and Dr Crowley's. But she said that Dr Towler asked her to *change* the hospital record, and to prove it she brought with her a true copy of the original. And do you recall how the defence tried to block this evidence? They tried to deal you a card from the bottom of the deck, slip you their own "doctored" version. And they almost succeeded. Someone took a pen, and what they accomplished physically to Deborah Ruth on the morning of May fourteenth, they finished off later, attempting to deny her her only right of recourse. Thank God for this little girl from East Boston and New York who had an inner conscience, knowing, as a nurse, what really happened to Deborah Ruth, who had the guts to get involved, or Deborah Ruth would never have had her day in court.'

'Now, I ask you to choose who is telling the truth. It's your duty. No one – the judge, the lawyers – no one but you can decide. I ask you to decide it for the right reason, based on the evidence you have seen and heard. Deborah Ruth asks no more than this.'

Galvin was on fire. The jury felt the heat. He almost wanted to stop right there. But now he had to assess money damages. And he knew he might lose the momentum.

He glanced towards the spectators. They were all there, lawyers, courtroom reporters, others. All had expected him to fall on his face. His eyes shifted past the sea of faces to a tall girl with blond hair. Donna St Laurent. Galvin sighed. Perspiration matted his hair and trickled down his cheek, staining his collar. He launched into his final plea.

'It is a painful duty that I have right now, talking like I'm buying and selling in the marketplace. But it's my duty. It boils down to this: What is the value of human life? What is a good life worth? Again, this is for you alone to decide.

'In many countries human life is the cheapest commodity available. Not so in this country. You know, in 1937 Amelia Earhart was missing with Fred Noonan out over the Pacific. Our government spent thirty million dollars trying to find her: search planes, patrol ships, men, manpower, day in, day out. It wasn't until Pearl Harbor Day, 1941, that we officially called off the search. In fact, unofficially the search goes on. Books are written even today, forty-three years later. New leads are uncovered.

'What was Deborah Ruth's life worth? What was the price tag? She was a cook, housemaid, buyer of food and supplies, seamstress, janitor, gardener, nurse, business manager, chauffeur, baby-sitter; a mender of hearts, of wounded knees; bowled a little on Tuesday nights, played a little weekend tennis, romped in the Vermont woods, climbed the Appalachian trail.

'A debt has been created. Deborah Ruth wants only just payment. What she is due. If you owed Dr Towler or Dr Crowley or Catherine Laboure a bill, say a hundred dollars, they and their attorneys wouldn't say to you, oh, well, pay only fifty dollars. They would exact full payment. A debt is owed by the defendants to Deborah Ruth Rosen. We have sued for five million dollars. Her hospital bill alone runs a hundred and twenty-five dollars a day, for four years, and will run for many, many years into the future. This debt should be assessed not to society, not to Welfare, not to you and me, but to those who created the debt, to the defendants and the defendant hospital.

'You know, someone once said, "Man is the only animal that laughs and weeps, because man is the only animal that knows the difference between what is and what might have been." And what might it have been for little Deborah Ruth Rosen? She was not great, as – unfortunately – we measure greatness. No Madame Curie or Florence Nightingale. But she was a woman. She was a vital human who enjoyed and lived life to the fullest. Loved to play a little weekend tennis, a little canoeing.

She was so young. No eagle, like Amelia Earhart, but a small sparrow knocked down on the wing. Thank you.'

No one spoke. No one moved. When Galvin sat down, his hair was wet and matted against his skull. He was exhausted.

'How can a man so immoral, so irreverent, be so eloquent?' murmured Monsignor O'Boyle to no one in particular.

26

The jury received the case at 7 P.M. There was no quick
verdict. They sent out for sandwiches and coffee. Eight
o'clock. Nine o'clock. Still no verdict. A few spectators came
and went. The tension stayed.

Judge Sweeney napped in his chambers. Galvin was in and
out of the men's room, heaving violently. Even the coffee
wouldn't stay down.

Concannon sat at the defence table, his hands clasped before
his eyes, staring hypnotically at some distant something. The
two young assistants kept a respectful silent vigil.

In the press row, they took a pool on the outcome. Porter
Fletcher of the *Herald American* wrote down a conservative
$385,000. Matt McIntyre of the *Globe* wrote $482,000. Karen
Zabilski of the radical *Beacon Underground* scrawled
$1,000,000.

At 9.30 P.M., the buzzer rang.

The word went up and down the corridors. In the coffee
shop, which stayed open late for night court, the participants
and spectators spilled out from the counters and booths.

'A verdict,' they whispered. 'A verdict.'

No one had to ask where, or what case. There was only one
verdict that they waited for that night. Only two and a half
hours. Too short, for such a complex case with such weighty
issues.

'Good sign for the plaintiff,' said one of the legal cognoscenti.
'The jury saw a clear-cut issue and didn't dawdle.'

'No,' said another. 'There was nothing to argue about.
When they're out only long enough for a free dinner on the
state, it's a defendant's finding.'

As they filed back in, after the judge had been roused and everyone else had assembled, the jurors looked grim. Their eyes were downcast.

Galvin tried not to throw up on the desk in front of him.

Concannon tried not to feel anything.

'Mr Foreman, have you reached a verdict?' Judge Sweeney asked Martin Edelstein.

'We have, Your Honour,' replied the short, nervous salesman who had been picked to lead the jury.

'Please let me have it.'

The foreman handed the envelope to the clerk, who passed it to the judge. The judge put on his reading glasses, stared at the document and then handed it back to the clerk.

'The clerk will now read the verdict,' said Sweeney.

'The finding,' said the clerk, 'is for the plaintiff against defendants Dr G. Rexford Towler, Dr Daniel Crowley, Nurse Carolyn Nevins and St Catherine Laboure Hospital in the sum' – but the buzz was so great that the judge had to gavel the room to order. 'In the sum of five million eight hundred dollars!'

'Oh, my God!' someone cried. A gasp and shudder rippled through the room as if it had one voice, one expression.

'So say you all, ladies and gentlemen?'

'So say we all,' answered the chorus.

Five million, eight hundred dollars! Eight hundred dollars more than the plaintiff's writ. Dr Towler sat rigid in his chair. Dr Crowley's head fell into his hands and he began to weep. Nurse Nevins made small, keening noises.

The two young attorneys, Gaynor and Kaplan, wrung their hands and glanced at Concannon out of the corner of their eyes. They did not dare look at him directly.

Concannon nodded twice and looked over at Galvin's table but found himself smiling at an empty chair. He arranged the papers inside his case very carefully, as if he were packing dynamite.

Galvin was nowhere to be seen.

'Where's Galvin?' yelled Mike Kellerman, dean of the trial bar, as if the matter of rehabilitation had been settled by the verdict as well.

Galvin was in the men's room with the dry heaves.

She watched him slouch out of the courthouse, lurching between the great pillars that held up the edifice. Nice, she thought. At first, she had considered catching up to him. Congratulating him. Patting him on the back and seeing how this man Galvin looked as a winner. But Donna thought better of it. She wanted to remember him just this way, staggering away from his greatest conquest.

There was a knock on Concannon's door, and before he could answer, Donna poked her head in.

'Come in,' he said.

'Are you upset?' she asked.

'Not even wounded, sir,' he replied. 'Just killed.'

'They lied,' she said.

'They lied,' he agreed.

'They should go to jail,' she said.

'They should,' he replied.

'But will they?' she asked.

'Unlikely,' he replied.

'Why not?' she asked.

'No evidence,' he said.

'The hospital records?' she said.

'Which records?' Concannon replied. 'They would never admit the photocopy. Not in a criminal trial. The rules of evidence are different. And on the originals you'd have experts up to your ears – some swearing that the records were forged, others swearing that no one could tell. But the most important reason is that it's too messy. No one wants to touch this anymore.'

She shook her head. She understood.

He was drinking brandy, and he poured her a glass. 'You know,' he said, 'I never even got a chance to meet Galvin. I have no idea what kind of man he is. What sort of man is he?'

She sipped her brandy and frowned. 'He is one of nature's noblemen. The luckiest of the luckless. He falls off the end of the world and snags his shirt on a limb.'

Concannon snorted a laugh.

'He manoeuvres through disasters like he's shooting the rapids,' she said. 'And he's unconscious. Don't get me started on Galvin.'

'You like him a lot.'

'Let's just say he amuses me.'

'Romantic entanglement?'

'No,' she said, sighing. 'There's nothing personal with Mr Galvin. We are both too preoccupied.'

He nodded and took another swallow.

'Now, you,' she said, narrowing her gaze, 'are something else. Something else entirely.'

He smiled an exhausted smile. He took it for a salute, a compliment, and raised his glass in mutual regard.

Early the next morning, a small group of professionals met in the conference room of Concannon's office.

Dr Towler and Dr Crowley punctuated each new arrival by pulling at an arm and swearing that Mrs Stampanatto had lied. No one believed them.

'We have our work cut out for us,' said Concannon. 'We will map an appeal and have one ready for the Massachusett Supreme Court by Friday. At the same time, we will present motion to set the verdict aside as clearly excessive. We wil start preparing for a new trial immediately. Next time ther will be no surprises.'

Concannon would not linger over a setback. He forced smile, and the young attorneys taking notes smiled back

There was, in his energy and direction, the strained optimism of someone telling you that cancer is not hopeless. And yet the sense of doom hung over the room.

Aloisi, the insurance man, kept writing down figures, dividing them, halving them, cutting them down, building them up.

'Where do we stand, Kaplan?' said Concannon, trying to exert some authority – trying to stem the rout.

'Sir, I have been over the transcript, and our exceptions are weak. Only four can be pressed, and they are not crucial. None would change the weight of the evidence, and none would appear significant enough to overturn the verdict. I'm afraid . . .'

Concannon nodded. 'I've already spoken to Judge Sweeney, and we both agree that there is little ground for an appeal on technical legal exceptions. But what he could do would be to let the verdict stand to the tune of five hundred thousand dollars. He would remit four million five hundred thousand eight hundred as excessive.'

'Would Galvin go for that?' asked Aloisi.

'He'd have to. If he didn't Sweeney could order a new trial . . .'

Bishop Brophey, Donna St Laurent and Roger Rutledge entered quietly and took seats in the corner. They stood back from the table – allowing the physical distance to speak for itself. There was a nod of recognition.

'The decision on whether or not to order a new trial is exclusively within the discretion of the trial judge,' continued Concannon, who then turned to the Bishop. 'We were just going over future tactics and possibilities, Your Eminence. We were saying that the judge could remit the verdict and offer Galvin five hundred thousand. Even if Galvin objects, the order would stand. The state Supreme Court would have to uphold Sweeney's ruling. They would find that the jury was swept away by passion.

'There's another thing,' he continued. 'A bill will be

introduced in the state Legislature next week that will render tort immunity to certain institutions and medical personnel.'

'Medical no-fault,' said Kaplan to the group by way of clarification. 'It was drawn up on the model of the Good Samaritan laws that have been instituted in over forty states to protect doctors who respond to accidents and emergencies.'

'This emanates from your staff?' asked the Bishop.

'It does,' replied Concannon. 'The bill can be regarded as insurance reform, charitable immunity. It would be retroactive to twenty-five years prior to enactment.' He looked at the Bishop carefully. 'An endorsement by Your Eminence will ensure passage.'

Concannon took a cigarette from young Kaplan. He had been smoking since the decision. He hardly even noticed it himself, but he could tell that the Bishop noticed.

'It is not only Catholic hospitals that we seek to protect,' explained Concannon. 'Charitable immunity will protect New England Baptist, Beth Israel and Massachusetts General, as well as a host of small-town medical facilities. The lobbying effort will be swift and decisive. In the event that Galvin refuses to accept Judge Sweeney's remitter, by the time his appeal reaches the Supreme Court, charitable immunity will be the law of the land. The case will be academic. He'll wind up with nothing.'

'You are a careful and thorough man,' said the Bishop. It did not sound like a compliment.

'Well,' said Aloisi, sounding for the first time relieved. 'I believe that I speak for both carriers by saying that we will be happy to offer the five hundred thousand.'

'No,' said Bishop Brophey, his voice now low and serious.

It was a jarring note. No one had expected anything but acquiescence from that corner. But it was as if the Bishop had pulled the emergency cord on a train that was just picking up speed.

'No,' he said with complete finality that meant he intended

severance of himself from this business. It was a 'No' from which there was no appeal. He leaned across the conference table and placed one hand over the other.

'I am impressed,' he continued. 'I'm going to read Cardozo after this. You get a little parochial in my job just reading Bellarmine and Thomas More. There's a whole lot more to read. There's Brandeis and Clausewitz.

'But I am not going to consent to any medical no-fault,' he said. 'This lawsuit has been an education for me. When we started out, I thought, as many of you did, that we were completely in the right –'

'But we are –' began Monsignor O'Boyle.

'Let me finish, Brendan. I found myself liking this man Galvin. I was sitting in his office and he was all the things that everyone said he was, and yet I liked the man. And you cannot dismiss the power of likeability. When you like someone, even if he's a scoundrel, you have to examine the reasons why.'

The Bishop paused. 'But I set those feelings aside and allowed the legal machinery to have its way. We had our day in court.'

Concannon stiffened. He knew what was coming, and he flinched against it.

'There will be no appeal. We will pay our debt.'

'We are talking about a lot of money, Your Eminence,' said the man from the insurance company.

'I do not think we can afford this,' said Monsignor O'Boyle.

'We can't afford not to,' said the Bishop. 'We were wrong, and we fought badly. For myself, I will use whatever influence I have to see that this matter ends, and that includes seeing those disbarment charges dropped. The Church's responsibilities go beyond this lawsuit.' The Bishop nodded to Monsignor O'Boyle, who gathered up their papers, and both of them left. As if on cue, Roger Rutledge and Donna rose to leave. Concannon walked with them to the door.

'I just wanted to say,' said Concannon to Donna, 'to quote

269

the good Bishop, "I'm impressed." '

She smiled courteously and left as quickly as she could.

'Well,' said Concannon to the remainder of the group. 'Do you think Mr Galvin will take a cheque?'

27

Miriam Katz was waiting outside the intensive-care unit. She looked drained. Her eyes were red and puckered. There were no more tears left. Galvin handed her a rose. The other twenty-three he handed to a nurse and told her to put them in a vase.

'He can't have flowers,' said Moe's wife.

'I know,' said Galvin. 'I wanted to bring them anyway.'

'Lovely. I always thought flowers were lovely. Even when I told Moe that he was crazy for throwing away good money on cut flowers that would be dead in a day. I always loved the way they looked and smelled.' There was something bereft in her tone.

'What's wrong?' said Galvin.

'He's had another stroke,' she said, looking up into Galvin's eyes. 'Early this morning.'

'Is he dead?'

'No. He's not dead. He's like your Deborah.'

They let Galvin in for a moment. The nurse was changing the bedding. The tubes and wires hung down and crisscrossed to the intravenous bottles and respirators and cardiac regulators as if he were an automobile engine. The nurse rolled him on his side and moved the sheet halfway home, then rolled him the other way, finishing up the job. She kept up a professional babble – a neutral patter somewhere between interest and humour. He might have heard or he might not. She called him 'dear' as if he were already gone.

Galvin stood by the doorway until they were alone. 'Just for a moment,' the nurse had warned. 'Mustn't get too excited. We need our rest.'

Galvin stepped closer to the bed and looked into Moe's eyes. They were blank.

'We won,' he said softly. 'We beat them! We got five million dollars and we walked away clean. And you were right, Moe. It was all your doing. I mauled them on the way down, just like you taught me.'

'He can't hear you,' said Dr Brooks. Galvin hadn't noticed when he had come into the room. The doctor was standing at the foot of the bed, reading the chart. He explained that Moe Katz was beyond hearing. 'Too much cranial-nerve damage.'

But Galvin knew better. 'He can hear me,' said Galvin. 'He only pretends not to hear. But he can hear what he wants to hear. And he wants to hear that we beat the bastards! Right, Moe? Right? . . .'